RUN
AWAY
WITH
ME

Also by Mila Gray

Come Back to Me

Stay with Me

RUN AWAY WITH ME

MILA GRAY

SIMON PULSE

New York   London   Toronto   Sydney   New Delhi

SIMON PULSE

An imprint of Simon & Schuster Children's Publishing Division

1230 Avenue of the Americas, New York, New York 10020

First Simon Pulse paperback edition November 2018

Text copyright © 2017 by Mila Gray

Cover photograph copyright © 2017 by Hill Creek Pictures/Getty Images

Also available in a Simon Pulse hardcover edition.

All rights reserved, including the right of reproduction in whole or in part in any form.

SIMON PULSE and colophon are registered trademarks of Simon & Schuster, Inc.

For information about special discounts for bulk purchases, please contact Simon & Schuster Special Sales at 1-866-506-1949 or business@simonandschuster.com.

The Simon & Schuster Speakers Bureau can bring authors to your live event. For more information or to book an event contact the Simon & Schuster Speakers Bureau at 1-866-248-3049 or visit our website at www.simonspeakers.com.

Series designed by Karina Granda

Cover designed by Steve Scott

Interior designed by Tom Daly

The text of this book was set in Chaparral Pro.

Manufactured in the United States of America

10 9 8 7 6 5 4 3 2 1

The Library of Congress has cataloged the hardcover edition as follows:

Names: Gray, Mila, author.

Title: Run away with me / by Mila Gray.

Description: First Simon Pulse hardcover edition. | New York : Simon Pulse, 2017. | Companion novels: Come back to me, Stay with me. | Summary: Seven years after a horrible event that caused Jake McCallister to move away and Emerson Lowe to lose credibility, the former best friends reunite on Bainbridge Island, but the future of their romance depends on their ability to confront the past.

Identifiers: LCCN 2017014378 | ISBN 9781481490962 (hardcover) | ISBN 9781481490986 (eBook)

Subjects: | CYAC: Rape—Fiction. | Love—Fiction. | Bainbridge Island (Wash.)—Fiction.

Classification: LCC PZ7.G7798 Ru 2017 | DDC [Fic]—dc23

LC record available at https://lccn.loc.gov/2017014378

ISBN 9781481490979 (paperback)

For Åsa

RUN AWAY WITH ME

Prologue

The woods are dark as a grave. Not a sliver of moonlight breaks through the firs and alders. The dank, loamy smell of wet leaves and earth fills my lungs and I draw it in deep as though I have been holding my breath underwater for the last twenty-four hours and have finally broken the surface.

I break into a run, stumbling over buried roots, ignoring the branches that whip my arms and face, ignoring the cold that slaps my cheeks and makes them sting, ignoring the damp that has soaked through my shoes and socks and jeans.

As I run, I can hear his voice echoing through the trees. He's chasing me, gaining on me. I run faster. I need to make it to the tree house. I'll be safe there.

"Em!" He calls my name again. This time closer. "Em!"

It sounds like he's right beside me.

I push on, sprinting now, desperate to escape him, but I can't because his voice is in my head and there's no running from it.

Fighting through a moat of ferns, I make it into the clearing, dart toward the tree house, and start scrambling up the ladder. A hand grabs my foot; another hand grabs my thigh. I yelp, kick out, almost fall, but manage somehow to keep climbing.

Dragging myself onto the landing, I lean over the ledge to look down. There's no one there. I'm imagining it all. It's not real. It's not real. It's only in my head.

I dig my fingers into the wooden boards I'm lying on—like it's the deck of a storm-tossed ship—and I hold on tight, until my breathing finally returns to normal and my heart rate begins to slow.

"Em?"

I jolt upright, scanning the forest floor, my heart bashing wildly against my ribs. There's no one there. Scrunching my eyes shut, I curl into a ball and press my hands over my ears.

"Shut up, shut up!" I scream at his voice in my head.

My skin prickles as if worms are crawling all over my body, leaving dirty, slimy trails in their wake. Another nest of worms writhes in my stomach. Why? Why? Why me? a voice mumbles over and over again, but there's never any answer. I must have done something wrong. That's the only thing I know.

Exhausted from crying and shivering from the cold, I finally open my eyes. My gaze lands on a half-empty packet of marshmallows. Have the Walshes been here? Or Jake?

A rustle in the undergrowth makes me jerk around in fright. Automatically, I cower backward into the shadows, holding my breath.

Is it my parents come looking for me?

Is it Jake?

Or . . . is it him?

Emerson

With my eyes closed and my face turned toward the sun, it's easy to pretend I'm somewhere else, like an island in the Caribbean, and not one in the Pacific Northwest. Though it's at least twenty degrees too cold for the pretense to last longer than a moment.

I stand there, hearing the water lapping the shore, trying to summon some images of my other life—the alternate version, that is. The one I planned for and imagined for years. The one where I get to escape from here—from this island that's turned into my very own version of Alcatraz, only with higher walls and not even the slightest chance for escape.

When the images won't come, I give up and open my eyes. The kayak still lies in the sand in front of me like a beached red whale. Sighing, I reach for it. And that's when I hear a voice behind me.

"Need some help with that?"

I spin around.

It takes a couple of seconds for my brain to confirm that it's actually him. That it's actually Jake McCallister standing in front of me and not a hallucination. My heart does this fierce smash and rebound against my ribs as though it's been violently woken from hibernation. I draw in a breath so big it feels like my lungs might explode, as if all that air is filling a vacuum and I'll never be able to let it out again.

I hate this feeling. Hate the way the adrenaline floods my bloodstream and tears sting my eyes. Hate the way my body reacts in a thousand contradictory ways at the sight of him, as though someone has plugged me into the wrong socket and fried all my synapses.

I have an impulse to throw myself at him, but I'm not sure if it's because I want to hug him or beat the living crap out of him. I drop the kayak, my hands fisting automatically at my sides.

I watch the smile on his lips fade when he notices the set of my jaw. His expression started off wary, but now I see him swallow and press his lips together, something he always does when he's nervous.

I take note of that and at the same time notice a dozen other tiny, insignificant, monumental details about this new old Jake. I see the faded white scar on his chin—the one I gave him—and the new scar cutting across his eyebrow. Then there's his height—we were always the same height, but now he's tall . . . much taller than me. His dark brown hair is the same, though—unruly, untamed, falling in his eyes. He's looking at me with the same mix of uncertainty that he looked at me the very last time I saw him.

I glance away, down at the sand. My whole body is shaking, and I can't seem to get it under control.

"Em?" I hear him say.

My head flies up before I can stop it. No one calls me that anymore. His voice is deeper, mellower. The inflection, though, when he says my name is still just the same . . . and instantly something inside me starts coming undone. Jake always used to say my name like it belonged to him, and only him.

I grind my teeth, steeling myself, and grab for the kayak and paddle, realizing only then that I'm wearing just my bikini and wet suit, which I've stripped to my waist. The arms are flapping freely against my legs and my bikini top is gritty with sand and sweat. My hair is plastered to my head, clinging in wet strands to my neck. Great. Just great. So many times I've imagined what I would look like, what I would say, how I would act if I ever met Jake McCallister again, and the universe does this to me.

Without looking at him, I start dragging the kayak up the beach, the blood pounding in my temples almost drowning out his renewed offer of help.

I push on past him, but as I do, the end of my paddle smacks him hard in the stomach. He grunts and stumbles back a few steps, hands pressed to his abs. I trudge up the beach, suppressing a smile, feeling his eyes burning into my back.

As I shove the kayak into its rack and ram the chain through the loop to lock it up, I'm aware of him watching me, the same way he used to watch his opponents on the ice, trying to figure out their play. Well, good luck with that, I think to myself. There's no way he's playing me.

I don't know what Jake's doing back in Bainbridge after all these years, but I do know that I am not going to let him ruin my life for a second time.

Jake

Shit. That went well.

I watch Em slam the padlock shut on the rack of kayaks and then shoulder open the door to the store. It slams behind her, rattling the glass, and I wince, rubbing my stomach where Em hit me with the paddle. Was that deliberate? No. If it were deliberate, she would have smacked me around the head with it.

I want to move. I want to follow her. But I don't. I head down to the water instead and stand staring out across the bay. What was I thinking? Coming here. Turning up out of the blue. What did I expect? For her to be happy to see me? Yeah. I laugh ruefully to myself. I guess that's what I had hoped for, deep down, but not what I had expected. I always knew it wasn't going to be that easy.

Damn. I reach for the oar she left by the shore and pick it up, still feeling a little winded.

So much time I've spent thinking about what her reaction would be to me, and I never once stopped to think about what my reaction would be to her.

But there it is. All those years between us are a chasm that probably can't be bridged. And there's a mountain of lies and pain and hurt that might be impossible to climb. But the fact remains that Emerson Lowe is still the only girl who's ever taken my breath away.

Emerson

'm shaking so hard I can't get my wet suit off. After a few attempts, I lean forward over the sink and take in a number of deep breaths. Why is he here? What does he want?

There's a knock on the door, and I startle.

"You okay in there?" Toby yells.

"Fine. I'm fine," I tell him, glancing up and seeing my reflection in the mirror. I'm lying. I'm so far from fine. I look like I've seen a ghost. Which in a way I have.

"Okay," Toby says, and I can hear the deep note of skepticism in his voice. "Does it have anything to do with that hottie you were just talking to on the beach?"

"No," I say too fast, too loudly.

I hear a chuckle from Toby. "Did he want a seal-watching tour of the harbor? Because, you know, I'd be more than happy to oblige if you're too busy."

I roll my eyes and start trying to peel off my wet suit again. "No!" I shout through the door. "He was just lost. Wanted some directions."

I am not going into details with Toby. He's about the only

person on the whole island who doesn't know anything about my past, and that's the way I plan on keeping it.

"I'm going to take a shower," I say, wrestling off my wet suit.

Jake

The store is pretty much how I remember it. Walking over the threshold feels a bit like taking a ride in the Delorean and hurtling back ten years into the past.

Em's family has owned this place since before she was born. Her parents used to be in business with my uncle, though now it's just them who run it. Em and I used to hang out here a lot when we were kids. I glance at the counter, where the Chupa Chup stand still sits like a balding porcupine. Her dad would turn a blind eye to our shoplifting every time we came in.

I smile despite myself and look around, feeling a jolt of nostalgia and a wave of sadness wash over me. It's as if I can sense the ghost of my ten-year-old self in here chasing Em into the stockroom waving a fistful of seaweed in my hand, can hear the echoes of her screams, our laughter.

Kayaks are propped against the far wall, and I notice that now the store is also renting and selling paddleboards, skateboards, and even skates. I walk over to the rack of Rollerblades and smile. I wonder if she still plays ice hockey? Emerson Lowe was the fiercest player on the Bainbridge Eagles team. She could have played at the state, maybe even the national level. It's just one of the many questions I want to ask her. Along with *Can you ever forgive me?*

Even the smell in here is familiar—board wax and musty, damp wet suits. I close my eyes for a moment and take a deep breath. Other memories flash through my mind, things I haven't thought about in years: Em's mom yelling at us when we took a kayak into the bay and almost got pulled out to sea, an argument over who got the last cola-flavored Chupa Chup that left me with the scar on my chin.

"Can I help you?"

I turn around. There's a guy in a LOWE KAYAKING CO. T-shirt standing in front of me. He's about my age, maybe a little older. Midtwenties at most. Tall, blond, athletic. I try to place him, but I can't. His name tag says Toby, and I don't remember any Tobys at school with us. Maybe he's not from around here. I've been gone seven years; who knows who's moved here in that time?

"You want to try those on?" he asks.

I frown and then realize I'm running my hand over a pair of skates. "No," I say. "I'm good. I was just looking for Em." As soon as I say it, I regret it. What am I doing? I should walk away, regroup, figure out a better approach.

Toby's eyebrow lifts and a sudden thought strikes me. What if this guy's her boyfriend? I've often wondered whether Emerson was dating anyone. I had heard rumors a couple of years back but had dismissed them, not wanting to think about it. I stopped asking people for news about her when it became too painful to hear the answers.

The guy crosses his arms over his chest and tips his head toward the storeroom door. "She'll be out in a minute," he says.

I nod and start flicking idly through a rack of T-shirts, glancing surreptitiously over my shoulder at the storeroom. Should I just leave? Why am I still here?

"You on vacation?" Toby asks.

"Yeah, kind of," I mumble. "Actually, I used to live here."

"So you know Emerson, then?" he asks.

"Yeah," I admit, nodding. "Since she was born."

He appraises me with narrowed eyes and I think I see a sudden flicker of recognition cross his face. He opens his mouth to ask me another question, but I quickly sidestep him and head toward the storeroom. I'll knock, walk in there, and get everything out into the open.

"Wait, I'm not sure . . . ," Toby calls after me.

Emerson

The door flies open just as I'm stripping out of my bikini and stepping into the shower. I let out a scream.

"Shit. Sorry. Sorry." Jake turns away, spinning on his heel, flustered.

I grab for my towel. "Get out!" I yell.

"I thought it was the storeroom. It used to be the storeroom," he says through scrunched-up eyes, searching for the door handle. Behind him I can see Toby with his jaw on the floor.

"Get out!" I shout again, kicking the door shut in their faces.

I turn off the shower and sink to the floor, wedging my back firmly against the door. There's silence on the other side of it. Is he waiting for me to come out? If he is, he's going to be waiting a long time. I'm not leaving here until he's gone. If that means staying in here until next Tuesday, I will.

I lean my head back and close my eyes. Instantly, and annoyingly, Jake's face flashes in front of me. Not this new Jake. But the Jake he was back then. The Jake who was, once upon a time, my best friend.

After a while—God knows how long—there's a timid knock

on the door. My eyes fly open. I'm still sitting on the floor of the bathroom in my sandy bikini.

"Emerson?"

It's Toby. I slump back with relief. At least I think it's relief. "Yes?" I ask tentatively.

"You can come out now. He's gone."

I take that in and then laugh bitterly under my breath. Of course Jake's gone. That's his MO. He gives you the surprise of your life, tips your world upside down, and then disappears without explanation.

Emerson

(Then)

I slip out of the girls' changing room, dragging my duffel behind me. It's stuffed with my uniform, helmet, and pads, but I'm pretending it's stuffed with Reid Walsh's big, fat body and bigger, fatter, uglier head. I'm still fuming over what he just said and wishing that I'd hit him harder . . . and with the blade side of my skate too. It would have been an improvement, that's for sure.

"Hey."

I freeze. It's Jake. What's he still doing here? I was sure that everyone, including him, had left by now. I hid out in the girls' locker rooms waiting, listening to the boys as they made their way out the building, laughing and joking as they went, slamming one another into lockers. After the door clanged shut for the last time and silence finally fell, I waited another full minute, counting off the seconds in my head, before slipping out into the hallway.

Clearly, I should have waited longer. Until next Tuesday even.

Jake's gaze drops to the ground. He toes his sneaker along the linoleum, making it squeak, and then looks up at me, brushing his hair out of his eyes and giving me an awkward half smile. "I figured I'd wait for you," he says.

He's wearing his ice hockey jersey and holding his skates in his left hand. He has a sprinkle of freckles across his nose, and I focus on those because I can't look him in the eye. Straightaway, I think about those man-made coral reefs we studied in science. They build them out of wire and then shoot a low-level electric current through them to encourage new coral growth. When the teacher explained it, I remember thinking that that was exactly how I felt whenever I was around Jake: like a low-level electric current was being zapped through me.

The first time I felt it, I was so appalled I ran away from him. Then I tried to avoid him. But that's impossible. I mean, we live on the same street, go to the same school, and play on the same ice hockey team. And when we aren't skating, we're out in the woods with our friends or biking over the island, climbing trees, trampolining in Shay's backyard, swimming off the beach, kayaking, or making stunt movies together. It doesn't matter what we're doing; the fact is, we do pretty much everything together.

There is no way of avoiding Jake, so I figured the only thing I could do was ignore the coral reef electrocution pulsing through my limbs and carry on as normal, hoping that one day it would just go away of its own accord—a bit like a stomach flu that's run its course. But it didn't. It hasn't. And now everything's ruined. Now Jake knows how I feel about him.

I'm such an idiot. I stare at the ground, silently cursing Reid Walsh with every swear word I know and simultaneously wishing for a sinkhole to open up and swallow me.

"You okay?" Jake asks as we walk toward the door.

"I'd be better if Reid Walsh had never been born," I mutter, still not looking at him. What if he no longer wants to be friends?

Jake mumbles agreement. No one likes Reid or his brother, Rob, though most people aren't stupid enough to say so within earshot of them. My mom says that when God was handing out brains, the Walsh brothers were at the very end of the line. Though they'd both pushed their way to the front of the line when the steroid-infused muscles were being handed out.

Jake and I start dragging our duffels toward the exit in silence. My face is burning hotter than the surface of the sun. What must he be thinking? If only Reid hadn't said anything. If only I hadn't reacted. It was stupid. It's not like I haven't heard it before. Jake and I have been teased about having crushes on each other since third grade. We've always ignored it. So why didn't I ignore it this time? Why did I have to flip out like that?

I can't stop hearing Reid's voice in my head yelling, "You love Jake!" His fat face honking with laughter. The sniggering of the whole team is now playing on repeat as the soundtrack to my life.

I came at him like a tornado. He didn't even have time to put his arms up to deflect me. My only regret is that Coach hauled me off him before I could get a second punch in.

Being the only girl on the team sucks. But today it sucked even more than usual. I blink away the tears before Jake can see them. I don't need him thinking I'm even more pathetic than he must already.

We've reached the first set of doors. Jake holds them open for me. I accidentally bump against him as I walk through and get that stupid surge of butterflies in my stomach. I shoot them down with a spray of bullets. Why do I have to feel this way about Jake, of all people? I hold open the door for him in turn so that he can drag his bag through, and as I let the door swing shut behind us, Jake unexpectedly grabs for my hand.

I'm paralyzed with shock. Jake and I don't hold hands. We don't touch. Ever. Unless we're clashing on the ice or playing thumb wars.

What is happening?

"Em," he says before breaking off. He swallows, pressing his lips together. I notice a glimmering shard of pure terror in his eyes. I've only ever seen that look once before, when he threw himself down Toe Jam Hill Road on his BMX before realizing his brakes weren't working.

Without warning, he darts forward, and before I know what is happening, his lips are mashing against mine.

I'm so startled I don't do anything. I don't even shut my eyes. I just stare at him. Up close, his freckles form a constellation. After a few seconds of nonaction on my part, Jake's eyes fly open too, and now the two of us are staring at each other in alarm, our lips still smashed together.

It's like a car crash.

My heart has joined my lungs and gone on strike, refusing to beat. And then, with a banging stutter, it starts again, exploding in my chest like a horse at a gallop.

I sense Jake about to pull away, extricate himself from the wreckage, and finally figure out that I should be doing something. I close my eyes in a hurry and part my lips, not even sure that that's the right thing to do but hoping it's enough. Jake hesitates for an excruciating beat and then the next thing we know, we're kissing. Actually kissing, that is. Inexpertly, messily, tentatively, yet somehow . . . perfectly.

It's my first kiss. I'm pretty sure Jake's, too. And when we break apart, coming up for air like two free divers, we're both so embarrassed and awkward that we just stand there for a few seconds in an epic, end-of-the-world-type silence, both of us contemplating the line we just crossed. It's wider and deeper than the Grand Canyon and the Mariana Trench put together.

I stare down at our interlocked fingers, struck by the strangeness of seeing Jake's hand holding mine—his hand as familiar as my own, both of us with bloody scrapes across our knuckles, doing something so unfamiliar. I'm not sure what comes next, so I look at him, feeling a flush spread across my face like an ice-pack burn. He's grinning stupidly at me, and I have to resist the urge to shove him in the chest and tell him to stop it.

It's then I notice the skates hanging from his other hand and remember I've left my own skates in the locker room. They're still on the floor, where I flung them after the Reid Walsh incident.

"Oh no," I say. "I forgot my skates." Because, yes, that's the best I can come up with after my best friend has kissed me for the first time and created a need for a whole new geographical feature to better metaphorically express the enormity of what has just happened.

Jake lets go of my hand, reluctantly it feels, and I start jogging back to the changing room.

"Want me to wait?" Jake calls out after me.

"No, don't worry," I say, spinning back around to face him. "I'll see you tomorrow."

He's still standing where I left him. "The usual place?" he asks, and there's a hint of uncertainty in his voice that I've never heard before. Jake's normally so confident it throws me to hear him sound so unsure.

I nod and start smiling. I must look like a total dork, but I can't stop the nodding or the smiling. I push my shoulder against the door to the girls' locker room, glancing back one last time and catching sight of Jake punching the air with his fist.

Jake

slam the car door, and after that doesn't make me feel any better, I punch the seat. Damn. Okay. It's not that bad. It could have been worse. I try and come up with ways it could have been worse. No. There aren't any. I lean my head back against the steering wheel and close my eyes.

I can't stop seeing Em's face when I opened the door to the storeroom (which is clearly no longer a storeroom—thanks for the warning there, Toby). And it's not just her face I can't stop seeing either. It was only a split-second glance, but oh man . . . For eight years I haven't been able to get Emerson Lowe out of my head, and now I know for certain it's going to be at least another eight before I can erase that particular mental image. Maybe longer, since I'm pretty sure my brain isn't going to work that hard on the erasing.

For a moment I feel bad for even thinking the thought, for allowing myself to go there, but my mind ignores me. It's already enjoying the playback of Em stepping out of her bikini. Not even a blow to the head with an ice puck could dislodge that image.

The last time I saw Em, she was thirteen and I was fourteen.

Her brown hair was cut to her chin—"hacked" is probably a better word for it since she'd cut it herself with some kitchen scissors, claiming that the hairdresser always tried to make her look like a girl. She was wearing a red ice hockey jersey that fell to her knees, and she had scrapes across her knuckles and her cheekbone from an earlier clash on the ice with Reid. She was the definition of a tomboy back then, desperate to prove that she was tougher and better than any of us boys. Which she was. She could skate faster than anyone on the team and scored more goals that first season than anyone in the league.

Now . . . Wow . . . She's nothing like the tomboy I remember. She's not much taller, but her hair is longer—to her shoulders now—and her face has lost any trace of girlhood, become more angular, her cheekbones sharper, her mouth fuller. And those legs . . . Hell, that body. She never used to fill out a bikini—in fact, I don't ever remember her even wearing one. She used to wear board shorts and baggy T-shirts—but not anymore.

Shit. I shake my head and pinch the bridge of my nose. Emerson Lowe grew up.

Emerson

have to go," I say to Toby. "Can you close up?"

"Sure," he says, frowning at me. I know I look a mess. I haven't showered. I just pulled a T-shirt and a pair of ripped jean shorts on over my bikini.

"I told my mom I'd get home and help with my dad," I say by way of explanation. "There's no time to shower."

Toby nods at me and I see that small smile of sympathy. "It's fine. You get home," he says. "I'll see you tomorrow."

"Thanks," I say, grateful for the fact he isn't asking me about Jake, and that he's agreed to lock up for me. We're understaffed at the moment, and Toby, who's only meant to work part-time, has been working overtime the last couple of weeks as a favor to me.

"Has anyone come in and asked about the job?" I ask, glancing at the HELP WANTED note I pinned to the front door a few days ago.

Toby shakes his head.

Damn. Sighing, I grab the keys to my bike lock off the counter. "See you later. Thanks, Toby."

The whole way home all I can think about is Jake. Why is

he back? Where is he staying? How long is he staying for? Can I avoid him for however long that is? A little voice in my head wonders if I should just seek him out and confront him, but this time on my own terms. And fully clothed. And with a speech prepared. But the thought of it, of what we would need to confront, is too much to contemplate. It's not just about what happened in the minutes that followed that very first kiss, it's about what happened in the days after. It's about the fact Jake left. That I never saw him again and never heard from him either. I don't know how to forgive him. Or why I even should.

I stand up on the pedals and bike furiously toward home. Thinking about the past makes it feel as if a giant hand is squeezing my rib cage so hard that my bones are going to splinter. Jake coming back has brought all the memories of that day rushing to the forefront of my mind, and I don't want to dredge through them. I want to shove them away where they were, firmly locked up in the darkest corner of my mind. I have enough to deal with right now with my parents and managing the store.

I pull into my driveway, noting that the grass needs cutting and that the garden is so overgrown it resembles a jungle. Our mailbox needs straightening too, but God knows when I'll get around to it. No, I decide, climbing off my bike and leaning it against the side of the house, I can't see Jake or talk to him. I have to focus on the present. I don't have any other choice.

As soon as I get inside, my mom walks out of the front room with a look on her face I recognize well. Her eyes are red-rimmed and she's holding a spoon in her hand. There's a streak of tomato sauce down her shirt that looks like a gunshot wound. Without a word, I take the spoon and walk by her into what used to be the living room.

My dad is sitting in his wheelchair. A bowl of spaghetti sits on a table in a puddle of sauce.

I take a deep breath. "Hey, Dad," I say, trying to sound upbeat.

He doesn't move. He stays staring out of the window, his body contorted into that unnatural shape that, however hard I try not to think it, always reminds me of a pretzel. One arm is bent and pressed against his chest. The other hand rests limply on the arm of the wheelchair.

"You want to try this again?" I ask, sitting down opposite him and fixing on my best customer service smile. He nods at me and I start to spoon-feed him.

"How was your day?" he asks with a slur, after he's struggled to swallow three mouthfuls of pasta.

"Fine," I say. I won't tell him about Jake. I worry that hearing the McCallister name might send his blood pressure through the roof.

"Your mom's angry," he says as I spoon some more pasta into his mouth and then reach for a napkin to wipe the dribble.

"She's fine," I say. "She's not angry at you."

She's angry at life. She's angry at the doctors, who tell us there's nothing they can do to stop the progression of this damn disease, and the insurance company, who refuses to pay for palliative treatment or occupational therapy or adaptive support for the house. And though she doesn't say it, she's mad at my dad, too, for missing our medical insurance payments in the months before he was diagnosed. I'm mad too. Not least because I've had to watch my athletic, healthy father turn into a wheelchair-bound stranger robbed of a future and struggling with debt.

My dad's hand suddenly jerks out in a spasm and knocks the spoon out of my hand. Spaghetti sauce splats against the wall.

I ignore the mess and go and pick up the spoon, eyes burning.

Blinking the tears away, I sit back down. "More?" I ask my dad, offering him another mouthful.

He nods and I spoon the pasta into his mouth, trying not to think about how dependent he is on us, and how my mom is struggling to cope, or about how we're going to pay the bills stacking up in order to keep the business afloat. I try not to think about all my peers and friends who've gone away to college.

I try not to think about anything. That's the easiest way to get through the days.

Jake

The place I'm renting for the summer is an artist's studio in the middle of the woods. It's small—just a living area, kitchenette, and bathroom. There's a ladder leading up to a tiny loft under the roof where a double bed is squeezed in beneath a skylight. A wood-burning stove, grill, and two wooden chairs sit on a deck that overlooks the forest. That's my favorite thing about living here.

I slump down into one of the chairs and put my feet up on the railing, drawing in deep lungfuls of air. The familiar dank smell of moss and fern and mulchy wet soil makes me smile, bringing all kinds of memories flooding to the surface.

It's approaching dusk and there's a damp chill in the air that makes me shiver. The forest of Bainbridge is a couple hundred years old, all towering pines, cedars, and thick-trunked firs. In places the underbrush is so dense you'd need a machete to cut a path through it. We're close to the Olympic Peninsula, which is one of the wettest places in all of North America, so even in summer the island has a fall feel to it.

I don't know if it's the high of seeing Em again or the forest calling me, but within minutes I've changed into my running gear. I start jogging through the trees, letting my feet choose the direction. I know where they're taking me, and for a few seconds I consider stopping and turning around, but I can't stop myself. I keep running, sweat trickling down my back and adrenaline pumping fiercely through my body.

About a quarter mile into the woods, the track peters out and I stop, unsure of where I am. It's been years since I've run in these woods, and the old landmarks that used to mark the route are gone. There was once a moss-covered tree stump in the middle of the path. I turn around, frowning, wondering if I ran by it already, but then I spot it almost entirely hidden by undergrowth. A sapling has sprouted from the center and is valiantly pushing its way toward the sky. Oriented, I fight my way through waist-height ferns, until I finally make it into the clearing.

For a minute I stare up in wonder. I can't believe it's still in one piece. The roof has collapsed in places, the wood looks rotten around the ledge, but the tree house is still standing.

I step closer and run my fingers over the slats of wood we nailed into the tree trunk to make a ladder. They feel solid enough, but from the derelict feel and the moss carpeting the wood, it seems as if no one's been here in a while.

I climb up, testing each rung before I put my full weight on it. An injury would be just what I need. I can hear my coach yelling at me for taking such a dumb risk, but whatever . . . I want to see inside. I need to see inside.

Once I reach the ledge, I step even more carefully. The wood is so rotten in places it's the consistency of papier-mâché. One wrong step and it's a six-meter drop to the ground. For a moment I stand there, dealing with a wave of vertigo that comes out of nowhere. I remember sitting here in the dark. Waiting. Hoping . . . I'd rather forget about that, though.

Ducking low, I walk inside. Instantly, I'm struck by how tiny the place is. In my memory it was huge. In reality it's about the size of my college dorm room—that is, about as wide across as a double bed. We all used to be able to stand up in here. Now I have to stoop to avoid smacking my head.

Em and I built this place, along with our teammate Denton and Em's other best friend, Shay. It took us a whole summer, ransacking yards and the forest for discarded bits of wood and tarp, stealing hammers and nails and even a power saw from Em's dad's shed.

The place was finally finished and we were all ready to start enjoying it when the Walsh brothers found out about it. They followed Em one day when she was dragging some old sun-lounger cushions through the woods for us to use as a sofa.

"Jake and Emerson sitting in a tree. K-I-S-S-I-N-G," Reid started singing from below.

Em reached straightaway for the hammer. I had to stop her from chucking it at their heads. Knowing her, she would have managed to hit both of them with just one throw. Thinking back on it, maybe I should have let her.

After that, every time we tried to use the tree house, we'd find Reid or Rob and their crew of friends already occupying it, piles of cigarette butts and smashed beer bottles littering the forest floor below. One time we found a porn magazine stuffed beneath the sun-lounger cushions, the pages stuck together with what Em loudly hoped was glue. Another time we caught Rob making out with some tenth-grade girl.

Em was so mad she wanted to tear the tree house down,

preferably while they were both still in it. She even stole an axe from her dad's workshop and marched off down the road swinging it. I had to chase after her on my bike and wrestle it from her hands. That was Em. She'd chop off her nose to spite her face before ever admitting defeat.

But then Rob started taking football more seriously and Reid began hanging out with a guy whose parents owned a boathouse. And just like that, the tree house was ours again.

We hosed it down with Lysol before we moved back in and burned the porn magazine in a victory campfire.

I smile as I stare around at the place, my eyes catching on the markings etched into the wall. There's Denton's name, and Shay's—both scratched into the wood with a blunt penknife. I cross to the other side of the tree house. Dusk is falling and I can barely see, but mine and Em's initials should be here too somewhere.

I take out my phone and shine the light on the wall, running my other hand along it. There they are. Or rather, there they *were*. Someone's scratched through our initials, hashed them out, scoring deep rents in the wood. It looks like whoever it was used a carving knife . . . or possibly an axe.

I exhale loudly. No mystery as to whom.

Emerson

There's something about the woods, about the smell—the sweet and musty dampness—and the way the trees creak in the wind as if they're talking to each other, that makes me feel calm. After everything happened and Jake left the island, I'd often escape here. It was the only place where I felt I could still breathe. The only place where I could be alone, where I didn't have to handle the looks I was getting or hear the snide whispers that followed me wherever else I went.

The tree house was also the only place I could go and cry. If I cried at home, my mom would talk about the idea of therapy, or my dad would start marching back and forth, shouting furiously and calling down every curse known to man. The fact that it reminded me of Jake was both a blessing and a curse.

Glancing up at the tree house, I instantly know someone has been here. In the next second I realize they're still here. Instinctively, I reach down and grab for the nearest object I can find—a rock the size of my fist—my heart starting to race despite the voice in my head ordering me to calm down.

I should turn and run. That's what my instincts are screaming:

RUN! Once upon a time, my instincts would have yelled, FIGHT! But that was years ago. Now they always shout, *Run!*

But not today. It's my tree house and I'm not going anywhere. There's a loud ruffle from inside the tree house, the wooden boards squeaking as the person steps out onto the ledge.

I draw in a sharp breath and take an involuntary step backward. It's Jake. Of course it's Jake. Who else would it be? For a second, I'm relieved that it's him and not some stranger trespassing on my property, but the moment passes quickly. I'm shaking with fury. My fingers tighten around the rock in my hand.

Jake hasn't spotted me yet. I watch him frown as he runs his hand along the railing. I wonder if he remembers how we used to sit up there on the ledge, feet dangling, surveying the forest like we were the rulers and it was our kingdom. He looks down just then, sees me, and trips over something, slamming his head into the doorway behind. I laugh before I can stop myself.

"I'll do it again if it means you keep smiling." He grins, rubbing his head.

I stop laughing and scowl at him instead. "What are you doing here?" I ask. I don't want him here. This is my place. My tree house. He abandoned it. He can't just walk back in and act like it belongs to him. It doesn't. Not anymore.

"I was just out for a run and—"

"And what? There's a whole island to run around, McCallister. You had to come here?"

He cocks his head at me and raises an eyebrow. A tremor of a smirk flickers at the corner of his mouth, and I know it's because I called him McCallister—something I only ever do when I'm pissed at him. Jake always found my temper hilarious.

"Sorry," he says. "I didn't realize it was private property. Never used to be."

He has me there. I grind my teeth and take a deep breath. I could turn around and walk away, but that would mean surrendering the tree house. What are you, Emerson, a fifth grader? This is not the Walsh Wars all over again.

As I stand there trying to figure out whether I'm staying or going, Jake starts climbing down the tree. I think about warning him that there's a rusty nail on the third rung from the bottom, but I don't. If he cuts himself, it would be karmic retribution.

I watch him descend, moving fast and fearlessly like always. My legs feel suddenly elastic, my stomach jittery. When did he get so . . . tall?

He jumps the last three rungs and then turns to face me. All the air leaves my lungs at once, like someone stamping on a set of bellows.

Jake stands opposite me, studying me with a serious expression on his face. Sweat is sticking his T-shirt to him in places, and though I try very hard not to, I can't help but notice the outline of his chest and shoulders. He's ripped. I know he's a pro skater, that he's already signed to the Detroit Red Wings, but, hell, how did he get that built? He must be in the gym or on the ice ten hours a day. To say that Jake is imposing is an understatement. I drag my eyes off his chest and back to his face, but it's somehow even harder to look him in the eye.

I fix on the scar on his chin instead, and on the day's worth of beard. Neither of us has said anything for a while. I'm not about to go first, though.

"I'm sorry," Jake finally says, his voice soft.

I blink. That wasn't what I expected to hear. At all. I narrow my eyes at him. Sorry for what, though?

Jake shakes his head and looks down at the ground before looking up at me through his lashes. Goddamn it. Why does he have to look at me like that? I steel myself against him. "You're sorry?" I say. My voice sounds robotic, cold as ice. I don't feel flustered anymore, just angry—it flushes through my veins like antifreeze.

A muscle in Jake's jaw pulses. He doesn't speak. He knows me too well. This was always his play. Let me burn off my anger, then say something funny when he knew it was safe enough for me to be defused. And it would always work. Except for this time. "You don't get to waltz back into my life, say sorry, and expect things to go back to the way they were."

He stays silent, staring at me with those deep brown Bambi eyes of his, and I think I see something buried in them, something like sorrow, but it's probably just pity, and it needles the heck out of me.

"Things aren't the way they were, Jake. Things have changed." I think about my dad and swallow away the lump that's materialized in my throat. "They're different now."

I'm different now, I want to add. I'm no longer the extrovert with the big mouth that he used to know, no longer the star skater for the Bainbridge Eagles, no longer the kid who used to dare him to do crazy stunts like swim across the bay in winter without a wet suit only so he would double dare me back. I'm not me anymore. I'm someone else, someone I barely recognize.

"I just want to be friends, Em," he says. There's hurt and pain but also a note of hope in his voice, and I can't bear to hear it, so I turn my back and start walking away.

"You don't get to be my friend anymore, Jake!" I shout over my shoulder. "And you don't get the tree house either!"

There's a pause. "How about we divide it in half?" he yells after me.

I can hear the laughter in his voice. He's trying to make a joke, trying to make me laugh. Trying to defuse me. And a little voice in my head tells me to let him. To laugh.

But it's like telling a rock to speak. I can't. It's been so long since I've laughed that I've forgotten how. And why should I laugh? Why the hell does he think he can turn up and act like nothing happened?

"Okay, then," Jake calls when I'm almost out of sight. "I'm down with that. You can keep the tree house. I won't come back again."

It's as if he's thrown a stone at my back. I almost stumble, but I don't. I keep on walking.

Jake

It's stupid. It's stupid. It's stupid.

But I'm doing it anyway.

Mrs. Lowe looks at me over the top of her glasses. "Are you sure, Jake?" she asks.

"Absolutely, Mrs. Lowe."

"Well, I know you don't need—"

I cut her off. "I have to do something over the summer to keep me out of trouble. May as well be this!"

She smiles at me and when she does, I see Em in her. They have the same eyes—the kingfisher blue of Crater Lake. "Well, okay, then," she says. "We sure need the help." She glances around the store with a little sigh, but it's big enough for me to guess that the business isn't doing so well. It makes me wonder how they ever managed to buy my uncle out, not to mention how they're keeping afloat during the nine months of the year when it rains in Bainbridge and the kayaks sit empty.

I didn't recognize Mrs. Lowe at first. Her hair's gone completely gray. But she recognized me the minute I walked in the door. She even darted out from behind the counter and hugged me for about five minutes, squeezing me so tight I thought I'd need a crowbar to pry her off me. I was kind of happy for the hug, especially after the reaction I got from Em.

"Does Emerson know you're back?" her mom asks me now, and there's no hiding the note of anxiety in her voice.

"Um, yes," I admit.

Mrs. Lowe shakes her head. "That's funny, she didn't say anything."

"Well, I'm not sure she's my biggest fan."

Mrs. Lowe smiles softly, a little regretfully, and then pats me on the arm. "She just missed you, Jake, that's all. We all did."

I clench my teeth together. "I didn't want to leave, Mrs. Lowe . . . ," I say, a little more forcefully than I mean to.

Mrs. Lowe says nothing. I glance at her quickly. My throat feels dry. How can she not hate me?

"Do you think she'll ever forgive me?" I ask.

"That's what you're here to find out, isn't it?"

I open my mouth to answer her, but the door behind me pings. "What's going on?"

Em's standing in the doorway, wearing the hell out of her wet suit. She's glaring at us as though she's just caught us robbing the store.

"Why are you wearing that?" Em asks me, staring at the T-shirt I've got on. Her eyes, flashing with fury, dart to her mother.

I take a step backward. Stupid. I knew this was a stupid idea. I should have explained to Mrs. Lowe what Em's reaction was to me yesterday. But if I had, she wouldn't have said yes.

"Because I offered Jake the job," Em's mom says before I can get a word in. "He's an employee now."

Em's eyes fly to the LOWE KAYAKING CO. T-shirt I'm wearing.

I give her a massive grin, but inside I'm busy calculating my escape route.

"Listen," I say, turning to Mrs. Lowe, my hands gripping the bottom of the T-shirt, ready to strip it off and hand it back. "Maybe this isn't such a—"

Mrs. Lowe cuts me off. "Emerson, you know we need help, and Jake's perfect."

Em's eyes go scarily round. Her nostrils flare. We're entering the danger zone here. I feel like warning her mother to take cover, maybe pulling her behind the counter for shelter.

"Perfect?" Em says, her voice the sound of a whip.

"Yes," her mother answers. "You can't manage all this by yourself."

I wince. Bad move. Never tell Em what she is or isn't capable of.

"I have Toby to help."

"Toby's only meant to be part-time."

"I can work extra hours."

"You know that's not possible." Her mother glares at her, reminding me exactly where Em gets her stubbornness from.

Em's jaw pulses like it's going into spasm. I back away, remembering the damage she did to Reid Walsh that time on the ice, and there are way more weapons on hand here than there were back then. My gaze lands on a row of steel fishhooks hanging on a rack just to her left. I hope to God she doesn't notice them.

Em glares at me and I ready myself for the fury that's about to be unleashed, but . . . There's no fight in her at all. Her shoulders slump. She turns and walks off, through the open door, not even slamming it behind her. I frown in astonishment. That's the first time I've seen Em back down from a fight. Ever. Some things *have* changed, then.

"Don't mind her," Mrs. Lowe says.

"Maybe it's better if I just leave," I say, clearing my throat. "I'm sure you can find someone else for the job."

"No," Mrs. Lowe says quietly. She's staring after Em, who is visible in the distance, striding down to the shoreline. "The job's yours, Jake. Emerson will come around."

I turn fully to face her. "You think?" I ask. I'm starting to doubt my so-called epiphany that I had this morning in the shower, remembering the HELP WANTED sign in the Lowes' store window.

In my head, it sounded ideal: eight hours a day in a confined space with Em . . . She'd have to talk to me. We'd have to work things out. It might take a day or two, but eventually we'd talk and figure things out and go back to being friends.

I let out a sigh.

It seemed like such a good idea at the time.

Emerson

"Excuse me? Hello?"

I startle and look around.

The man behind me in the kayak is waving his arms, and there's an urgency in his voice that pulls me back to the present. He gestures toward the island and my eyes widen. I'm almost at the far end of the bay, paddling furiously toward open water, the shore a blur on the horizon. I smile, make a joke, and quickly steer the kayak one eighty, feeling the ache in my arms and the intractable pull of the current trying to tug me back out toward the ocean.

Tired, I lead the three tourists who are with me back toward the bay. This is my third tour of the day. I've been an automaton, pointing out seals and the skyline of Seattle, all the while unable to stop thinking about Jake and the past. But now I force myself to focus on the job, playing the role of enthusiastic tour guide, a role that doesn't fit me at all well.

I left Jake and Toby to manage the store, but I've decided I'm going to draw up a schedule that puts Jake on a different shift from me—that way, we'll never have to be in the same room together. The only thing is Jake doesn't know the tours or the spiel that goes with them, so that makes it difficult. I don't want to have to teach him. I curse under my breath, furious at my mother for putting me in this position.

As we approach the shore, I spot Jake out the front of the store helping a little kid try out a skateboard. I watch the kid fall off. Jake picks him up off the ground, grabs the skateboard, and, much to the kid's delight, executes a perfect kickback. Show-off. I taught him that. He hands the skateboard over to the kid, who high-fives him in delight. Jake takes off his cap and shoves it on the kid's head, yanking down the rim. The kid grins up at him like he's the Messiah. I roll my eyes.

We hit the shore and I jump out of the kayak, pulling on my customer service face like it's a latex mask. Everyone seems happy at least, busy taking photographs. That's something. I just hope they leave good reviews online. A rival kayaking company has just opened up in town, so I'm having to pull out all the stops at the moment, and customer service, as Toby so frequently reminds me, is really not my thing.

But it's obviously Jake's thing. The kid's dad is inside, standing at the cash register as Toby happily rings up a sale.

Jake's standing in the doorway outside the store, hands shoved deep in his pockets. He's watching me. Our eyes catch. I see the silent plea in his. For a brief moment, something catches inside my chest and I feel an invisible pull toward him. But then I turn around and grab a kayak, pushing it out onto the water, jumping into it the moment it becomes weightless.

My muscles burn from the last tour, but I push out into the deeper water and make for the headland, wanting to disappear around it as fast as possible. I don't want to feel his eyes on me.

That's what I'm constantly trying to hide from. Judging eyes. What I'm constantly running from: Shame. Embarrassment. Guilt.

Even after all these years, though I know I have nothing to feel ashamed for at least, I can't stop those feelings from crippling me. And knowing that Jake looks at me and sees a liar is too much to bear on top of all that.

Jake

(Then)

*S*he walks toward the locker room and I stand there as if Mr. Freeze has just turned me into a statue. I just kissed Emerson Lowe.

Yes!

I punch the air. She sees me do it. Good move, McCallister. Very cool. But I don't care. She's smiling at me. And it's a different smile from any of her other smiles—almost shy—which weirds me out because "shy" is the very last word anyone would ever use to describe Em.

She bashes through the door into the locker room, and I stand there, completely incapable of moving, my lips tingling. I press my fingers to them and realize I'm grinning like an idiot.

Em's been avoiding me for months, making sure that we're never alone together, dragging Shay along to everything except ice hockey practice. I worried it was because she'd figured out that I liked her and was embarrassed about it, but when Reid teased her earlier, her overreaction suddenly made all her behavior make sense.

"You want Jake's babies!" Reid laughed. "You love Jake!"

We've heard stuff like that for years—I mean, people have always teased us for being friends, and we've always ignored it. This time, though, Em launched herself at Reid and would have shaved his nose off with her skate if Coach hadn't dragged her off of him.

Em powered off the ice, face beet red, refusing to look in my direction. I watched her go—knowing she's like a campfire that needs to cool down before you can cook over it—while Reid smacked me in the ribs with his elbow and said, "Told ya."

That was when it occurred to me that maybe, just maybe, Reid was (for once in his life) right. It made a few other things make sense too, like how I caught Em glaring at Lucy Deckers just the other week when she gave me a Valentine card. And the other time a month ago, when I refused to play Spin the Bottle at a party and Em went uncharacteristically quiet, got up from the game too, and said she wanted to go home.

Em likes me. I repeat it in my head just because it's still so crazy unbelievable. I kissed her. She kissed me back. It's the most amazing feeling ever. Like the Eagles winning the championships and the Detroit Red Wings winning the Stanley Cup and me winning the lotto, all at the same time.

I'm still staring at the door to the locker room. Where is she? She's taking her time. How long does it take to pick up a pair of skates?

A sense of dread comes over me. What if she's hiding? Waiting until I'm gone because she doesn't want to face me? What if she's freaking out—regretting what just happened?

No. No, I tell myself. Play it cool. She said she would see me tomorrow at school. She smiled at me. I'm being paranoid. If she sees *me waiting out here for her like a stalker, though, she might have second thoughts. My mom's probably wondering where the hell I am anyway.*

I heft my bag over my shoulder and start trudging toward the door, slowly, looking back a few times over my shoulder in the hope I'll see Em running to catch up with me, but she doesn't.

Jake

L ooks like she's not coming back," Toby says.

"Not until I've gone, at least," I answer, scowling after the disappearing dot on the horizon that is Em. "Maybe I should go after her," I muse.

Toby pats me on the shoulder. "I'd take a harpoon gun for protection if you do," he says.

I follow him back into the store. He hops up onto his stool behind the counter while I meander through the aisles, tidying up stock. So far my plan is failing miserably. Em has spent the whole day out on the water, ignoring me. I'm starting to think it was a big mistake coming back.

"You know," Toby says now, cocking his head at me, "you look really familiar. I swear I've seen you somewhere."

I clear my throat. "Oh yeah?"

"Yeah . . ."

I angle my face away from him. "So where are you from?" I ask, trying to change the subject.

"Well, originally I'm from Bend, Oregon, but I'm studying at Washington State."

"What are you studying?"

"Architecture," Toby answers, busily tapping away on the store's computer. "You're at Boston College, right?" he asks. "What's your major?"

"Engineering with a minor in Environmental Studies."

Toby nods, looking impressed.

"Hey," I say, frowning as I realize what he just said. "How did you know I'm at Boston College?"

Toby swivels the laptop in my direction. Shit.

"Google," he says with a grin. "It's an amazing tool. What did people do before its invention?"

"Enjoy their privacy?"

"I knew I'd seen you somewhere," Toby says triumphantly, slapping the counter.

I cringe as he flicks a tab and a picture pops up of me posing on a beach wearing just a pair of board shorts and some sunglasses. Two girls in bikinis are draped over me. I look like a total tool.

Without warning, Toby jumps off the stool and runs around to the magazine rack in front of the counter. *Don't do it!* I want to yell out. *Don't do it.*

He pulls out a copy of *Snow & Skate*.

I exhale loudly. Here we go.

"Yes!" Toby cries, and thrusts the magazine under my nose. It's the same picture as on the screen, except this one is the glossy print version.

"It's really you," he says, staring between the picture and me.

I grimace. Yep, it's me. It was my first fashion shoot for a major sportswear company. They signed me a couple of months ago after offering me stupid money to endorse their product and model for them. They flew me to Hawaii and made me stand around on a beach all day posing in swim shorts, holding a surfboard. The fact I'm an ice hockey player didn't seem important. My teammates haven't stopping teasing me about it. Everywhere I go on campus, I find that picture torn out of magazines and pinned up on walls, usually inventively graffitied.

I've had girls as young as twelve asking me at matches to sign copies of *Snow & Skate* and even *Vogue*.

"Did they make you wax or are you really that smooth?" Toby asks, frowning over the picture.

"Photoshop," I say, turning my back and starting to hastily reorganize the T-shirts.

"Seriously?" Toby asks.

"Yeah. I look nothing like that in real life."

"Are you sure?"

"Yeah. Pretty sure."

"I think you need to prove it to me," Toby says, resting one hand on his hip and offering me an arch smile.

I laugh. Nice try. Toby being gay was one of the best pieces of news I'd heard all day because it meant he couldn't be Em's boyfriend.

He sighs and goes back to the counter and starts typing into a search box. Oh man. I hate the Internet. After a minute, I hear him clear his throat.

"*Jake McCallister, twenty-one, hails originally from Bainbridge Island, Washington. At six two and one hundred eighty-seven pounds, McCallister is the top-ranked NHL prospect.*"

I duck my head, embarrassed, wishing he'd shut up.

"*McCallister is on a full athletic scholarship to Boston College,*" Toby continues, reading off from the article. "*A gifted* player and slick puck handler . . .'" Toby bursts out laughing. "Puck handler?"

I grimace at him.

"'. . . with excellent playmaking skills . . .'" He looks up. "Are they talking about ice hockey here or about something else?"

I shake my head, still grimacing.

"'McCallister shows immense promise and has the potential to be a future hockey champion. The only issue he faces is a propensity to recklessness and risk-taking, which, though it's paid off in these early years of his career, may land him in trouble when he hits the big leagues next year.'"

I scowl at the rows of T-shirts. My coach says the same thing about my risk-taking. Thing is I don't know any other way to be anymore. Once upon a time I used to play with a lot more caution, but not lately—not for the last seven years, in fact.

"So how come you're back here, in Bainbridge?" Toby asks, finally closing the laptop lid. "Aren't you supposed to be training or something over the summer? Or do they let you have a break?"

I turn my back to him under the pretense of straightening up the water bottles. "It's . . . uh . . . I'm on summer break."

I'm grateful that for the moment there's nothing about the real reason for my training break on the Internet. I guess it hasn't leaked yet. Maybe it won't. Here's hoping.

"And you decide to come back to Bainbridge and take a job earning minimum wage even though you could earn millions standing around on a beach with an oiled torso."

"It wasn't that much," I mumble.

"Don't hockey players earn millions, though?"

I shrug awkwardly and turn away. He's right. They do. Most

players in the National Hockey League earn seven figures, and that's before all the money they can earn from endorsements, but I'm not about to tell him that. He's probably already Googled it anyway.

"So come on, then," Toby says, breaking the silence. "Why does Emerson hate you so much? She won't tell me."

My back stiffens. I'm pleading the fifth. Sticking to silence.

"Did you guys used to date?" Toby presses.

"No," I say with a frustrated sigh.

"But you had a thing?"

I turn and look at him, frowning. "What?"

"A thing. You know, a thing. It's obvious. No one gets this mad at someone unless they had a thing. Love, hate. Thin line. The only people I ever experience total blind raging fury at are my dad and my ex-boyfriend."

"Em and I didn't have a thing," I say. "We were just friends."

"So you never kissed, then?"

He's got me there. "Okay," I admit. "We kissed. But just one time."

"With tongues?"

I roll my eyes. "Yes. I don't really remember. I was fourteen. It was my first kiss." That's a lie. I remember it like it happened yesterday.

"Wow," says Toby, looking impressed. "I was eleven when I had my first kiss. Eliza Seltzer. She turned me gay. Or at least that's what everyone went around saying when I came out two years later."

I've lined the water bottles up in perfect formation. But now I start all over again. Out of the corner of my eye I notice that Toby has picked up the copy of *Snow & Skate* again and is idly flicking through it.

"What about Em?" I suddenly hear myself asking. "Has she . . . you know . . . got a . . ." I break off.

Toby glances up over the top of his magazine. "Boyfriend? Are you asking me if Emerson has a boyfriend?"

I shrug. "Maybe."

He makes a face at me. "Why don't you just ask her?"

"Because, in case you hadn't noticed, she's not talking to me. Besides, I don't want her thinking—"

"Thinking what?" Toby cuts in. "That you have a thing for her?"

"I don't have a thing for her."

Toby gives me a raised eyebrow. "Aha. Whatever you say, Slick."

Slick? "So does she?" I ask, feeling frustrated but trying not to let it sneak into my voice.

Toby lays his magazine down. "Depends what you mean by 'boyfriend.'"

I frown and open my mouth to ask him to clarify, but the door pings open before I can. I turn around and find myself face-to-face with Rob Walsh.

He does a double take when he sees me, his mouth falling open. He rams it shut. "Jake McCallister," he says with a snide smile.

I'm two inches taller now, and I've probably got ten pounds on him too, but even so, my memories of Rob Walsh rise to the fore and I feel a momentary spurt of adrenaline before I quickly shake it off, laughing at myself. Rob Walsh no longer has any power over me. We're not kids. There's no pissing contest happening over a tree house.

"Walsh," I say, appraising him in the same coolly disdainful way he's appraising me.

He's still flying the jock flag, wearing a varsity football shirt and his sunglasses pushed up high onto his head. His dirty blond hair is crew cut just like it was in school. He's still built, but I'm not intimidated by him anymore, because I know I'm stronger. And faster. You don't make it into the college hockey leagues and to the top of the draft prospect list by sitting around drinking beer. I train three or four hours a day. Hard. The realization that I'm more than a match for Rob Walsh is something of a revelation. A happy one.

"What are you doing back?" he asks, frowning.

"Thought it was about time," I say.

I can see Rob's having a few revelations of his own. He licks his lips dryly, eyeing me. My back straightens under his gaze. I stare back at him, unflinching. The last time he saw me I was an underdeveloped fourteen-year-old and he was an overdeveloped seventeen-year-old. People used to wonder if he was taking steroids. He was the only kid in school who was shaving a full beard by tenth grade. I barely reached his navel back then. It's somewhat satisfying to see him recalibrating me in his mind. *Do that*, I think to myself as I stare him down.

"You still playing hockey?" he asks.

I nod. "You still playing football?"

His face contorts into a scowl. "Nah," he grimaces. "Tore a ligament in my knee, second semester of freshman year." He shakes his head. "Game over."

"I'm sorry," I say. And I mean it. It's an athlete's worst nightmare. That or being busted for something really stupid and getting thrown off the team.

He nods. "I'm going through the police academy, actually. In the fall." He lifts his chin as he speaks, his back straightening.

My eyebrows shoot up and I have to stop myself from laughing out loud. Rob Walsh is going to be a police officer? That's one of the funniest things I think I've ever heard. He spent most of his teenage years smoking weed and beating people up. Then I remember his father is the chief of police here in Bainbridge. I guess it figures he'd follow in his footsteps.

The door pings again. It's Em this time. She's wearing her wet suit zipped all the way to her chin, but all it does is accentuate every curve. Even Rob notices. His eyes drop the length of her, and I feel an overwhelming urge to push him into the rack of skates.

The minute Em sees Rob, she freezes, her eyes going wide like a rabbit caught in the crosshairs, and I have to resist the instinct to step between her and Rob.

Em glances at me—is that a nervous flicker in her eyes?—and swallows before quickly ducking her head and trying to move past us.

Rob grabs her wrist and yanks her toward him, sliding his arm around her waist and pulling her roughly against his side. I open my mouth ready to yell at him to take his goddamn hands off her, but the words get stuck in my throat when I notice that Em isn't protesting.

With his eyes fixed on me, Rob lifts Em's chin up with his free hand and plants a loud kiss on her lips, his other hand grabbing her ass.

"Hey, babe," Rob says. "I missed you."

Babe? The ground rocks beneath my feet. I look between them. They've got to be joking. This cannot be true. Rob Walsh and Em? She hates his guts. I blink, trying to clear my vision, convinced I've got to be seeing things, hallucinating. Why is his hand on her ass? Why isn't she telling him to get the hell off her? Why isn't she kneeing him in the balls?

Em wriggles out of Rob's hold and pushes him away. "Get off me, Rob," she says. Finally.

Relief rolls off me in powerful waves. They aren't together, then. Of course they aren't. I almost laugh out loud. But seriously . . . the guy needs a talking-to. I'm about to suggest we take it outside, in fact, because if she won't call him out on his behavior, I will, but then I see Rob is scowling at Em.

"What's up with you?" he grunts.

Em strides past us both without even looking at me. "Nothing's up with me," she hisses.

"You weren't complaining last time I kissed you!" Rob yells at her departing back.

Em walks into the storeroom and slams the door shut behind her.

"Women," Rob mutters under his breath, seemingly for my benefit.

I turn slowly back around to face him, feeling as if I'm dreaming. He smiles at me, the glint of triumph brightening his eyes.

Emerson

What the hell is Rob doing here? Damn. I told him to leave me alone, but he never takes me seriously. This is my own stupid fault. If I stopped yo-yo-ing back and forth with him and actually told him once and for all that it was over, I wouldn't be in this situation.

Jake is out there and he thinks there's something going on between Rob and me.

And what does it matter if he does think that?

I tell myself I don't care, but I do. Just picturing Jake's face when he saw Rob kiss me . . . I bury my head in my hands as shame drenches me.

Jake hates Rob. Rob hates him right back. Maybe I shouldn't leave them outside together. I move to the door before stopping myself. No. They're both adults. I'm sure they're okay. And why would Jake even care about who I'm dating or not dating? I bet he has thousands of girls throwing themselves at him. I mean, women are paid to drape themselves over him like tinsel on a Christmas tree, after all.

I make a point of never Googling Jake. I don't have Facebook or Instagram accounts and stay off social media. But Shay sometimes lets something slip in conversation about what he's up to and how well he's doing, and when the pictures of Jake came out in *Vogue*, Shay bought a copy. I took a quick look, saw him sandwiched between two girls wearing thong bikinis, and then tossed it into the trash. And then, because I couldn't stop glancing at the trash can, I took it out and fed the entire magazine through the shredder.

I press my ear to the storeroom door but can't hear anything. Are they still out there? Are they talking? No. Don't be stupid. What on earth would they be talking about? The only thing they have in common is a Y chromosome. As I'm trying to listen, my gaze lands on the shiny new lock attached to the door.

That wasn't there this morning.

Goddamn it. It's got Jake written all over it. . . .

When we were building the tree house, he'd always do things like this, surprising me with small details he'd thought up: a cup holder he'd screwed into the railing to stop our Coke cans rolling off the deck, a hidden compartment beneath the floorboards where we could hide notes for each other and sticks of gum.

Slowly, I run my fingers over the lock, sliding the bolt into the catch and then back again. Goddamn him.

I take a scalding shower, and when I slip out of the bathroom, thankfully I find only Toby inside the store, serving a customer. He nods at me and I walk to the door and peer out.

Rob has left—his truck's nowhere to be seen—and Jake is down by the shore, bailing water out of the kayaks. He looks mad. His face is set, his lips pursed, the muscles of his shoulders and forearms are working furiously beneath his skin. I've never seen him mad before. He was always so chill as a kid.

I fight the urge to go to him and explain about Rob. Why should I have to? He never gave me the same courtesy. He just up and left town the day after we kissed, the day after it happened, and I never heard from him again. I owe him nothing.

"Toby?" I say, when he's finished with the customer. "Are you okay if I take off for a while? I'll be back to close up."

Toby nods. "Sure. Are you going to talk to Slick out there?"

"Slick?" I ask, frowning at him.

Toby laughs and points at Jake, who is still outside, scrubbing down the kayaks now, scowling.

"No," I say, turning away. "I'm going to see Rob."

Jake

finish cleaning the kayaks and drag them up the shore. I saw Em take off on her bike about thirty minutes ago. Toby told me she's gone to see Rob, and the thought of it, of her and him in the same sentence let alone the same room, doing whatever it is they're doing, makes me slam the lock down so hard on the chain that it catches my thumb.

"Shit!" I yell, shaking out my hand and cursing some more under my breath. I kick the nearest kayak, forgetting I'm barefoot. "Shit," I say, hopping now on one foot while waving my hand in the air.

"Don't take it out on the kayak. It's not the kayak's fault Emerson has terrible taste in men."

I turn around. Toby is leaning against the door, watching me.

"Sorry," I grumble. Then I shake my head. "I don't know what I was thinking—taking this job. It was stupid."

Toby doesn't say anything—he probably agrees with me.

I take a deep breath, glancing at the water, back at the kayaks, at the sign on the door saying LOWE KAYAKING CO., and then I take hold of the bottom of my T-shirt and strip it off over my head. "I'm done," I say.

I push past Toby into the store and walk over to the counter where I've stashed my bag. Giggling alerts me to the fact that there are customers in the store. I turn around. Two girls are over by the swimwear section. They can't be older than fourteen, and they're staring at me wide-eyed, nudging each other in the ribs. I turn back around, blood pounding, and reach inside my bag for a fresh T-shirt.

Toby is suddenly in my face. "You lied," he says.

"What?" I say, pulling a Boston College T-shirt on over my head and trying to ignore the girls in the corner who are now whispering frantically between themselves.

"They didn't Photoshop you."

I grab my bag and head straight for the door.

"Don't quit," Toby calls out after me.

"Too late," I answer.

I jump in my car. If Em's gone to see Rob (don't think about it, don't think about it), then that means she won't be home, so now's the perfect time to go speak to her mom and tell her I'm quitting. It was stupid of me to ever come back here. What was I expecting?

On the way to Em's I pass by my old house. I hit the brakes and crawl past, noting the swing set on the lawn. The new owners have painted the veranda a vile green color. A pang of nostalgia punches me hard in the gut at the sight of the place, but it's tainted, like most of my family memories are now. Pulling up in front of Em's house a few minutes later makes me feel even sadder, bringing with it another wave of anger. Or sadness. I don't know what it is, only that it feels as if fire ants are marching beneath my skin.

Em's house looks as worn as Mrs. Lowe. The paint is peeling, the gutters need clearing out, and the mailbox stands at a drunken angle. I climb out of my car—a Prius rental I picked up in Seattle—noticing with a twinge of guilt that Em's mom is still driving the same car she had when Em was a kid: a beat-up Ford. Her dad's truck is nowhere in sight. Hopefully, he's out. I'm not sure I want to see him again or what I'd say if he answered the door.

I knock, but no one answers, and I'm about to give up and get back in my car when the door finally swings open.

Mrs. Lowe looks flustered, as well as surprised to see me. "Oh, Jake," she says, her hand moving instinctively to smooth down her hair. "Hi. What are you doing here?"

"Um," I say, words deserting me. Yeah, I should have planned this better.

"Here, come in, come in," she says, and ushers me inside with a distracted smile.

I feel more comfortable standing outside on the veranda, but I can't say no, so I follow her inside and wait for her to shut the door behind me.

"Is something the matter?" she asks. "Emerson isn't here."

"Oh, um, no," I say. "I just wanted to tell you that I can't do the job anymore."

Her face falls. She looks at the ground, then back up at me, her blue eyes piercing right through me like a pair of knife blades. "You're quitting?"

Oh man. She sounds just like my coach. I take a deep breath and blow it out. "Not exactly," I say. "I just . . . I'm not sure it's such a good idea after all."

Mrs. Lowe studies me for a moment and then pats me on the arm. "Come on in and have a cup of coffee, Jake."

"I . . . ," I say, glancing over my shoulder at the door. "I don't know if I should." I don't want to be here when Em gets home.

"Don't worry," Mrs. Lowe says from the kitchen, where she's already reaching for mugs. "She won't be home until six."

I cross the threshold into the kitchen and stand there, hovering, looking around. There's the table I used to sit at with Em when we were toddlers, pressing out cookies, while our moms stood leaning against the counter drinking tea. There's the refrigerator that used to be covered in our finger-painted masterpieces. There's the ceramic flowerpot Em painted for her mom for Mother's Day. There's the back door that I put my hand through when I was ten and Em slammed it in my face. I still have a jagged scar running up the inside of my arm from the twelve stitches I needed as a result.

Most of the scars on my body were given to me by Em, I realize now. I'm not sure why that fact makes me smile, but it does. They're like war wounds, but all from battles that I wanted to lose.

"Sit down, sit down," Mrs. Lowe says, ushering me toward the table.

Feeling awkward and too big for the kitchen, I pull out a chair and sit down.

"You've gotten so tall," Mrs. Lowe says, smiling at me fondly.

I squirm a little under her gaze. I wonder what she really thinks of me? Of my family? She and my mom were best friends—they met at the doctor's when Em's mom was pregnant and I was six months old—but now they don't talk. There's so much I want to say and ask her, but I can't seem to find the right words.

Mrs. Lowe busies herself with making tea and I stare around at the kitchen feeling awkward. A cabinet door is hanging at an angle. Where's Em's dad?

"I've been keeping up with all your news," Mrs. Lowe says.

I look up sharply. She has?

"How are you finding Boston?"

"It's good," I say, running my thumbnail over the groove in the table where Em once tried to carve her name with a butter knife. She got to EMERS before her mom discovered her and grabbed the knife from her hand. My finger traces out an invisible ON.

"And top of the draft prospect list. That's great, Jake."

I give her a wan smile.

"Your parents must be so proud of you," she says, opening the refrigerator and reaching in for the milk. Is she fishing for information?

"Yeah," I mumble. "I guess."

"How's your sister?"

"She's okay. She just finished tenth grade."

"And your parents are still in Toronto?"

I nod.

"And your grandmother?"

"She passed away a few years ago."

I watch Mrs. Lowe pouring out the tea and I wonder how they managed to stay in Bainbridge after. How did Em cope? My face suddenly blazes.

If I were any kind of a friend, I would know the answer to that.

Emerson

Rob's watching TV in the basement apartment of his parents' house, where he's lived ever since finishing college. I walk in without knocking and find him watching ESPN. . . . Rob tosses the remote aside and flashes his alligator grin when he sees me, the smile he uses when he thinks he has a chance of getting some. I flare my nostrils at him in reply.

"Rob," I say, putting my hands on my hips and delivering the lines I rehearsed on the way here. "It's over. We are over. You can't keep coming around and acting like I'm still . . . yours."

I was never yours, I want to add.

He's on his feet instantly, his arms coming around my waist, pulling me close. My body tenses, and I squeeze my eyes shut. "Rob," I protest. "Get off me."

"Awww, babe, come on." He nuzzles his lips against my neck and I jerk away. "What is it?" he asks, frowning at me. "Are you on your period or something?"

I shove him hard in the chest and he stumbles back toward the sofa, laughing. "Guess that answers that. Why don't you go away and come back in three to five days?"

For a few seconds I stare at him dumbfounded. It's as if the veil has finally been lifted from my eyes. What was I on? What did I ever see in this person? Jake's expression when he saw Rob pawing me was the catalyst. He was horrified. And now I am too. Horrified that I ever let Rob touch me or talk to me this way.

"How can I get it through to you that we are over?" I say.

Rob smirks again. "You always say we're over. You said it a week ago and then three days later you came running back, just like you always do."

"I did not!" I yell. I need my head read. Why did I ever start dating him?

Because you had to, I remind myself. Because it was the only way to stop the noise. And because I was lonely. I hate to admit it, but it's true.

Rob Walsh made all the gossip and the bullying and the name-calling go away and he distracted me from thinking about Jake. That's why I started dating him. But why am I still dating him? We have nothing in common, and after three years together neither of us has ever said the L word. It's not that kind of relationship. I'm not sure what kind of relationship it is. One of convenience, I guess.

The truth is it felt like Rob was all I deserved. Most people told me it was more than I deserved. But comments like that were nothing compared to the nasty things hurled toward me up until then. Comments I won't think about. Can't think about. And from Rob's perspective, he probably saw me as easy, in more ways than one. He's never had to put in any effort, which was probably the appeal for him.

Rob drops down onto the sofa and reaches for the TV remote.

He turns off the game and looks up at me, his expression unusually serious. "Is this about wonder boy?" he asks me.

"What?"

"Jake. Is this about him?"

I swallow. What? "No."

He narrows his eyes at me. "Really?"

"Why would it be about Jake?"

"Because you guys were always hanging around when you were younger. You were best friends, weren't you? And now he's back and suddenly you're breaking up with me."

"I'm not suddenly breaking up with you. I already broke up with you last week. And probably a half dozen times over the last three years. It's not like this is coming out of the blue."

"Yeah, but you never mean it. We've established that."

"Stop telling me what I do and don't mean! You're always doing that."

He rolls his eyes at me, his sign for *whatever*. That's another thing he always does: makes me feel like I'm some hysterical, nagging girlfriend all the time. "So if it's not because of Jake, is it because I forgot your birthday?"

"You always forget my birthday."

"No, I don't."

My eyes roll of their own accord. "Listen, we've broken up," I say. "We're not getting back together again. Ever. Okay?"

The puzzlement on Rob's face is a picture. He frowns at me, his nose wrinkling. "Like, never ever?"

"Like, never ever," I say, feeling as if I'm channeling Taylor Swift.

He studies me for a beat, slowly nodding to himself. "I was going to dump you anyway. You just beat me to it." He reaches over and picks up the remote, switching the game back on and racking up the volume until the walls vibrate.

"Okay, then," I say, my words instantly swallowed by the noise from the TV. "I guess I'll see myself out."

I head down the driveway, feeling a weight roll off my shoulders. As if I'm Atlas and someone just lifted the world off my stooped back. Why the hell didn't I do that sooner? I think about texting Shay to let her know. She'll be so thrilled. I can picture her doing her happy dance, whooping for joy.

As I'm unlocking my bike, I hear the angry growl of an engine and turn in time to see Reid Walsh howling up the street in his truck, music pumping through the open windows. He screeches into the driveway, missing me by bare inches, and hops out, twirling his keys in his hand.

"Haven't seen you around in a while," he says in the affected drawl he's experimenting with.

"I've been busy," I say, stuffing my bike lock into my bag. There's still no love lost between Reid and me, though thankfully I don't have to see him much these days as he's at college in San Diego.

"How's your dad?" he asks.

I turn to him. It looks like he's smirking; his lip is turned up at the edge. My body quivers with rage. I step forward, hands clenching into fists. Reid feigns fright, backing into the car, holding up his hands in mock surrender.

"What?" he asks. "What did I say?"

Breathing hard and fast, I get within a step of him. My blood boils and my hand itches to ram itself into his smug, stupid face, but he's taller than me and built like King Kong.

"Don't ever talk about my father," I growl at him through my teeth.

He laughs. "I hear it's him who can't talk."

He pushes past me like I'm a piece of trash and heads toward the house, walking with a swagger that would, under normal circumstances, make me laugh.

My arms start shaking. My legs, too. Tears sting my eyes, threatening to fall. It's the same feeling I had in the locker room all those years ago. I can't move, can't speak. I'm paralyzed.

"Asshole," I finally manage to whisper as he slams the front door shut behind him.

Jake

An angry shout from the front room makes Mrs. Lowe jump, splashing boiling water from the kettle over herself. I'm halfway out of my seat, but she waves me back down with a short smile and hurries past me.

"It's fine, don't worry," she says as she disappears into the hallway.

I stare after her. More noises issue from the front room. What the hell is going on? I get up and follow after her.

As soon as I push open the door, I see that the dining room is no longer the dining room but has been converted into some kind of bedroom. There's a bed where the table used to be, and, over by the window where there used to be a sideboard, there's a small table with a wheelchair pulled up to it.

It takes me several seconds to reconcile the shrunken, gray man with the twisted body sitting in the chair with the image I have of Em's dad. What the . . . The breath slides out of my body. Jesus.

Mrs. Lowe is bent over the wheelchair talking quietly to her husband.

I hover in the doorway, unsure what to do, but then Mrs. Lowe looks up at me. "Come and say hi, Jake," she says.

She must see the look on my face.

"He was diagnosed with MS a couple of years ago."

MS?

"Hi," I say, trying to smile but aware that the horror of what I'm feeling must be reflected in my expression.

"Jake's back for the summer," Mrs. Lowe explains to him. "He's working at the store."

I shoot her a glance. I just quit, or doesn't she remember?

"Em needed some help managing things," she explains with a strained cheery voice as she fixes Mr. Lowe's pillow so it supports his head at a better angle.

"I'm just going to get a glass of water for him," she says to me, and before I can offer to do it for her, she's gone.

I stand in front of Mr. Lowe, feeling like a soldier facing a firing squad.

"Sit," he suddenly barks at me.

I'm so stunned I drop straight into the chair behind me. His words are a little slurred, but I can see the intelligence in Mr. Lowe's eyes, along with the frustration and anger that's so obviously eating at him.

"Why back?" Mr. Lowe slurs. Straight to the chase, then. That was always his way.

I feel like I'm strapped to a chair in an interrogation cell. I consider lying to him, but I can't. I look him in the eye. "I wanted to see Em," I tell him.

When my mom asked why I was going back to Bainbridge for the summer, I told her it was to see old friends. When my coach asked, I told him it was because I wanted to get back to my old training ground and reconnect with what I loved about the sport.

Really it was because I wanted to see Em. I couldn't put it off any longer.

"Hockey?" he asks next.

I nod. "Yeah, I'm still playing."

"Top prospect."

I frown in puzzlement. He would have to be following my career to know that. "Yeah," I say. "For the moment." It's as easy as sliding on ice to drop from being top prospect to being a nobody, is what I'm thinking. Just ask Rob Walsh. An injury is all it takes. Or one stupid mistake.

"You signed already?" Mr. Lowe asks.

I nod. "Yeah, to the Red Wings." I was a first-draft pick. When I finish college, I'll hopefully start playing for them. Mr. Lowe nods as if he's hearing this for the first time, but something about his smile tells me he already knew this bit of information too.

"Em faster," Mr. Lowe says now, and a bit of spittle appears on his bottom lip.

"What was that? I didn't catch it," I say, grinning.

He laughs.

"She might have been faster than me then, but not anymore," I tell him.

He nods his head, but the laughter has died. I notice the spittle hanging from his lip is still there and impulsively grab the tissue from the table in front of him and lean forward to dab it away. "Does she still play?" I ask.

Mr. Lowe turns toward the window and grimaces.

No, I guess she doesn't still play. I often wondered if Em had

quit hockey. I couldn't imagine how she'd be able to keep playing after what had happened. "So," I say after a long quiet pause,
"Rob Walsh, huh?"

I try to keep my tone light and conversational, but when Mr.
Lowe turns back to face me, there's no disguising the sneer pulling up his top lip. I'm kind of happy to see it there.

"I just—I don't get it," I say, shrugging at him.

He studies me for a long, hard moment. "You weren't here,"
he finally says, struggling to enunciate the words clearly.

I turn away and stare out the window at the wonky mailbox.
Is that true?

I wonder how long Em and Rob have been dating. I wonder
even more what the hell she sees in him. She must have had
dozens of guys after her. I mean, we're talking about Emerson
Lowe. Every boy at school was equal parts terrified of her and in
love with her. Or maybe it wasn't love. Maybe it was awe. I know
I felt all those things and more.

"How on earth did they end up dating?" I ask, though it's
more a whisper under my breath.

Mr. Lowe turns from the window to look at me. "He was the
only one who was nice to her."

I frown at him. The only one that was nice to her? Were things
really that bad? I can't imagine how bad they must have been for
Em to think Rob Walsh was her best shot at happiness. Pretty
goddamn horrific is the only answer I can come up with.

I look up then and notice Mrs. Lowe standing in the doorway holding a plastic sippy cup of water. How long has she been
standing there?

"I should go," I say, making a move to stand.

She smiles at me. The lines around her eyes crinkle. "Thanks for staying to talk." Her gaze drifts to her husband, and I wonder how many visitors he gets. He was always a really proud man—Em took after him on that score. I'm sure he hates people seeing him like this.

Em's mom walks me to the door and just as I'm leaving, she says, "So, do I need to look for a new member of staff or not?"

I shake my head at her, embarrassed now that I even came around and told her that I was quitting. They clearly need as much help as they can get, and I'll do whatever I can to not make their lives more complicated. I owe them that at the very least.

She takes my hand and squeezes it. "Thank you, Jake."

I nod, feeling a lump rise up my throat—at her kindness, at what she and Em are dealing with, at how unfair everything is.

"By the way," she says as I walk out the door, "have you been up to the labyrinth?"

"The what?" I ask.

She smiles again. "You have to see it. You'll like it. It's one of Emerson's favorite places to go."

I shake my head at her, confused. What labyrinth? What's she talking about?

"You remember where the Ollendorfs used to live?"

I nod. "Near Blakely Harbor?"

"Yes. Just go past their place and up the hill. It's there on the right. You can't miss it."

"A labyrinth?" I say.

She nods and I leave.

Emerson

After the run-in with Reid and fleeing Rob's place, I head back to the store to lock up. Toby is sitting behind the counter, engrossed in a well-thumbed copy of *Snow & Skate*.

"Where's Jake?" I say, noting that the store looks like it's had a spring clean in my absence.

Toby looks up and shrugs. "He quit."

"Quit?" I say, my blood running slow and cold at the news.

Toby shrugs and makes a face—a *what did you expect?* kind of face.

I turn away. Damn. I quickly correct myself. Not damn. This is a good thing. This is what I wanted in the first place. So why, then, don't I feel happy about it? I kick the shelf in front of me and a dozen water bottles topple off. I wish I could just quit so easily. I wish I had that option.

Toby picks up the fallen water bottles.

"I'm sorry," I say, bending down and helping him. "I know you can't keep working overtime."

Toby doesn't reply and we start rearranging the bottles in

silence. He has an internship with a top architecture firm in Seattle and college work to be doing. He can't keep pulling extra hours to help me out. "I'll find someone else," I tell him. "I promise."

Toby puts a hand on my shoulder. "You know, you could do a lot worse than Jake."

"Huh?" I turn to him. "What are you talking about?"

"For the job," he says. "He's a really good salesman. And since the tweenage population of Bainbridge discovered that he works here, we've had a constant stream of customers through the door."

"Twelve-year-olds. The last of the big spenders." I laugh, though something inside me twists painfully tight at the thought of a stream of girls passing through the store checking Jake out.

"They dig the Chupa Chups," Toby says, nodding his head in the direction of the counter. I glance over and see that the Chupa Chup stand is bald. "But where twelve-year-olds go," Toby continues, "their moms follow. We've sold four pairs of inline skates today, three skateboards, and we're all out of the LOWE KAYAKING CO. T-shirts in extra-small."

"What?" I say, astonished. We barely sell any of those things.

Toby nods. "A fact that may or may not have anything to do with it being modeled by the hot guy you just made quit. We should get new ones printed up ASAP with Jake's face on them. Or maybe just his naked torso. Have you seen it?" His expression goes all dreamy.

I frown. Yes, I've seen it. In the *Vogue* pictures, not in the flesh. I open my mouth and then shut it again, noticing the balled-up T-shirt on the counter. Toby follows my gaze. "Is that—" I start to ask.

"Yep," he says, snatching for it. "He took it off when he announced he was quitting, much to the enjoyment of the fan girls in the store. I'm saving it. Figured I could auction it off."

I stare at him in bewilderment.

"Kidding," he says, and throws it at me. "You can keep it."

"I don't want it," I protest.

"Well, if you want my advice," says Toby, "take that T-shirt, go find Jakey-Jake, and plead with him to put it back on. We need him."

I do not need Jake, so I don't go to find him. Besides, I have no idea where he's staying.

On the way home I decide to stop by one of my favorite places. It's a traditional Tibetan prayer wheel sitting inside a beautiful landscaped garden overlooking Eagle Harbor.

Right alongside the park is a labyrinth made out of stones inlaid into the ground, and when I pull up on my bike, out of breath from the uphill ride, I see a familiar figure standing at the start to the maze.

What is he doing here? How does he even know about this place? For God's sake. For seven years, I don't see hide nor hair of him, and now he's around every damn corner. Wherever I turn, there he is.

Jake hasn't noticed me yet. He's too busy studying the stones. I watch Jake start to walk the circuit, making his way toward the center, which is marked by a stone sun. I could turn around and ride off, but I'm struck by the look of concentration on his face, the furrow between his eyes, and I find myself rooted to the spot. I'm intrigued by this new Jake, by how different he is, how grown-up. I wonder if he thinks the same about me? That

I'm the same but different too? How could he? I'm nothing like the way I used to be.

Halfway around, he looks up and notices me staring at him. He falters and for a moment we both stand there watching each other, neither of us speaking. Finally, he says, "I'm lost."

"You took a wrong turn," I say, pointing him back.

He nods and turns around, following a new path toward the center. "Remember that time we got lost in Islandwood?" he says without looking up.

"Yeah," I say, stuffing my hands in the pockets of my jeans. We were on a four-day overnight program with school. Jake and I wandered off when we were supposed to be collecting pond critters. We had heard there was a really old cemetery some-where in the grounds, and we wanted to see if we could find it. But we got lost and wandered into a bog. They had to send out a search party for us.

"You were so worried," Jake says now with a smile, glancing my way.

"I was not," I argue.

He cocks an eyebrow, still smiling.

I frown, hating the way my pulse quickens in response to his smile. "So were you."

His half smile becomes a full-on grin, revealing his dimple. "I wasn't worried," he says, turning his back on me as he walks around the labyrinth. "I wasn't lost."

Huh? What does he mean by that?

"So when did they build this?" he asks, pointing at the laby-rinth.

"Last year," I tell him. "It's meant to represent the different circuits of the planets. The sun is in the middle."

Jake studies it and nods. Taking a deep breath, I try to calm myself. Being around Jake is sending me into a tailspin. I don't know whether to be mad at him still or to let it all go, to walk toward him or walk away from him. There are so many conflicting voices in my head, so many conflicting feelings battling it out.

I watch him in silence as he winds his way into the center, where he stops and looks over at me. "Where do I go now?"

"Now you come back," I say. As soon as I say the words, I look away. Looking at him is like looking at the actual sun. I can't keep my eyes on him for longer than a second. When I do dare a quick glance, I notice that he's still staring at me as though trying to figure something out. My breathing speeds up in response and my skin starts to warm under his gaze.

"I wanted to, you know," he says quietly.

"Wanted to what?" I ask, my voice hoarse.

"Come back."

He holds my gaze, and this time it's too difficult to look away. I don't know what to say, though. Is it worth even having this conversation? It feels far too late. And it's not a conversation I even want to have. If he didn't want the truth back then, why would he be prepared to listen now?

Finally, I manage to wrestle my gaze away. I turn my back and walk toward the prayer wheel. A few seconds later, I hear Jake's footsteps following. He stops an inch behind me. A shiver runs up my spine, making me frown and cross my arms over my chest.

"What's that?" Jake asks.

"It's a Buddhist prayer wheel."

"When did Bainbridge get so hippy?" His voice is filled with amusement, and it takes me straight back to when we were kids. Jake was always laughing. We were always laughing.

"What's it for?" he asks.

"You turn it nine times while saying a prayer, and then, when the bell sounds inside, the prayer is released to the universe."

"You come here often?" Jake asks, one hand resting on the bell.

I give him a sideways look and see he's grinning at me.

My stomach flips over on itself.

"Sometimes," I say, walking off. It's hard to be near him, to be close to him. Harder than it should be.

Behind me, I hear Jake start to turn the wheel.

What would he think if I told him that I come here all the time? That I ring that bell almost every day? I've been ringing it for years. I've prayed for my dad to get better. I've prayed for the business to stay afloat. I've prayed for other things too. Lots of things. The universe never listened. My prayers were never answered.

Until now.

Jake came back.

Jake

The bell rings, echoing out and splitting the silence in two. I open my eyes and look around. Em's walked off.

She's standing looking down over the water, a sad expression on her face. I walk toward her slowly, enjoying the chance to observe her. Summer has tanned her face, but she has dark bruise-colored shadows beneath her eyes that I want to brush away. Sadness hangs over her like a fog. She doesn't smile anymore. Not like she used to. How long has she been like this?

I want to bring back the old Em, the one with the dangerous tinder spark in her eyes, the wicked grin, and the manic laugh that sounded like a donkey braying. I want to breathe life back into her. Because this Em is a pale, broken imitation of the Em I once knew. Can she get that spark back, or is it gone forever? Did I help snuff it out? Or was it the sum of everything? Of everything that happened and everything that didn't? I can't help but wonder too what part Rob might be playing in her unhappiness. Every time I think about them together, I grimace and have to stop myself from confronting her about him. It's not my place.

There's a bench a few feet away from her and I amble toward

it. She doesn't follow. I sit. And I wait, wondering if she feels it too—that pull that I've been feeling ever since I saw her again. Maybe she doesn't. Maybe I'm imagining it. She's forever walking away from me, refusing to look me in the eye.

But just as I'm about to stand up again, she sits—as far away from me as she can possibly get without falling off the bench, but it's something.

"I'm sorry about your dad," I say after a minute.

Em's head flies instantly toward me.

"I went around to see your mom, to tell her I quit," I explain quickly.

Em looks away, a frown line furrowing her forehead.

"I had a good conversation with him."

She turns to look at me again, frowning this time. "What?"

I shrug. "We talked, about hockey and stuff."

"Stuff?"

"Yeah."

Her mouth tightens. What's she angry about?

"When did he get diagnosed?" I ask.

Em doesn't speak for a second, and I wonder if she's going to, but then she sighs heavily. "Three years ago."

There's a catch in her voice and her nostrils flare.

"Is there anything the doctors can do?" I ask.

Em shakes her head. "No. It's the most progressive type. It's just going to keep getting worse until . . ." She breaks off, biting her lip.

I inhale softly. Shit.

"Em . . . ," I say, trailing off. What is there to say? Without thinking, I reach over and take her hand. At once she stiffens. I glance down at my hand resting on top of hers. Does she feel the same electric heat that I do? God. I think about sliding her palm over and threading my fingers through hers. I want to do it. I'm about to do it. But before I can, she pulls her hand out from under mine and swipes at her eyes. She's angry. She always hated people seeing her cry. And perhaps I should have thought twice before reaching out to her. I have no idea how she must feel about people touching her without permission. It was a stupid thing to do.

"Can you get any help?" I ask her.

She shakes her head again, shoving her hands under her thighs. "No, the insurance company won't pay up."

"What?"

"They won't cover any home assistance. They won't even cover all his meds or help us adapt the house for a wheelchair. We're completely on our own."

It takes a few seconds for me to process what she's saying. They won't cover his medical needs? It's no wonder her mom looks so worn-out. No wonder too that Em looks so defeated. It's just her and her mom looking after her dad and the house and the business. I also figure something else out, stupidly late. "What about college?" I ask her. "Is that why you never went?"

Em turns to me, eyebrows raised, and laughs—a short, bitter laugh that cuts like a knife because it sounds so wrong coming from her, so unfamiliar.

"Who else was going to help my mom look after my dad? And besides, there was no way—" She breaks off abruptly.

"No way what?" I press.

She glares at me, her cheeks flushed. "There's no way we could afford it. My college fund went to medical bills."

With that, she stands up and starts walking rapidly back

toward the road. I chase after her. "Em," I say, darting in front of her to block her path.

"Listen, Jake," she says. "It is what it is, okay? It's fine. It's not your problem."

"But . . . ," I argue. "I want to help."

She takes a deep, angry breath in. Her eyes glance off me and out across the bay. Finally, she releases the breath. "If you really want to help me," she says, "then don't quit. At least, not until I can find someone else to—"

"I didn't quit," I interrupt.

She looks at me in confusion. "But Toby said—"

"I went around to your house to tell your mom I was quitting, but I didn't get around to it in the end."

"Oh."

"I'm not going to quit."

She nods. "Thank you. I'll put an advert in the local paper tomorrow."

"You don't need to. I can stay for the whole summer."

She frowns again. Her nostrils flare. "Okay."

What does that "okay" mean? Are we friends again? Does she want me to stay for the whole summer? Our eyes stay locked. It's the first time Em's looked me in the eye for longer than a couple of seconds, and it feels like a breakthrough of sorts. I can't read her expression, though—there's too much going on beneath the surface. It reminds me of the riptides you sometimes get in the sound, invisible fast-flowing currents churning beneath a seemingly calm, flat ocean. It bothers me. Em was always so transparent. She could never hide what she thought of anything or anyone. She was famed for her flaring nostrils and for telling it like it was. When she was eleven, she told a famous ice hockey pro who came to guest coach the team that he was "full of bullshit" after he said that girls couldn't play goaltender as well as boys because of their size.

Time stops still as we stand there and my hand itches to reach for her hand again. I try to tell her just through a look that I'm sorry, but she tears her eyes from mine and starts marching toward her bike.

I walk alongside her, aware—so aware—of her bare arm close to mine, of how much my body is trying to veer toward her—but careful not to touch her, to respect her space.

Em stops by her bike and bends to unlock it. She swings her leg over the saddle, and now I have to try not to stare at the long, lean length of her bare thighs. I fail.

"I'll . . . um . . . see you tomorrow, then?"

She nods and cycles off, but then she slows and looks over her shoulder at me. "Jake?" she says.

I nod, blood quickening, hope flooding through me.

"I'm glad we talked."

I smile. The weight rolls off my shoulders. My lungs fill up with air. Maybe there's a chance . . .

"But just so we're clear," she adds as she pedals off, "we can be civil, we can work together, but that's it. We're not friends anymore."

Emerson

I walk into the girls' locker room with my lips burning, my heart exploding in my chest and excitement bubbling through my bloodstream like an invading virus. We kissed! What does it mean? Are we still friends? Or have we crossed over into some strange new world where we're more than just friends? Are we boyfriend and girlfriend? The thought makes it feel as if a flower is blooming at high speed in my chest.

I pull up short, my smile dying. "Hey," I say, startled at the sight of a grown man in the girls' locker room. What's he doing in here?

"You forget something?" He smiles, holding up my skates.

I smile back automatically, but something tugs on my gut. All the excitement I was feeling just a second ago, thinking about Jake, vanishes into thin air. There's something odd, something not quite right, but I can't put my finger on what exactly. And then it comes to me. He called me Em. Only my friends call me Em. Adults only ever call me Emerson.

A worm of discomfort wriggles through my insides.

He's still standing there, holding my skates. I'm being stupid. Of course nothing is off or weird. He just took me by surprise. I thought everyone had left the building already.

"You want them or not?" he asks, dangling my skates like a carrot.

His smile is weird, I think to myself as I step toward him. It says one thing, but his eyes say something else. They're not smiling.

It hits me then. Did he see me and Jake kissing? Is that why he's acting so weird? Blood rushes to my cheeks at the thought he witnessed it. I don't want anyone to know. The teasing would be even worse than it is now.

The voice in my head is getting louder, saying something to me. I can make out the urgency in the tone, but I can't make out the words.

Emerson

It takes me a week before I notice what's changed. The mail-box has been straightened. It takes me another week to notice that the gutters have been cleared and the loose step up to the front door nailed down. Even then I just figure my mom has finally gotten around to working through the list of chores that has been stuck to the refrigerator door for over a year. It's only when I come home early from work one day and find Jake, with his shirt off, mowing the lawn, that I realize that he's the handyman.

I screech to a halt on my bike, almost throwing myself over the handlebars. Partly it's the shock of seeing him mowing the lawn mingled with embarrassment that he's doing jobs around my house. But, if I'm being totally honest, it's mainly the sight of him without his T-shirt on.

My inner voice yells at me to get a grip. Jake hasn't heard me over the sound of the lawn mower's engine, and my eyes linger on his back rippling with muscle and coated in a sheen of sweat. He turns, and I catch a brief glimpse of the rigid lines of his stomach, my eyes wandering to the shadows that dip below the waistband of his low-slung jeans. He looks up and catches me staring. I spin around to face the door. Shit.

The lawn mower engine cuts out. "Hey," he calls.

I dart a glance over my shoulder. He's using his forearm to wipe the sweat off his brow.

"Hey," I answer, trying to sound aloof.

"I didn't think you'd be home until six," he says.

Is that what he's been doing? Coming around when I'm not here? Why didn't my mom say anything? I narrow my eyes. Maybe because they both knew I'd be pissed about it.

"You don't have to do this," I say, gesturing at the garden while trying not to look at him.

"It's cool," he says. "It needed doing."

"I was going to get around to it this weekend," I mumble, wheeling my bike toward the house. I lean it against the garage and head up the front steps, still trying not to look in his direction.

Jake jogs up to the porch and reaches for the glass of water sitting on the ledge. I drop my keys and have to stoop to pick them up. Jake reaches for them at the same time and I get hit of the way he smells—of cut grass, and sweat and something else—something that makes my throat go dry and my stomach do a triple somersault. I stand up way too fast and my head spins. Jake hands me my keys, and when I take them, our fingers touch. My hand jolts violently, almost making me drop the keys again. Does he notice? I could kick myself.

"It's hot," he says, downing the glass of water.

I can't tear my eyes off him, off the beads of sweat rolling down his neck and glistening on his shoulders. For God's sake! I force myself to look away. I'm thirteen all over again, but luckily Jake seems oblivious.

I point at the door. "I'm going to, uh, go and see if my mom needs anything."

"Okay," Jake says. "I'll finish the lawn."

Once inside the house, I lean against the front door, my heart stuttering and starting like an old car backfiring.

"Oh!"

I jump. It's my mom. She's frozen halfway across the hallway. Her eyes dart to the front door in fright. "You're back early."

"Yeah," I say, rounding on her furiously. "What's Jake doing?"

"Mowing the lawn." She glances through the side window and smiles. Oh my God! Is my mom checking Jake out?

"He had an audience earlier," she tells me. "Little Kerrie Dean from across the road and her friends kept riding past on their bikes."

Kerrie Dean is not little. She's fifteen. And for some reason, hearing this makes me mad.

My mom bustles into the front room. I follow behind her.

"Hey, Dad," I say, stopping to kiss him on the head.

"Hi," he slurs.

I notice that there's a deck of cards on the table in front of him and a pile of quarters. Who? What? Are my dad and Jake playing cards?

"We're paying him, right?" I say.

"Who?" my mom asks.

"Jake," I say, going over and helping her change the sheets on the bed.

"I tried to pay him, but he won't accept."

"Well, make him accept it. Add it to his pay packet or something," I say.

My mom sighs and whips off the pillowcases. "Emerson, when are you going to give him a chance?"

I gather up the dirty sheets in a bundle and cross to the door. "Emerson?" she calls after me as I walk out.

I take the sheets down to the basement and shove them in the washer. I know my mom's got a point, but when I told Jake that we couldn't be friends, I meant it.

The last two weeks, I've managed to schedule it so that Jake and I only have a few afternoons working in the store at the same time, and thankfully we've been so busy during those times that we haven't had to talk.

Toby was right. Jake's presence has been good for business, annoying as that is to admit. Not only is he a draw because of who he is—national athletic champion and Bainbridge's prodigal son returned!—but he's also supernaturally great at customer service. Toby and I watch him from the sidelines in awe.

Merchandise, especially skates, seems to fly off the shelves. The cash register rings out like church bells at Christmas. I've had to reorder twice this week alone. Jake's even started doing impromptu skateboarding and inline skating lessons down at the park. Toby swears that by the end of summer he'll have his own cheerleading squad made up of both boys and girls. Kerrie Dean will probably be leading them.

I add the laundry detergent and punch the buttons. The lawn mower hums in the background, and the smell of cut grass wafts through the open basement door. I close my eyes and breathe in deeply. Jake's torso, sweat-streaked and looking like it belongs on the front cover of an erotic novel, flashes before me like a neon sign.

I have to erase it. I can't let myself think about him. At all. And definitely not in the way that Kerrie Dean and my mother are thinking about him. I'm angry at my brain for even going there.

When I come upstairs, I find my mom in the kitchen making a salad. "Oh, Emerson, can you set the table?"

"Sure," I say, walking to the cutlery drawer.

"For three," she adds.

"Hasn't Dad already eaten?" I ask. He usually eats earlier than us because he gets so tired. I'm guessing he's already asleep, in fact.

"Yes," my mom says. "I invited Jake to stay for dinner."

My hand freezes halfway to the knives. "What?"

"He's just outside firing up the grill."

I look out the window and see it's true. Jake is out in the back fiddling with the gas canister. He's put a T-shirt on. I'm both disappointed and relieved, getting used to the constant state of contradiction I feel around him.

"Are you okay?" my mom asks.

I press my lips together and reach for the extra cutlery. No, I'm not okay. I'm furious as hell that she's invited him to dinner. I don't want to sit and eat with him. I don't want to be around him. "It's just difficult, that's all," I mumble.

My mom pauses. "Have you talked to him yet? About what happened?"

I shake my head vehemently. No. No way. My mom puts her hand on my arm, and I notice that I'm shaking.

"Maybe it would help to clear the air."

I set the table, throwing Jake's cutlery down. "I know what he thinks. I don't need to talk to him about it."

It's not just that I don't want to hear his excuses, it's also that I hate conflict. I run away from it usually, or fall silent. I find it hard to articulate myself. I've learned it's easier to say nothing. Do nothing. Then people leave you alone quicker.

"I think you should," my mom says. "I think it would do you both good to get things out into the open and talk them through."

Jake strolls through the back door just then. He looks faintly bashful and uncertain when he sees me. He hesitates on the threshold, his shoulders almost the width of the doorway. "The burgers are almost done," he says.

"Great," my mom says. "Emerson, have you finished setting the table?"

I look up and meet Jake's eyes. A hot sun rises in my chest. I quickly smother it to ash.

We eat mainly in silence. Or rather, Jake and I eat in silence. My mom won't stop chatting. It's as if someone has pulled a stopper. I guess she doesn't get out all that much these days and we rarely have company.

"We got three more bookings today," she informs us.

"That's good news," says Jake, sawing into his burger.

"Two half-day tours around Blakely Harbor."

I sigh. I'm getting so tired of pointing out seals to tourists.

"I'll do them," Jake says quickly, noticing my shoulders slump. "Toby's taught me the whole routine," he adds, noting I'm about to protest.

"It's fine," I say. "I can do it." I don't want his help. I don't want to get used to it either.

"Well, actually," my mom says, giving me an apologetic wince, "they asked for Jake."

"Oh," I say.

There's an awkward silence as I push my salad around my

plate and Jake clears his throat and fills my mom's water glass.

"The other good news," my mom says, forging on, "is that we've got six people booked in for a three-night, four-day trip to Blake and Vashon next week." My mom is beaming. The longer tours are worth a lot of money. "It's a bachelor party."

I freeze with my fork hovering over my plate. "We can't do it. We need two guides for a tour that size," I say. "And Toby can't come. He has to be in Seattle next week for a conference." And there's absolutely no way I'm doing it on my own. Even the thought of being around a group of rowdy drunk guys makes me feel sick.

"I know," my mom says smiling at me reassuringly. "I thought you and Jake could take them."

"And who'll look after the store?"

"I'll manage," my mom says. "I'll get help with your dad."

"From who?" I ask.

"I'll manage," she says again, firmly. "We can't turn it down." She widens her eyes at me, a sign that she wants me to drop it. I know we need the money, so I have no choice.

"Sounds fun," Jake says. He's looking at me with the beginnings of a smile on his lips and a dare in his eyes. "Don't you think?"

Jake

The sun's barely up, but I've been at the store already for an hour making sure we've got everything we need for the trip. Toby pulls up in his car as I'm dragging the kayaks to the shore.

"Hey," he says, coming over to help.

"Hey," I say.

"You all set?"

"Yeah, I think so. Did you double-check the bookings?"

Toby slaps me on the shoulder. "It's all good. Tents will be ready when you get there, and all the provisions, too."

"Great. Thanks." I drop the oars alongside the kayaks and the waterproof bags.

We're kayaking light with just water and energy bars. It's a couple of hours' paddle across to Blake Island, a state park with a few campsites dotted around it. We're staying there overnight before crossing to Vashon the day after. Toby's been in charge of the campsite bookings and arranging supplies.

"I've put you and Emerson in separate kayaks," Toby tells me now, giving me an arch look. "I thought it was the wisest decision."

I frown at him, but he's already heading toward the store.

Once I'm done organizing the kayaks, I head into the store and find Em has arrived. She's wearing just a pair of shorts and an oversize LOWE KAYAKING CO. T-shirt over a long-sleeved top. Her hair's down, hanging past her shoulders in just-got-out-of-bed waves. I immediately picture her just getting out of my bed. She catches me staring and looks away fast. Shit. Did she catch me perving?

"Toby put us in the same kayak," I tell her.

She looks up startled, no disguising the look of horror on her face.

"Joking," I say quickly.

Is that a flash of disappointment? Or is it just plain old relief?

"Are we all set?" she asks.

I nod. "Think so."

A car pulls into the lot. "That'll be our group."

Em quickly rearranges her features into a smile as a bunch of rowdy guys in their thirties tumble out of the SUV. The first guy is unshaven and wearing a rumpled T-shirt. He holds up a hand and squints against the rising sun. It looks like they've had beer for breakfast. I step past Em and head to greet them, so she's not in the firing line.

As I suspected, all of them have bloodshot eyes and five-o'clock shadows, and three of them are clutching half-empty bottles of Bud. It's like my hockey team the morning after a big game.

"Gentlemen," I say. "You ready to hit the water?"

They cheer in answer and clink their beer bottles.

Toby hands out Clif Bars and cups of coffee in a vain effort to sober up the group. I go around and make double sure they've signed the insurance disclaimer forms. Em slips into the storeroom and comes out a minute later wearing her shorts and a blue bikini top. She pauses in the middle of the store to pull her hair up into a ponytail. I must make a sound—a sigh perhaps, hopefully not a groan—because she whips around.

"What?" she asks, a flash of defiance in her eyes.

"Nothing," I say, looking hastily away and catching Toby smirking at me.

Maybe it's best she goes in another kayak after all. If she's in front of me, there's a real danger I'll be so distracted I'll steer us into the shipping channel. I turn around and see one of the bachelor party guys staring at Emerson with his mouth hanging open like he's watching Kate Upton perform a striptease.

I step in front of him, blocking his view, and scowl until he looks away, abashed.

Em grabs two life jackets off the counter and tosses one to me. "Ready?" she asks.

"Definitely," I say, pulling it on.

She gives me a questioning look, and . . . is that the very start, the tiniest hint, of a smile?

Emerson

Because we have to sober up the clients first, we don't get to Blake until after lunch. We pull the kayaks up onto the spit. The men are still in high spirits thanks to the constant stream of energy drinks and Clif Bars we kept feeding them en route. I climb out of my kayak, gritting my teeth, and walk over to Jake, who is laughing about something with one of the clients. Seeing my expression, though, he instantly breaks off his conversation and strides toward me, his smile fading, replaced with a deep frown of concern. "You okay?" he asks.

"Yeah, fine," I say, glancing over my shoulder at the sun-burned, drooling idiot I just spent three hours stuck in a kayak with. "But tomorrow I'm in a kayak with you."

Jake stares past me, a dark look transforming his face. "What did he do?"

I glance up at him in surprise. Is he being all alpha male protector-y? I'm not sure how I feel about that. I don't need anyone to look out for me. I can look out for myself. But at the same time, there's something about the gesture that makes me almost smile.

"Nothing," I say in a hurry. "He just would not stop talking about how much money he makes and how awesome it is to be him, and how women are constantly throwing themselves at him. I swear the only place I wanted to throw myself was out of the damn kayak. He didn't shut up. Three hours," I say. "Three whole hours of him talking at me. And he has no idea how to steer, either."

"It's okay," Jake says. "Tomorrow we can put Casanova with Captain GoPro over there."

I smile and gesture at the guy in the wet suit and thousand-dollar diver's watch who's now unstrapping his GoPro camera from the special helmet he's wearing.

"The guy thinks he's Bear Grylls. He spent three hours telling me about the time he nearly got eaten by a bear while white-water rafting in Alaska right after he nearly got killed by an anaconda canoeing in the Amazon."

"Let's call Toby and get him to arrange a bear attack," I say, but secretly I'm worried. What if they think this trip is lame and don't give us a good review? Maybe I should try harder to smile and act like I'm interested in Casanova's stories.

"I'm just going to find out which are our tents," Jake says to me.

I nod, watching him as he strolls through the campsite, and shake my head in wonder. If anyone had told me even three weeks ago that Jake McCallister and I would be in charge of a drunk bachelor party and camping together on Blake Island, I would have told them they were high. But here we are. And for the first time since my mom told me about the trip, I'm glad that Toby had a conference to go to in Seattle.

That all changes when Jake comes back ten minutes later

with a very worried look on his face. I excuse myself—I've been caught by Captain GoPro, who is eagerly telling me all about the time he wrestled the anaconda—and walk over to Jake.

"Do you want the good news or the bad news?" he asks, looking nervous.

"What is it?" I ask, steeling myself.

"Well, the good news is that lunch is ready. Plus Toby ordered three cases of beer, so these guys are going to be very happy campers."

"And that's good why?" I ask, thinking of the hangovers we'll have to deal with tomorrow.

"Because hopefully they'll pass out and we won't have to listen to any more anaconda stories and humblebrags."

"Okay," I say, seeing his point. "And the bad news?"

"The bad news is that Toby only booked four tents."

I take a deep breath in. "Are you sure?" I ask.

Jake nods. "And before you ask, I checked. They're fully booked. I even had them call the other campsites. But they're all fully booked as well."

I turn to stare across the water back toward Bainbridge, visible as a blurry green outline in the distance. Damn.

"Look," Jake says. "It's just one night. It's warm enough. I can sleep outside."

I frown at him. "It's okay," I mumble. "We can share a tent."

Jake follows my lead and stares back across the water toward Bainbridge. He takes a deep breath and then turns back to me. "No," he says, "I'm not sure that's such a good idea, Em."

What's that supposed to mean? I'm about to ask him, but before I can, the bachelor comes over, wearing a neon yellow mankini. Because the bachelor is short, stocky, and hairier than a Yeti, the effect is stunning, and not in a good way, but in a stupefying, rendering-sentient-creatures-speechless kind of way.

"I have to get a stranger to autograph my butt," he tells us, swaying slightly on the breeze.

Jake and I stare at him and then at each other.

"Please?" the guy slurs. "It's a dare. I have to do twelve dares or else they're going to make me kayak naked for the rest of the trip."

"I'm not touching his butt," I say, shaking my head.

Jake sighs and grabs the proffered Magic Marker from the guy's hand. The guy turns around, and Jake and I both flinch backward. The mankini is a thong, and it's riding between his butt cheeks like a strand of yellow dental floss.

Taking a deep breath, Jake scribbles his name across the guy's butt. His friends all cheer. The bachelor walks off, unsteadily, waving his arms in victory.

Jake's right. After a lunch of grilled fish and potato salad and a dozen more beers, the bachelor partiers all crawl into their tents and pass out, including the buck, still wearing his mankini and now missing half of his back hair thanks to the others performing an experimental waxing session on him. His screams still ring in my ears.

"I'm going to take a walk," Jake says to me as I'm unfurling my sleeping bag and mat and laying them out in the tent. He pauses. "Do you want to come?" he asks.

"I . . ." I stop. I was about to say no, but something about the way he's looking at me makes the words dissolve on my tongue. There's a yearning in his eyes, and it makes a shiver run up my spine. "Okay," I say.

Emerson

(Then)

I take a step toward him, reaching for my skates, but he pulls them out of my reach. I frown and reach for them again. He jerks them even higher out of my way. I glare up at him, confused, ignoring the voice in my head that I can hear clearly now—the voice that's telling me to turn around and run out the door. To catch up with Jake.

I don't listen because I convince myself that I'm being stupid. It's just Coach Lee.

But then he strokes his free hand across my cheek. It burns as if he's pressing a hot poker to my skin. I can feel my heart beating in my throat as though it's stuck there, and I think for a moment I'm going to throw up. My brain tells me to move. To say something. To do something. But I don't move. I can't move.

He's just being friendly, I say to myself. Be polite. Don't cause a scene. Don't embarrass yourself.

He moves his hand so his thumb is resting against my bottom

lip. I shudder and turn my head, trying to make it seem like I'm not freaking out.

"Can I get my skates?" I ask.

"How about we trade?" he murmurs.

I frown up at him, not understanding, yet starting to.

"A kiss," he says, smiling, "in exchange for the skates."

My stomach drops with leaden weight to the floor. What's he talking about? He's the same age as my dad. He's Jake's uncle. He owns half the kayaking business, alongside my parents. I have known him all my life. Why is he asking for a kiss?

I shake my head.

His expression alters. It's subtle, as though a light has flickered on behind his eyes, and I don't know what it means, but I do know that I'm scared, that panic is starting to drag its claws down the inside of my rib cage, and that I'm also frozen solid and my voice has vanished.

His hands are there, on my collarbones. What's he doing? He pushes me back against the cold metal lockers. I can't breathe. Where's my voice? The combination lock digs into my shoulder blade. This isn't happening. It can't be happening. What is happening? I don't understand.

Coach looms over me. His breath is minty and also fumey—it reminds me of my granddad after he's had his nighttime bourbon. Coach's fingers are like blunt screwdrivers and they're digging into my waist. And still I say nothing. My brain has shut down. It's as if I'm watching it happen from a distance to somebody else.

"Saw you out there with Jake just now," he says, smirking. "Don't play innocent with me, Em."

His hand starts stroking my hair. He tucks a loose strand behind one ear, and I hear a whimper that I don't at first recognize as coming from me.

"Oh, come on, Em," he says in a husky voice.

Come on, what? I want to say, but before I can, his mouth is on mine.

It takes a few seconds—how many, I don't know—before I react. Finally. And it's more because I can't breathe. He's suffocating me. His hands all over me like an octopus, pushing and groping and grabbing.

I push him in the chest. He stumbles back and starts laughing, a soft chuckle that grows into a full-throated laugh. But then the smile vanishes, replaced with a heavy-lidded, ice-cold stare.

He strides toward me and I can't even scream because his hand is over my mouth and he's shoving me up against the lockers once more. My head slams against the metal, the sound ringing deafeningly in my ears.

I start to struggle, adrenaline surging through my bloodstream, but he's holding me tight and he's too strong and he starts whispering, "Shhhh, shhhhh," and I stop struggling because it's useless and because I think maybe if I do, he'll stop and let me go and I can walk out of here and pretend this never happened and everything can go back to normal. But he doesn't stop. His other hand slides beneath my clothes. His fingers—calloused and rough against my skin—start prodding and squeezing. . . .

Tears well up and start to fall. My body tenses. If I squeeze my eyes shut, maybe I can pretend this isn't happening. Maybe I can block it all out and pretend I'm somewhere else. But it doesn't work. I'm still here.

His hand crushes my mouth. His lips, wet and gross, are on my neck. My lungs burn. My vision blurs.

"Em?"

Coach Lee springs away from me as if he's been electrocuted.

It's my mom. She calls my name again, and I almost burst into sobs I'm so relieved.

I want to shout out, call to her, but I can't find my voice. I'm pressed up against the lockers, shaking. A geyser of vomit rushes up my throat, and I barely swallow it down. I have an urge to rip my skin off. Everywhere burns as though I've been stung by a jellyfish. A sharp, stabbing pain echoes through me even though he's no longer touching me.

My mom sticks her head around the door. "There you are!" she says. Then she sees Coach Lee and stops. Her smile fades when she looks back at me and sees my tearstained face. A furrow appears between her eyebrows.

"Hi, Audrey," Coach says to my mom in a totally ordinary voice.

I dare a glance at him. He's acting so normal. Did I just imagine what happened? How can he stand there and sound so normal?

"I was just giving Emerson a little pep talk. She got in a fight with one of the Walsh boys, hurt him pretty good."

My mom frowns at me. Coach Lee gives me a look and I know he's telling me to go along with it, to keep quiet. Or else.

"I told her she can't behave like that if she wants to stay on the team." His eyes stay glued to mine. "Isn't that right, Em? It's all about being a team player."

I just stare back at him, barely breathing. This can't be happening. Say something. Say something! But I can't. I can't speak. Tongue-tied. Now I know the meaning of the word.

He turns to my mom. "Well, I'd best be going. See you next week at practice, Em. And mind you work on your attitude."

My mom steps aside to let him through the door, and then he's gone and I suck in a breath and then another.

"Em?" my mom asks.

I sink to the ground as if the bones have evaporated from my legs, and my mom races toward me and catches me, sinking to her knees, still holding me.

"What happened?" she asks.

Emerson

For at least ten minutes, we say nothing to each other. We just walk in silence through the forest. I guess you could call it a companionable silence.

"I miss this," Jake finally says, throwing his arms wide and tipping his head back to the sky.

I smile, but a little tightly. You can only miss something if you have the opportunity to leave it in the first place.

"What do you miss most?" I ask as we keep walking through the woods. There's a sense of warmth flooding through me at the familiarity of being with him, of walking beside him through woods.

He glances in my direction briefly, then looks away fast. "The sky. And the trees. And the water." He pauses again. "Do you remember that time we planned to run away together and camp out here?"

"Oh my God." I laugh as the memory comes back to me. "I'd forgotten about that. How old were we?"

He shrugs. "Eight? You got into trouble at school—"

"And I was too scared to tell my mom and dad!"

"So you made a plan to steal a kayak and run away—"

"And you agreed to come with me."

"I was worried you wouldn't make it in the wilds on your own."

I turn to him, surprised. "Really?"

He shrugs. "Yeah. Plus, you had a big bag of marshmallows. I'd follow you to the ends of the earth for a bag of marshmallows."

I fall silent. Jake does too. We keep walking.

This could be the moment. I remember what my mom said about talking about what happened, but as soon as I contemplate it, my throat squeezes shut as if someone is strangling me. I know what I want to say to him. I want to ask him whether he thinks I'm a liar. I want to know why he left and never got in touch. I want him to know how much it hurt me. But there's no way I can put any of that into actual words.

"It would have been cool," Jake muses. "Setting up home here. Living on berries and marshmallows."

I smirk. "We would have lasted a night before you got hungry and made us go home."

"I would not."

For a moment I can almost hear the eight-year-old versions of us arguing, their voices echoing through the woods.

Without realizing, I have slowed down so he can catch up with me. We walk alongside each other again, arms almost brushing. "Why didn't we run away in the end?" I ask Jake.

"Your dad busted us trying to sneak a tent and a bag of marshmallows into a kayak."

"Oh yeah." I laugh as the memory comes back to me. "You tried telling him we were just acting out a scene from *Huckleberry Finn*, but you're such a bad actor he didn't believe you."

Jake laughs. I almost do too.

"What did I even do? Why was I in trouble? I don't remember."

"That particular time?" Jake answers, raising his eyebrows at me in amusement. "Who knows? Was that the time you glued Tanya Hollingsworth's hair to the back of her seat?"

A smile bursts across my face. I'd forgotten that, too. "The temptation of a hot glue gun. I put some on Reid's hockey stick too. Do you remember? His hand got stuck to it."

Jake glances sideways at me. "Remind me never to get on your wrong side."

Another awkward silence descends. His smile fades. Mine too. I think about turning around and making an excuse about needing to get back, but I find my feet are following him. Push, pull. Push, pull. I'm a magnet that can't work out its charge.

"Why did you choose Boston?" I ask him when we're almost a mile down the trail.

Jake gives me a one-shouldered shrug and a half smile. "Full scholarship. Great hockey program. Interesting choice of major."

Makes sense, I suppose. "Do you think you'll stay in the game?"

He draws in a deep breath, then lets it out. "For the moment. It's tough sometimes," he explains, "trying to balance the academic side with the athletic side. They don't cut us much slack."

"But is it what you want to do? After college, I mean?"

"I've got a contract already to play. So yeah, I think so."

"You think so?" I ask, surprised.

"I love the game. It's what I want to do. For now. But, you know, I'm not going to be able to play forever."

"What will you do after? Any ideas?"

"I don't know. I'm thinking about something like architecture, like Toby, but with a focus on sustainable design."

I nod.

"Maybe it's thanks to having grown up here," he says, gesturing at the woods around us, "among so much nature. I want to get back to it. Hockey's all about the buzz. Everything's about the kill. About winning. Out here it's just about the quiet. Winning doesn't matter so much. I like that."

"It was the tree house," I tell him.

"What was?"

"That was what inspired you to want to build stuff."

He laughs. "Yeah, it probably was."

"I guess we can share it," I say, increasing my pace so I'm ahead of him once more. "You did build most of it, after all."

He catches up to me and bumps my shoulder with his arm. "And there I was on the verge of calling in the lawyers."

I smile despite myself.

"So, what about you, Em?"

He's done it again. He keeps calling me Em. There's a piercing joy to it. No one has called me that in such a long time. I didn't want anyone to at first—insisted, in fact, that people call me Emerson—but hearing Jake call me Em, I feel a desperate sadness that I let Coach take my name as well as everything else. "What about me?" I ask quietly.

We're strolling side by side again. Jake's hands are swinging free by his sides, and I can't stop focusing on them and on his forearms, no matter how hard I try not to. There's just something about the strength in them that I'm drawn to. I can't stop myself from imagining what it would be like to be held by him. How good it would feel.

There's no more denying that I'm attracted to him. I can barely breathe whenever he's nearby; every time we come into contact, lightning tears a path through me. I can feel my pulse beating in my belly, against my ribs, in my throat. Everywhere. I remember the way he was looking at me earlier in the store when I walked out in my bikini top. Am I reading into the way he keeps looking at me? Is it possible he likes me? The thought makes my heart race—though whether that's panic or excitement, I can't tell. Angrily, I remind myself that he can't possibly feel that way about me.

"If you didn't have to stay and help with the business and your dad, where would you go? What would you do?" he presses.

"What?"

"What would you do if you could do anything, go anywhere?"

I come to a halt, no longer focusing on his hands or his arms or on the possibility he might like me. Did he seriously just ask me that question? I shake my head and march on.

Jake chases after me. "I'm sorry. I didn't mean to—"

I stop and stare at him, frustration biting at me. "It's just a stupid question, Jake. What's the point of having dreams like that? Some of us don't have the luxury of planning for the future."

"It doesn't have to be this way, Em," he says softly, almost an entreaty.

"Oh, really? Do you see another option? Because I don't."

Jake chews his bottom lip and doesn't say anything.

I exhale loudly and kick a pile of sticks lying on the ground. "I guess I'd study journalism and I'd go somewhere like Washington State," I hear myself say after a few seconds. "Somewhere near home."

"Is that because of Rob?" Jake asks. He throws it out there like a casual comment, but I sense that he's holding his breath on the answer. The forest seems to fall silent waiting too.

I make a face at him, my heart starting to beat faster. "Rob? I couldn't care less about Rob."

"But—" Jake says.

"We're not dating anymore," I blurt.

Jake takes that in. He tries to suppress a smile, but he can't, so instead he turns his head so I can't see it. Will he ask when we broke up? Or why? "It's over," I say. "For good this time." There, I've told him. "How about you?" I ask, then straightaway wince, wishing I could take the question back.

"How about me what?" Jake asks.

I shrug and look away, cringing.

"Am I dating anyone?" Jake asks.

My cheeks scald. Is he teasing me? I can't bear the thought that he might think I care if he's dating anyone.

"No," he says quietly. "I'm not dating anyone."

I shoot a quick glance in his direction, surprised at the news. He looks me in the eye. Is he a player? Is that why he doesn't date? Because he has too many girls throwing themselves at him, so why bother limiting himself to just one?

I try to shake the idea off—Jake wouldn't even play Spin the Bottle when we were kids; he'd get up and leave the room—but that was then, and this is now. I don't know him anymore. I don't know who he is. We've been apart for seven years. Look at how much I've changed in that time. Maybe he's sleeping with a different girl every night.

He's still watching me as though waiting for me to say something. He won't look away. And I find that I can't either.

Jake

It's cold. I'm used to subzero temperatures from playing hockey, but when I play hockey, I'm wearing layers and I'm constantly moving around. Stupidly, I only thought to bring a light sweater with me on this trip. Toby managed to also not book a spare sleeping bag, so I'm managing with an old, musty-smelling blanket the campsite manager found in a storeroom and using a life jacket for a pillow.

Em tried to argue with me about staying in the tent, but she sounded about as enthusiastic as a person climbing the steps to the guillotine. I said no and then went and joined the bachelor party to see if they had all they needed. They were busy covering the bachelor in layers of fake tan (I'm wondering what's next—a little tarring and feathering?). I know Em thinks I'm being stubborn. I don't know whether she's guessed the real reason I can't sleep in the tent with her. I hope not. The truth is, with her lying beside me, there's no way I'll get any sleep.

Having said that, it's not like I'm going to get much sleep out here, either. The wind has picked up and what seemed at first like a pretty cool way to spend the night—under the stars, on the beach, listening to the waves crash against the shore—is swiftly becoming a nightmare as reality sets in. It's cold. Loud. Buggy. I have rocks poking into my ass and sand in places it's going to take a jet shower to remove.

I punch the life vest beneath my head, trying to fashion it into a more comfortable pillow, and stare resolutely up at the starless sky. The clouds have rolled in, blanketing out the moon. It's pitch-black; the lights of Seattle glittering across the bay are the only sign of life, a terrestrial version of the Milky Way. There are muffled sounds coming from the campsite: a few thundering snores, someone coughing, the stag party singing off-key Aerosmith songs.

I think about Em. Is she managing to sleep? I'm lying about fifteen feet from her tent. Call me overprotective, but I wanted to be close in case anyone from the bachelor party accidentally, or on purpose, decided to involve her in one of their pranks. I've been noticing their frequent glances in her direction, especially when she went for a swim earlier in her bikini. I'm not sure she has any idea the effect she has on men, which is to literally render them speechless . . . even Captain GoPro, who fell into the smoldering remains of the fire earlier—barefoot—when Em waded out of the shallows. I even caught him surreptitiously trying to film her while she toweled off, and went over and started asking him all about his Alaskan rafting trip, putting myself through a twenty-minute play-by-play of the bear attack he single-handedly fought off, until Em was dressed and out of shot.

I think back to our conversation earlier in the woods. All day, I've been puzzling over the fact she broke up with Rob. I wanted to ask her when and why but couldn't without it being really obvious. The fact that they're over, though, makes me happier than if I'd scored a winning goal in a playoff game. I tell myself it's because she deserves better than an asshole like him, but that isn't the whole truth.

She smiled at me too. It was the first smile I've had from her since I got back. It's as if the steel door she uses to keep out the world had been pushed ajar. I'm just scared now that I'll say or do something that will make her slam it shut again.

Without warning, I flash back to the time we kissed all those years ago. I waited months for that kiss. Em doesn't know it, but three girls had propositioned me before then, one of whom was Tanya Hollingsworth—the most popular girl in school. I turned them all down. I used to walk out of parties when they brought out the bottle to spin because I didn't want to play the game and risk my first kiss happening with some other girl. I wanted it to be with her.

There was only ever Em. Since we were kids. As stupid as it sounds, even when she was six years old and I was seven and we were playing Star Wars in my backyard I never wanted to play Luke. I always wanted to be Han to her Leia. Except Em never wanted to play the part of the princess; she always wanted to be the rogue rebel Han. So I always had to suck it up and be Luke or Chewy.

A raindrop hits me in the face. I blink. Another lands on my arm. Damn. I wait for a few seconds, hoping it will blow over, but it doesn't. It becomes a full-on downpour. I jump to my feet, grab the blanket and life jacket, and head toward the bathroom block at the far end of the campsite. There's a bench outside that's sheltered by the roof. I lie down on it and watch the rain come down, harder now, enjoying the drumming sound of it as it fills my head with white noise.

After a few minutes, I catch the beam of a flashlight strobing through the campsite, and a few seconds later the flashlight lands on my face, blinding me.

"I was looking for you," Em says, breathless. She's been running.

She drops the flashlight to her side. The light from the bathrooms illuminates her. She's wearing a rain jacket with the hood pulled up and she's bare-legged.

"Come on," she says, beckoning me.

I watch her. To be honest, I can't take my eyes off her legs. The jacket barely covers the tops of her thighs, and her skin is gleaming in the light.

She stops ten feet away and glances over her shoulder at me. "You can't stay here all night," she says. "Are you coming or not?"

I get up slowly and follow after her, jogging through the rain toward the tent. Em unzips the door and ducks inside. I hesitate for a second before following after her.

Inside, there's barely room for two people to lie down. Maybe if we were both Em's size, it would be okay, but I'm about twice her size, so this is going to be a squeeze. An awkward one. There's hardly any space to maneuver, so when Em unzips her jacket and pulls it off, I find myself pressed up against her. She hastily balls up the jacket and throws it into the corner of the tent. She's wearing an extralarge LOWE KAYAKING CO. T-shirt, and when she wriggles to get inside her sleeping bag, I get a glimpse of her underwear. I turn away fast and make a show of zipping up the tent door.

When I turn back, Em's cocooned inside the sleeping bag, which she's pulled up to her chin. I lay out my damp blanket and then drop down onto it, staring up at the tent roof.

Em switches off the flashlight, plunging us into darkness. In the cave of the tent, our breathing amplifies. Neither of us says anything, and I wonder after a while if Em's fallen asleep. There's no way that's even a possibility for me. My whole body is tense, my muscles elastic bands that are stretched to breaking point. I can feel the heat of her body radiating toward me, and my senses are swimming with the scent of her—her shampoo, maybe, or body lotion. I just want to turn my head toward her and inhale.

"Are you warm enough?" Em suddenly asks.

"I'm fine," I say, though I'm not. It's cold, and as soon as she asks the question, I start wishing we were sharing the sleeping bag, and maybe some body heat too. I curse myself out silently. If I want Em and I to be friends again, I can't keep allowing thoughts like that one to hijack my brain.

"Don't you love the sound of the rain?" she asks.

"Yeah," I murmur, though truthfully I hadn't even noticed the sound of the rain pattering against the canvas roof of the tent. I'm glad for it now, though, as it's helping drown out the sound of my heartbeat, which I'm sure must be louder than the Aerosmith karaoke from earlier.

"I used to go and sit in the tree house when I knew a storm was coming."

"Yeah?" I ask, propping myself up on one arm so I can see her better.

She nods, still staring up at the roof. "I like how it drowns out everything, even the sound of your own thoughts."

I watch her, tracing her silhouette with my eyes. I'm scared to move or say the wrong thing in case this house of cards it feels as if we're building gets blown to smithereens. I wonder what kind of thoughts she's talking about—ones no doubt concerning my uncle. Is she ever going to talk to me about that?

When Em accused my uncle, it didn't even get to court. Insufficient evidence. Em's word against his. With no previous convictions, a stellar career, and character references from a number of influential people, my uncle was never punished for what he did.

He died six months ago in a hunting accident. Apparently, there was a huge turnout at his funeral. He was buried in his coaching kit. I didn't go, of course.

The Lowes almost lost their business because of what happened. My uncle owned half of it, and Em's parents cut their ties with him, walked away, and were forced to start over from scratch. I wish I could talk to her about it all, but I don't want to seem like I'm prying into her family's affairs, and I also don't want to bring up my uncle in case I trigger her. I need to wait for her to do it.

She turns her head away, sensing me watching her. There's a glimmer in her eye. Tears?

"Em?" I whisper, reaching for her before I can stop myself.

She flinches when I put my hand on her shoulder, and I pull it away, angry at myself for overstepping her boundaries. "I'm sorry."

She turns to me. "For what?"

I open my mouth to answer her and then shut it again. The question seems too loaded.

"I'm sorry I left. I'm sorry for what happened. I'm sorry for everything."

Her bottom lip starts to tremble and her nostrils flare as though she's holding back tears or anger, maybe both.

"You just disappeared," she says.

"What?"

She blinks, and her voice gets small. "You didn't even bother to ask me if it was true or to hear my side."

"What?" I ask again.

"You just left. You never came back."

She rolls over so she's facing away from me, and it's as if she's put up a force field between us. All I can do is stare at her back and replay the conversation in my head. I will her to turn around, wishing I could reach out and touch her, frustrated that we never seem to be able to get everything in the open.

Shit. After a while her breathing becomes deeper and more regular. Has she fallen asleep or is she faking it?

Letting out a sigh, I glance up at the ceiling of the tent, listening to the rain patter against it, wondering if it might have been better if I'd just stayed outside.

Emerson

I wake before dawn, and instantly I'm aware that Jake's not there. I roll over and see that I'm right. The bed is cold. He's gone. His blanket is lying discarded on the ground. I sit up. Where's he gone? Panic starts to bubble through me. He's left again. It's my fault. I should have said something last night. I should have opened up about everything and told him how much it meant to me to hear him say sorry. I should have told him I forgave him. But I found myself in the same place as always, unable to speak, unable even to find the words to voice just how I was feeling. What if it's too late, though? What if he's left?

I wriggle out of my sleeping bag and rummage through my bag for a pair of shorts, pulling them on as fast as I can.

Unzipping the tent, I race outside barefoot. The campsite is quiet in the predawn light. The bachelor party boys are still fast asleep, their snores almost drowning out the sound of the surf. I scan the beach and spot Jake at the far end, sitting at the water's edge, his forearms resting on his knees, staring out at the horizon. Straightaway, I feel a jolt in the pit of my stomach, like someone's zapped me with a cattle prod. Relief. It's just relief that he's still here. The panic that he'd left me in the night subsides, but in its place comes a dizzying wave of adrenaline.

Jake doesn't notice me approaching, and from a distance I get to study him. He's gazing out at the water with something of a scowl on his face. Even from here I can see the dark shadows beneath his eyes and the set of his jaw. It gives me pause, but my feet keep moving anyway. I try to work out what I'll say when I reach him.

He looks up when I'm a few feet away, though, and the scowl disappears instantly, giving me another shot of relief. "Hey," he says, his smile reaching his eyes.

"Hey," I answer, and sit down beside him, my legs almost giving way. I still haven't figured out what to say to him. My heart is a butterfly struggling out of a cocoon. It's only when I'm sitting beside him that I remember I'm wearing his T-shirt. It's the one he took off and left in the store. I never returned it. I gave him a new one. It was stupid. I'm not sure why I did it, not sure either why I've been wearing it every night since. Hopefully, he won't realize.

Jake shifts in the sand and picks up a stick. I watch him start to play with it—watch his hands—finding it hard to look away from them. I should say something, make a reference to last night at least.

"Have you been awake long?" I ask, forcing my gaze to the water.

He laughs under his breath. "A little while."

"Have you called ahead to the campsite in Vashon and checked the booking?" I ask, cringing that all I can find to talk about are safe things, practical things, when really I want to look him in the eye and tell him thank you. "Yeah. It's all good," he says.

There's an awkwardness to our interaction. Jake seems tense.

Absentmindedly, I rub at my neck. Jake glances over. "You okay?" he asks.

"Yeah, just a sore neck. I'll take some painkillers. It'll be fine."

He nods to himself, then moves to stand up. "I'll go see about starting breakfast."

I open my mouth, ready to say something, but then I stop myself. Instead I just nod and watch him walk back toward the campsite, aware that the ache in my shoulder and neck has now spread outward, downward, into my heart. My feet itch to run after him, but I force myself to stay sitting. It's better this way.

He's going to leave again. In six weeks' time, to be precise. If I give him a chance, I know he'll wheedle his way in. The door's already ajar. If I let him knock it wide-open, then I'm done for. I have to stay here in Bainbridge. He's moving two thousand miles away. Jake's world and my world are like two planets in separate solar systems, at opposite ends of the cosmos. We're on different trajectories. He's moving forward, heading for the brightest spot in the universe. I'm stuck here for the foreseeable future, possibly forever. If I let him in, if I get used to that feeling, if I give him that power, what will happen to me when he leaves?

After breakfast, the bachelor party lies half-comatose around the campfire, emitting the occasional grunt and groan. I've handed out Tylenol, but it doesn't seem to have made much of an impact.

Jake walks into the tent just as I'm walking out with my bag, and we bump into each other.

"Sorry," Jake says, moving quickly out of my way.

"It's fine," I say, rubbing my still-sore neck.

"Is it still hurting?" he asks, casting a quick look my way.

"Mmm," I say.

Jake frowns. "Turn around," he orders.

"What?"

"Turn around."

"Why?"

"Because you can't kayak with a sore neck, and I can fix it." He flushes. "If you want me to, that is."

"Um, okay." I turn around.

He places his hands on my shoulders. His touch is enough to paralyze me, and even the muscles that weren't locked up sure as hell are now. Every nerve in my body seems to have repositioned itself beneath Jake's fingers, so when he starts to massage my shoulders, I almost jump high enough to hit the stars.

"Wait," he says, stopping suddenly. "This will be easier if you sit. There's not enough room in here."

I sit, so wobbly legged it's more of an ungainly collapse to the ground. Jake kneels behind me. I close my eyes, feeling a heat wave travel through my body as he starts kneading my neck muscles.

Holy shit. I try to stop myself from groaning out loud as his thumb moves and starts rubbing circles over the ridges of my spine. He pauses for a moment to brush my hair over one shoulder, and my stomach constricts corset-tight.

"Is that too hard?" he asks, his voice a husky murmur in my ear.

"No," I manage to stammer. "It's good."

"This might hurt," he says, and next thing I know, he's digging his thumb into a really sore spot in my shoulder blade. I let out a yelp that's as much in response to the pain as it is to the pleasure.

"Sorry," he says.

"No," I say, my stomach squeezing even tighter. "Don't stop."

Jake keeps going, and I let out a loud groan, then laugh in embarrassment to cover it up. "Oh my God, this is so good," I say. "How did you get so good at this?"

"Practice," says Jake, and I can hear the smile in his voice.

"On whom?" I immediately ask, and then wish I hadn't as I'm now picturing him giving some oiled, naked cheerleader a full-body massage.

"I get massages all the time. We have a full-time physio on the team." Jake slaps me on the back. "There, how's that now?"

I have to stop myself from leaning back against his chest and begging him to keep going. I roll my shoulders instead and stretch my head from side to side. "Good. Better," I tell him. "Thanks."

"Yeah, no problem." He reaches for his blanket again and suddenly he's acting distant and professional. "We should get going."

I nod. The heat from his hands is seared into my skin. "Yeah," I say, grabbing my bag and following him outside.

As soon as I exit the tent, I spy all the bachelor party sitting around the ashes of the fire, staring at Jake and me with amused grins on their faces.

"You guys have a good time?" Captain GoPro asks.

"What?" I ask, my face turning the color of a ripe beetroot.

"It sounded like you were." He winks at me.

Oh my God. What is he suggesting? They're all grinning at Jake now. I even see the one with glasses, the one we've nick-named Clark Kent because his skinny frame belies a secret athletic prowess and abs of steel, give Jake a sly thumbs-up. I spin on my heel, bumping into Jake in my haste to get away. They clearly think we were just . . . oh God . . . I rush toward the kayaks, ignoring the laughter that follows me.

A few minutes later, as I'm readying the kayaks, still fuming with embarrassment, Jake comes over. He helps me tip the kayak over to empty out the rainwater that's collected in it overnight. "I set them straight," he says, without looking at me.

I make a mumbling sound at the back of my throat.

"So you still want to paddle with me today?" he asks.

"Um," I say. I'm not sure anymore. I do and I don't. There's that contradiction thing again.

"It might be better," Jake says, finally meeting my eye. "That way you can rest if your neck starts to bother you."

I raise my eyebrows. As if I'm letting him paddle for the two of us. "I'll be okay," I tell him.

Jake nods and moves to the second kayak, rolling it onto its side.

"But yeah," I say. "Maybe it's best we stick together."

Jake

There are bikes ready for us at the rental place near the harbor. It's a twenty-minute ride from there over to the campsite where we're staying on Vashon. The men all seem in fairly good spirits thanks to the coffee they've just drunk, which I suspect they may have laced with something stronger than milk.

Em and I ride along at the front, side by side. It reminds me of old times, when we were kids and Bainbridge Island was our adventure playground.

"You remember Toe Jam Hill?" I ask her.

Em looks over at me, grinning, and the sight of that grin makes me almost swerve into a ditch. "I remember the blood." She smirks.

We're holding each other's gaze, and I find myself weaving toward her across the road on my bike, almost knocking into her.

"Watch it, Slick," she says, braking to avoid me.

"Slick?" I ask as she pedals back alongside me again before speeding past. I smile to myself. She always had to be in the lead. She grins at me once more over her shoulder.

"I'm going to kill Toby," I say, standing up on the pedals to increase my speed. Damn him for kick-starting that whole nickname.

"It has a good ring to it, though, don't you think? Slick."

"No," I say, pushing level with her. "I never want to hear it from your lips again."

"Or what?" Em asks. Now we're racing each other. Beads of sweat appear on Em's shoulders and neck, and I'm instantly swamped with images of pinning her to the ground and tickling her until she declares she'll never say that word again. "Or I'll put you in a kayak tomorrow with the bachelor."

She laughs. Finally. She laughs. Not quite a braying donkey sound, but I'll take it. "How many dares are there left to go?" she asks, nodding her head at the buck.

"About eight."

We both shake our heads. The poor guy is the color of an Oompa Loompa after the fake tanning session last night. He's orange all over except for the patch on his lower back where they used masking tape to spell out the words KICK ME.

"Do you think he'll make it down the aisle?" Em asks.

"Yeah, but I'm not sure his fiancée will agree to marry him if he's still that color. Does that stuff wash off?"

We keep talking, laughing about the dares they've made him do and speculating on what more possible humiliation lies ahead for him. Then we get to chatting about the dares we used to put each other through: swimming across Eagle Harbor in January without a wet suit, riding down the almost vertical Toe Jam Hill Road on our bikes—first to hit the brakes the loser. Em laughs as I point out the scar on my knee. I argue that I still won the bet.

She asks me how I got the scar through my eyebrow, and I tell her I had a run-in with a stick last year on the ice. A stick attached to the number two on the draft prospect list—a Finnish guy called Koskela. Things at college level get way more violent than they used to when she and I both played for the Eagles. But then I remember the way Em tackled Reid that time and reconsider. Maybe Koskela could learn a thing or two from her.

The conversations we had yesterday seem to have changed something between Em and me. Even though she still hasn't said anything or acknowledged my apology, she's looser, more open. She's smiling! And laughing. This is progress.

Maybe I'm imagining it, but I also feel like there might be something more there too. I know I haven't stopped feeling it: this faint buzzing around my sternum, a bruising kick to the gut every time I catch her looking at me, a sharp hit of adrenaline straight to my bloodstream each time she gives one of her rare smiles. I'm not going to risk ruining things by trying to talk to her again about what happened.

She told me she broke up with Rob, and that has to mean something. I don't want to get my hopes up, and I really don't want to mess things up with her just as our friendship is starting to heal . . . but the fact remains that whenever Em and I are within reaching distance of each other, all I want to do is pull her into my arms. All I'm aware of the entire time she's around me, is her. She's not even a distraction, she's the sole object of my attention. And a day ago, I thought it was just me who felt this way, but now I'm not so sure. It's like being fourteen all over again, wondering if I should kiss her, tell her how I feel, risk . . . everything.

"I'm going to check on the tent situation," Em tells me when we get to the campsite.

As I watch her walk toward the reception area, blowing her hair out of her face and wiping at the sweat on her forehead, I get that same gut-twisting feeling I catch right before a game: a mix of excitement and apprehension about what's possibly to come.

"So are you guys, you know, an item?" the fifth member of the bachelor party asks. This guy we've nicknamed Thor because even though he's not particularly tall and not in the least bit godlike, at the last campsite he spent a long time trying to impress a group of female campers by hammering in their tent pegs with a wooden mallet.

"What?" I ask, turning to him.

Thor nods his head in the direction of Em.

"Er . . . ," I say.

"Because if she isn't your girlfriend, then you need to up your game," he tells me, slapping me on the shoulder.

"Thanks for the advice," I tell him, walking off before he can offer any more suggestions on my game.

The campground covers over a hundred acres: teepees and cabins dotted throughout woods and meadows. It would be the ideal place for a romantic weekend away. I laugh under my breath and think back to last night and being squeezed into a damp tent with Em. At least tonight I should get some sleep—that's one thing.

But within two seconds of seeing Em return from the reception area, I have a feeling that that's not going to be the case. She strides toward me wearing a face like thunder. When they see her marching toward us, even the bachelor party, who are all busy raiding the store's snack bar selection, fall silent like school kids caught stealing.

"Don't tell me," I say when Em stops in front of me, hands on hips. "Toby forgot to book enough tents."

She nods, grimacing, and I take her elbow and steer her away from the bachelor boys.

"What the hell is he up to?" she hisses.

I bite my lip. I think it's pretty clear what Toby's up to. He's done this on purpose. And the reason is so obvious I wonder how Em can't have figured it out.

"They can't be fully booked," I say, making a move toward the reception area. There has to be a way to fix this.

"I checked and double-checked," Em says, stopping me. "Apparently, they had two last-minute bookings."

I turn back to her, all out of ideas. "Why don't you catch the last ferry back to Bainbridge?" I say. "I can get the group back tomorrow by myself. Your shoulder's hurting anyway."

Em frowns and shakes her head at me. "It's fine," she says, and I'm not sure if she's talking about her shoulder or the tent situation.

"The bachelor party has the cabin," she says. "We've got the fire teepee."

"A fire teepee?"

Em looks at me with an expression I remember from when she was a kid and was deeply unimpressed by something—usually a losing result at a hockey match, a bad draw in the opposing team, or Reid Walsh's existence.

"It's the honeymoon teepee," she mumbles, not meeting my eye.

"What, do they scatter rose petals across the bed?" I ask, laughing. "Do we get a fruit basket and a bottle of champagne?"

"I don't want to know," Em says, her hands fisted at her sides. "I'm going to kill Toby."

"Em, I can sleep outside," I say. "It's fine—"

"Jake?" she interrupts.

"Yeah?"

"Shut up."

I nod, trying not to smile. It's the old Em. Right there. Standing in front of me. At long last.

"Okay," I say. "I'll show the guys where the cabin is and get them fixed up for the afternoon. Tell me, Toby did at least organize that part?"

Em nods. "Yeah. The wilderness expert will be here at three."

I shake my head. "Good, because I do not feel like standing in and teaching these guys how to make fire."

"Don't they need opposable thumbs for that anyway?" Em asks.

I glance sideways at her. "Did you just make a joke?"

Em looks away, a flush creeping over her sunburned cheeks.

"I knew the old Em was in there somewhere," I say.

"Don't get too used to it," she mutters, and walks off. But she's still smiling. I can tell.

Emerson

I watch Jake's eyes widen as he enters the tent. He stops dead in the doorway and takes in the bed, scattered with red silk cushions and a half-dozen throws, including a faux fur one. His gaze falls next on the twinkling lights they've strung around the inside of the tent, before moving on to the fire pit in the middle where logs have already been laid in preparation for the night. He doesn't, however, look at me, which is good because I'm struggling very hard to strike a casual yet cool pose.

"Wow," Jake says, his eyes settling again on the double bed. There's a shadow of alarm on his face that he hurries to hide.

"I tried calling Toby," I tell him. "I can't get through. There's no signal."

Jake gives me a look. I know what he's thinking. Because I'm thinking it too. Toby set this up. And I'm going to kill him when I get back.

Jake tosses his bag to the ground and then bends to pull something out of it. It's a bag of marshmallows. He gives me a tentative half smile, one meant to break the tension, and I can't help but smile back.

"You remembered," I say.

"Of course," Jake murmurs.

He hands me the bag and for a brief second our fingers touch and I wonder if he feels it too—the small jolt of electricity that zings up my arm. Does the lightning feel the shock in the same way that the earth does? Or is it all one-sided?

While the bachelor party is off on their foraging and wilderness skills course, Jake takes a nap.

I sit outside the tent and try to write while he sleeps, though my attention won't stay on the page and every so often I look over my shoulder through the open door of the tent and catch myself staring at him. He's sleeping on his front, with his head turned in my direction, his hair flopping into his eyes. He isn't wearing a T-shirt, and I let my eyes linger for way too long on his bare shoulders and back. I still can't get used to seeing this new Jake—all muscle, tight sinew, stubble—and I can't stop myself from thinking about what it would be like to stroke my hand over his skin.

My phone vibrates, startling me, and I quickly pull it out of my pocket. It's Shay.

How's it goin'? she asks.

Good.

How r things with Jake? she asks, and I know she's digging. We had a conversation last week where I told her everything, including my breakup with Rob, which as predicted, made her break out the happy dance.

I hesitate, unsure what to tell her about Jake and me. I settle on **OK.**

?

My stomach squirms. My fingers hover over the keys. I turn my phone off and shove it back in my pocket. I don't want to lie to my best friend, but I don't know what to tell her. Shay was never a fan of Rob, but she's not exactly a fan of Jake's, either.

I wish I could allow myself to fall for him. Too late, I think to myself ruefully. Permission doesn't come into it. I already have fallen for him. I fell for him a long time ago, years ago, in fact, and when you fall that hard, you never really get back on your feet.

My eyes scan the few lines I've managed to write in my notebook, determined to focus on that, but it's all a blur. It may as well be written in Mandarin. Writing has always been my escape. Though I always struggle to formulate the words I want to speak out loud to people, somehow when I pick up a pen and put it to paper, the words appear, as if the pen is some magical catalyst that's doing the thinking for me.

But not today. The words won't fall onto the paper. The sheet stays blank, and when I try to focus, I can't. All that fills my head is Jake. All I'm aware of is him lying behind me asleep, and the growing desire I have to walk over there, lie down beside him, and just rest there with my head on his shoulder.

Jake

(Then)

I don't sleep, and I'm early to school the next day. My stomach has shrunk to the size of a raisin. I couldn't even manage a slice of toast for breakfast. My mom almost kept me home, she was so concerned at this unusual loss of appetite. I wonder if maybe I am sick. My stomach doesn't feel too good and my palms are sweating as if I have the plague.

However, I also recognize these symptoms. I get the same way before a big game. Which means it's likely nerves. Or excitement. Possibly both.

I wait by the gym, where I always meet Em before first period. I've got my basketball with me, and I lean against the wall with it tucked under my arm, but I feel self-conscious all of a sudden. Awkward. I rearrange my stance, straighten my T-shirt, and run through what I want to say to Em when she gets here. I was awake most of the night rehearsing it, when I wasn't running action replays of the kiss, that is.

I get a lurch in my chest as my brain does yet another replay. It's followed swiftly by another lurch—this one more like the feeling I had when I failed to score a penalty in our last game and we lost. What if she didn't like it? What if she was just being polite? What if she told me she'd forgotten her skates just to get away from me? What if she doesn't want to be friends anymore? I'll be straight-up honest, tell her how I feel but give her an out. If she just wants to be friends, then we'll just be friends. I can do that.

I think.

I glance at my watch, anxious. She's late. Em's never late.

Denton and Shay round the corner of the gym as I'm frowning at my watch.

"Hey," Denton says, nodding at the ball in my hands, "you want to shoot some hoops?"

I shake my head at him, wondering how I can get them to leave without being rude. I can't talk to Em with an audience.

"Okay," Denton says, looking at me oddly.

"Why are you standing like that?" Shay asks, giving me side-eye.

"Like what?"

"Like you're posing for a Calvin Klein ad."

"I'm not," I say, shifting positions as casually as I can.

Shay smirks at me. "Are you waiting for Em?"

She knows. Damn. She knows. Blood rushes to my face. I shrug, aiming for nonchalant. Did Em talk to her last night and tell her what happened?

Shay starts rooting through her bag. She doesn't say anything else. Maybe Em didn't tell her after all. I'm fairly sure that if she had, Shay would be ribbing me about it.

"I gotta go," she says. "I have a book to return to the library." She pushes her glasses up her nose and rushes off.

"Bye!" Denton shouts after her. "See you at lunch." There's a *note of hope in his voice that makes me narrow my eyes at him for a moment, but then I'm back to staring at the road, scanning the mass of kids, trying to find Em among them. I know she isn't inside already because I was the first kid here this morning. I made sure to be.*

The bell rings. I jump.

Denton heads to the door. "You coming?"

I frown. There's still no sign of Em. Where is she? Did she decide to play hooky because she's too embarrassed or worried about facing me? My insides squirm at the thought.

"We're going to be late," Denton calls over his shoulder.

Reluctantly, I pick up my bag. The parking lot is empty. Everyone's inside, apart from a few late stragglers, none of whom are Em.

I follow Denton inside, shoulders slumped.

Where is she?

The gossip at first is just a murmur, a faint stir that I don't even notice because I'm too caught up in my own worries about Em and me and why she isn't at school. But by the afternoon it's a full-on hurricane.

"Did you hear?" Reid Walsh blurts in the middle of the cafeteria. "Em's saying Coach Lee assaulted her after the game last night."

I look up from my lunch tray and catch Shay's eye. Next second I'm on my feet. "What did you say?" I demand.

Reid snorts. "Em's saying Coach Lee attacked her in the locker rooms."

I blink at him before lunging. "You lying piece of shit!"

Denton grabs me by the arm and drags me back. Reid laughs. "I'm not the liar!"

I swing around and come face-to-face with Tanya Hollingsworth in her cheerleading outfit. "She's making it up."

"What are you talking about?" Shay demands of her before I can.

"Oh, come on, as if Coach Lee would do something like that." Tanya says it with an air of absolute authority, tossing her ponytail over one shoulder like a whip. "I heard it's revenge because Coach benched her for tackling Reid."

She tries to walk by, but I move to block her path. Her lunch tray bumps my chest and a milk carton falls off, spilling milk all over the floor and our shoes. I ignore it, as well as her squeal of indignation. "What did you say?" I ask.

Tanya raises her overplucked eyebrows at me and shoots me a look of pure scorn. "What's your problem, McCallister?" she asks. "If she's not lying, then your uncle's a pervert. Which version do you prefer?"

I glare at her, words jumbling in my head, trying to come up with a response, and all the while I can feel the entire cafeteria staring at me . . . waiting for my comeback.

"Jake?"

It's Denton. He's pulling on my arm. "Come on," he murmurs. "Let's get out of here."

I let him tug me away, out of the cafeteria, out across the playing field. Shay is on my other side. The three of us keep going until we're at the far end of the field.

"Shit," Denton says, running his hands through his hair.

"I have to call her," Shay says. "We have to find out what happened."

I nod, but there's a part of me that hesitates. Because what if it's true? Em would never lie about something like this. But my uncle? He wouldn't do anything like that. Not Uncle Ben.

There's an angry buzzing in my head as though a swarm of hornets is hovering around me. I can't hear what Shay and Denton are saying through the deafening hum. It must all be lies. A mistake. A stupid rumor someone's started. And when I find out who . . .

"Whoa!" Denton and Shay both grab for my arms.

"Where are you going?" Shay asks.

I realize that I've started marching back across the playing field. "To find Reid and figure out who started the rumor. Because it's bullshit."

"Hold up," Denton, ever the calm pragmatist, says. "Let's just calm down."

"What if it's true?" Shay whispers.

"It's not true!" I shout, turning on Shay in a fury.

Her eyes go wide. "Okay," she says, glancing at Denton, who gives her a small shake of the head that he doesn't think I notice.

"He's my uncle. He wouldn't do that."

"So you think Em would make this up?" Shay spits back.

I glare at her, blood smashing into my temples with the force of a hammer. No. She wouldn't. But I don't think my uncle could ever do something so horrible either.

Denton gets between us. "Guys, guys, come on . . . Until we know the facts, let's not argue, okay?"

The bell pulls us back to school.

I sit through afternoon classes, unable to concentrate, trying to block out the whispers whipping around me, gathering speed and volume.

As soon as the final bell rings, I grab my bag and sprint for the door. In the hallway I pass a group of juniors and hear something that sends me into a skid.

I turn around and march up to them. "What did you say?"

The junior looks me up and down scornfully. I'm a foot shorter than him. "I said Emerson Lowe's a slut."

Before he even finishes the sentence, my fist is slamming into his jaw. He doubles over with a grunt, groaning. His friends freeze in *shock and disbelief, and then in the next second they're leaping into action, coming at me.*

I spin on my heel and tear off down the hallway, dodging around people hovering by the exit, bashing my way through the doors, and leaping down the steps.

I can hear them hot on my heels, yelling about what they're going to do when they catch me, but I'm faster than all of them. I've got reason to be.

Jake

can sense her looking at me. Although I fell asleep the moment I hit the pillow, my sleep was restless, filled with dreams, mainly about Em, the past blending into the present in a disorienting blur. We were riding bikes together up Toe Jam Hill. Em was pushing on ahead of me, and I was trying to catch up to her, but she always stayed frustratingly just out of reach. I woke at the point she looked at me over her shoulder and smiled and I swerved into a ditch.

Through half-closed lids I watch her now. She's sitting on a rug just outside the tent, in a patch of late-afternoon sunlight. She's writing in a journal or something, though the pen stays poised above the page as though she's lost for words. She tucks her hair behind one ear and then turns to look over her shoulder.

She startles when she sees I'm awake.

"Hey," I say, my voice hoarse with sleep.

"Hi," she whispers back, gently closing her book and resting it on her knees.

"How long have I been asleep?" I ask.

"A couple of hours."

I watch as she puts the book down and slowly rises to her feet. She seems uncertain for a moment, unbalanced, but then she walks inside the tent, bringing all the warmth and the sunlight with her.

I sit up and reach for a T-shirt. Em drops her book on top of her bag and rummages through it for something, biting her lip, and that's all I can focus on: her lips, the bottom one fuller than the top, and how badly I want to kiss her.

Suddenly, the tent feels too small, too hot—not a fire teepee but a sauna—and I need to get outside and away from her. Grabbing my wash bag, I hustle my way toward the exit. "I'm going to take a shower."

I make it a cold shower, but even so, when I head back toward the tent and see Em standing outside among the bachelor boys, who have just returned from their wilderness course jubilant and keen to display their newfound hunter-gatherer skills, I almost have to turn around and take another one. But then I get this overwhelming feeling of protectiveness at the sight of all those guys surrounding her. I want to march over there and put myself between them and her. I never knew I had so much caveman in me. Shit. I have to get a handle on it. Learning not to be impulsive is one of the things on my to-do list.

The men cook their own food over an open fire—using sharpened sticks to impale the store-bought burgers. As we're sitting around the fire eating dinner, Thor sidles up and offers me a beer.

"No thanks."

"How old are you?" he asks.

"Twenty-one."

"Wow," he says in an appraising kind of way, looking me up and down. "I thought you were older."

I shake my head at him, my gaze falling on Em, who's sitting on the opposite side of the fire, laughing at Clark Kent as he shows her how to tie a rabbit snare with a piece of wire and manages to catch his own thumb in it.

"You need to tell her."

"What?" I say, turning back to Thor.

"You're mooning over her like some lovesick teenager. No offense intended."

"I'm not mooning."

"You're not eating," the guy says, pointing at the uneaten burger in my hand.

"That's because I don't want to die of E. coli poisoning."

"Dude, it's not the burger. It's love. I know. I've been there. Several times. I'm on my third marriage."

"So obviously I should be taking advice on love and relationships from you."

He slaps me on the shoulder. "Take the bull by the horns, my friend, tell her the truth, tell her how you feel. From where I'm standing, it's pretty obvious she feels the same way."

That gets my attention. She does? I study Em, remembering how she stormed off this morning when the guys laughed suggestively after they heard her groaning in the tent. It reminds me of the time she rushed off the ice after Reid teased her for having the hots for me.

A light bulb goes on. I start grinning. How did I miss the signs?

"What's the worst that could happen?" Thor whispers in my ear.

I chew my lip while looking into the flames and pondering that question. No one's ever had to tell me to take the bull by the horns before. Usually, they're yelling at me to let the damn bull go. Why am I so hesitant to take a risk now? I never usually am. If I could manage it when I was fourteen, what's stopping me now?

Emerson

All evening I've been feeling jittery—as if the blood in my body has been replaced with strong black coffee. My body is buzzing. The bachelors have gone back to their cabin for the night and now it's just Jake and me left. We circle each other inside the tent like two chess players—every move seeming calculated and self-conscious. I'm still not sure what he wants or how he feels about me, but then again I'm not sure what I want or how I feel, and it's all confusing the hell out of me. When I try to process my thoughts by writing, I come up blank too.

Defeated and anxious, I go to the shower block to brush my teeth and put on my pajamas. When I get back to the tent, I can see that the flaps are down and there's a warm orange glow coming from inside. Jake must have lit the fire. I stop where I am, a hundred feet from the tent, and take a few deep breaths. I'm nervous, and I hate myself for it.

When I finally summon the courage to walk inside, I find Jake crouched down by the fire making s'mores—sandwiching chocolate and melting marshmallows between two graham crackers. He looks up and grins at me, that one-sided smile that makes my insides feel exactly like the marshmallow he's holding. "Dessert?" he asks.

"I just brushed my teeth."

His smile fades.

"But hell yeah," I say, dropping my wash bag and reaching for the s'more he's offering.

We sit down in front of the fire to eat—though I'm careful to leave a good foot of space between us, a space that feels as wide as the universe and as tiny as a molecule all at the same time.

"How's your shoulder?" he asks when we've eaten the entire pack of crackers and licked the chocolate, the foil, and our fingers clean.

"Hurts," I say.

Jake glances at me. "You want another massage?"

"Um," I say. Suddenly, the heat from the fire seems to increase by a thousand degrees. I hear Shay in my head yelling that the correct answer is YES.

"No," I say. "It's okay."

Jake nods and stares into the fire, his elbows resting on his knees. "Okay," he says. "I guess maybe it's time to turn in." He looks over his shoulder at the bed. "Which side do you want?"

Awkward. "I don't mind," I mumble.

Jake gets up. "I'm going to go brush my teeth," he says quickly, and exits the tent.

I brush my teeth again too, not bothering to go to the bathrooms but spitting into a mug. Then before he can get back, I crawl beneath the blankets.

When he does return, slipping into the tent quietly, head down, I close my eyes and pretend to be asleep. I hear him banking up the fire, wood crackling and hissing, ash settling, and then after a few more seconds I register his weight as he sits down on the mattress. He slides beneath the blanket and suddenly my breathing is so rapid that my arms start to tingle from lack of oxygen. I can smell him—the citrus smell of soap and shampoo masking the warm, woodsier scent of his skin. I draw in a deep breath and then another.

"Em?" I hear him say after a minute.

"Mmmm," I murmur, my back to him.

"I need to tell you something."

He doesn't say anything more, so I roll slowly over, my heart pounding, and find myself face-to-face with him. He's tanned, but I can still see the smattering of freckles across his nose. His expression is serious, anxious almost, and I feel my throat constrict.

"You remember you said you didn't want to be friends?" he says.

I nod, unable to find my voice.

He licks his lips and swallows. "Well, I don't want to be friends with you either. I want more." He's looking directly in my eyes as he speaks.

Slowly, I let out the breath I'm holding. Everything inside me is vibrating as if my body is a note on a piano that's just been struck.

"And I think you do too," he says next.

My breath becomes jagged and uneven.

"Tell me if I'm wrong."

I still can't speak. I wasn't expecting this at all. I didn't want this. Or . . . who am I kidding? Of course I wanted this. I want this. I want him. I can't tell him he's wrong, even though part of me knows that it would be the sensible thing to do. The right thing to do.

His hand finds my cheek. His palm is warm, his fingers strong, soft, gentle, just as I imagined they would be. The buzzing feeling kicks up a gear and now I'm tingling all over, almost shaking.

Jake waits a beat, as if checking my reaction, before he draws me gently toward him. I don't fight it. Can't fight it. I need this.

"I'm going to kiss you if that's okay?"

Why is he even asking? *Just kiss me!* I want to yell.

"Is that okay?"

I haven't breathed in at least thirty seconds. My lungs are paralyzed. Jake's studying me intently, and I notice the flicker of doubt pass across his face when I don't answer him. His hand drops from my cheek. He's starting to pull back. Do something! I nod frantically.

He stops. His lips twitch into a relieved half smile. He takes my face in his hands again, slowly, carefully, and draws me toward him. And I still haven't taken a breath yet. My nervous system has gone into meltdown; current surges through me, electrifying my nerve endings.

This. This. This moment. Isn't it what I've been waiting for all along? Was it that simple all along? I let out the breath I'm holding, and as I do, years and years of unhappiness dissolve in the space of a heartbeat so that when I finally draw in a new breath, it's as if I'm filling my lungs for the very first time.

I close my eyes. . . . There's a pause that seems to last a lifetime, and then, finally, I feel his lips on mine, soft and warm. And his kiss is hard and gentle at the same time and has the exquisite promise of something more—something much more—behind it.

It's a kiss that could go either way—a tentative beginning.

We're resting on the edge of something—a line that's bigger than the Grand Canyon—and I can feel my willpower slipping away, my body catching fire as his thumb slowly caresses along my jaw. I hear the groan building at the back of my throat, feel his hands tightening on my shoulder blades. God, it would be so easy to fall into him, to let myself go, to lose myself in this feeling and his arms and this hunger I can feel growing inside me.

I want nothing more than to pull him on top of me, feel his weight pushing me down. My hands itch to press themselves against his stomach, trace the taut lines of muscle I've so far only looked at from a distance. I long to taste him and get to know him, really know him, in ways I've only imagined in my dreams . . . but with a monumental surge of willpower I pull away from him, struggling out of his arms.

My eyes flash open in time to see the frown cross Jake's face.

"I'm sorry," he says, rolling onto his back, running a hand through his hair. "I thought—" He breaks off abruptly.

"No," I say quickly, not wanting him to get the wrong idea. "It's okay." I want to reach for his hand and pull him back toward me. I want to kiss him again. I want to show him just how much I want him. It would be so easy. But I can't.

Jake rolls away from me, swinging his legs off the bed. His voice is husky, filled with emotion. "I'll go sleep somewhere else. I didn't mean to—"

I sit up and grab for his hand. I can't bear it that he thinks he did something wrong. "Jake," I say. "It's not what you think."

The muscles across his shoulders and back are tense. I want to rest my cheek against them, wrap my arms around his waist and anchor him beside me, but it's too late. He's on his feet, moving toward the door.

"I liked it," I murmur. I liked it too much.

He turns to look over his shoulder, uncertain, as though he isn't sure whether to believe me or not. I swallow hard, the butterflies in my stomach flitting lower. Jake's framed by the firelight, but I can see the confusion on his face and the faint flicker of hope in his eyes. I look away, down at the ground. Why is it so goddamn difficult to speak to him and tell him how I feel and what I'm thinking?

Suddenly, I feel Jake's hand against my cheek. I look up, drawing in a breath that catches between my ribs like a fishing hook. He strokes my hair gently behind my ear. "Then what is it?" he asks.

"I . . ."

"Is it Rob?" His jaw tenses as he says Rob's name.

"No," I say, shaking my head and laughing. He has no idea. That kiss . . . that five-second kiss Jake and I just shared was more perfect, more incredible, than anything I ever shared with Rob in four whole years. And that's part of the problem.

"You're going to leave, Jake," I say, the words finally tumbling out of me. "Again."

He frowns. He doesn't get it. How can I trust him? He left me before; what's to stop him from leaving again? I can't handle any more hurt or betrayal.

"I can't do this," I say, smarting at my choice of words. I'm assuming that this is even something. What if it's nothing for him? Just something to do to fill the time while we're stuck out here in the middle of nowhere.

I twist away from him, but he takes my face in both his hands, forcing me around to look at him. His expression is fierce, and when he speaks, his voice is even fiercer. "Em," he whispers.

"You're the reason I came back. Yes, I'm going to leave the island again. But I swear to you, I'm never going to leave you again."

How can he mean that? How can he even know that? That's an impossible promise—one he can't keep. His words are a magic spell I want to believe in—but I know better by now than to believe in fairy tales. Real life isn't like that. The princess doesn't get rescued from the tower. She has to stay there forever. Sometimes she gets eaten by the ogre. And why should she expect a prince to rescue her anyway—when she can't even rescue herself?

"Jake—" I start to say, pulling away again. I can't do this when he's so close. I can't think straight. I can't find the words. I stand up, my legs filled with pins and needles, and head to the fire, needing to put space between us. I crouch down beside it, keeping my back to Jake because I can't look at him anymore. It's too hard. I hear him, though, as he gets up and walks toward me, sense him come to a stop just behind me.

"Em, I mean it," he says. "I haven't stopped thinking about you for all these years. About us. About what might have been."

I laugh through my nose. "We were thirteen, fourteen— nothing would have been, Jake."

"You don't know that," he says, his voice a whisper in my ear that sends a long shiver down my spine.

I stand up. He's an inch from me and the pull is so great it takes everything I've got to not press myself up against him. I try not to, but my attention falls straightaway to his lips. My stomach muscles tighten at the memory of them on mine. Goddamn it. Why did I give in and let him kiss me?

And why must there always be this contradiction when it comes to Jake? This constant urge I have to run from him conflicting with an intense yearning to give in and draw close to him?

"Em," he says, shaking his head, "if all that's holding you back is the thought of me leaving, then that's not a good enough reason."

I take a step back, but there's nowhere to go except into the fire, so I just cross my arms in front of my chest instead in an effort to keep him at bay. He stays where he is, and I realize he's challenging me. He knows exactly what his proximity is doing to me. The heat from the flames behind me is nothing compared to the heat building between the two of us. I can feel my defenses melting, and he can feel it too. I know from the victorious, challenging look in his eye. He'd look like that as a kid when daring me to do something he knew he'd win at—like hundred-meter sprints.

He always did know how to play me, and the thought drives me insane. I don't want to let him win. But it's not a game, I remind myself. It's not a dare. It's my life, and Jake winning doesn't mean that I have to lose. We can both win.

"I can't get you out of my head," he continues.

I am this close to caving in, but I dig in my heels.

Jake is waiting, watching me, but he finally seems to realize I'm not going to back down, that I'm resolute on this. He nods, almost to himself, his shoulders slumping, and then he takes a step backward. I take a deep breath in, feeling the distance between us as a physical ache. Another step and the ache becomes a stab to the gut—a ripping feeling in my chest as though someone has my heart in their hands and is tearing it into pieces.

"I guess then," he says, smiling sadly at me as he reaches the door, "I'll just have to settle for being friends." He runs his hand through his hair. "It's more than I hoped for." A pause. "But it's less than I want."

His words knock something loose in me, jolt me into realizing that it's less than I want too. The voice in my head screams that I can't let him go, that I need to trust him not to hurt me again.

He's over by the door to the tent, lifting the flap, when I grab his hand. I'm almost as stunned as him, as I don't remember having moved across the tent.

Jake turns, surprised, but in the next second I'm in his arms and we're kissing, not tentatively this time but as if time is running out on us, as if those lost years need to be caught up on in the next five minutes.

It's so strange after Rob to kiss someone else, to be held by someone else, and I wonder now in total bewilderment how I ever thought Rob and I had any kind of connection or chemistry. I never even knew that a kiss could feel like that, and it's frankly blowing my mind.

We sink to our knees together, Jake's arms around my waist holding me close, my hands in his hair. He pulls me onto his lap in one swift move, and we're still kissing, any lingering thoughts and doubts blasted away by the heat of his lips on mine, feverish and frantic. After a few minutes, though, he stops and rests his forehead against mine and takes a deep, shaky breath in. I'm still pressed against him, can feel his heart hammering beneath my palms. His own hands are gripping my hips and my whole body is trembling. It's as if we're standing, teetering, on the very edge of a precipice after almost running headlong into an abyss. I can sense him trying to inch back from it, and I'm poised, every nerve ending humming, as I wait to see what will happen next. And then I realize that I'm in control of what happens next. I don't have to wait and see.

I run my hands around his neck and pull him closer and keep kissing him.

Jake sighs, his hands stroking up my spine, pulling me closer against his body. "I really want to take you to bed," Jake murmurs in my ear. He pauses and I wait for the "but" . . . and then it comes. "But I don't think we should, you know, have sex or anything."

I pull back, giving him an archly amused look. That's not what his body is telling me. Far from it.

"I mean, I do," he says. "Absolutely, I do want to have sex." He gives me a winsome shrug, a blush spreading over his face. "I just . . . I want us to take it slowly. Do it right."

"Me too," I say, feeling both frustrated and, I must admit, a little relieved at the same time. I want him, but I don't want to rush things either. I've only ever been with Rob up until now. What if I'm not good enough?

"Besides," he adds, "I don't have any protection with me."

I smile. He didn't plan to get me into bed, then. I'm glad about that. I rest my head on his shoulder and he strokes his hands gently down my back and kisses my shoulder.

"We've waited so long I think we can wait a little longer," I tell him, kissing him back. "And I think you can still take me to bed."

"Really?" he asks, his voice strained.

I nod, stroking my fingertips along his jaw, feeling the stubble and marveling at how much more there is to get to know about this new Jake. "I mean," I say, "we don't have to have sex."

He interrupts me. "I don't intend to have sex with you, Emerson Lowe, ever. I intend to make love to you."

And with that, he picks me up and stands. I wrap my legs around his waist and let him carry me over to the bed.

Jake

I lay her down on top of the covers and then slowly start to undress her, first pulling off her T-shirt and then inching down her pajama bottoms. Her skin glows in the firelight, and I stroke my fingertips over her stomach, watching it flutter in response. Shit. She's beautiful, her skin smooth and flawless. And she's here, with me, staring up at me with a look that makes me pause. I see the desire in her, the way her skin is flushed with heat from the fire and from my touch, but I also see the vulnerability in her eyes, the shadow of fear lurking there, and there's a hard punch in my chest cavity as my heart thuds against my ribs.

God, I want her. She's biting her bottom lip, her hair all disarrayed, looking sexier than I've ever seen. I lie down beside her, pressing up against her. She reaches for the bottom of my T-shirt and pulls it over my head. Her hands slowly start to trace their way over my shoulders and down my chest, until I'm driven so crazy that I have to swing my leg over her waist and pin her wrists to the bed.

She laughs and arches her back in response. I kiss my way

down her body, starting at her neck, making my way down, down, down, taking my time, listening for the rising moans and the hitched breathing, loving the way her body arches higher and higher as I make my way lower and lower.

I reach the waistband of her underwear and she holds her breath, her back still arched. I pause, enjoying the sight of her— eyes half-closed, head thrown back—wanting to drink her in and remember this moment forever. I start to ease her underwear down and off and her fingernails imprint half-moons into my shoulders. I laugh and she swipes at me with her hand, growling. I kiss her stomach. She laughs in response, but I silence her with my tongue between her legs. She gasps loudly and her body stiffens, but I push her legs farther apart and kiss her more until she relaxes and lets out a moan. Her free hand twists the sheets into a knot.

I keep going, loving the feel of her, the taste of her, the sound of her cries, coming faster and faster. Slowly, I start to explore her with my hands and tongue, wanting to take my time, to show her how much I want her.

It's not often I've got the upper hand with Em, and I'm enjoying it, reveling in the way I can make her writhe and move against me, but suddenly she shifts her body, wriggling free of my grip, and rolls herself so she's on top of me, still breathing hard, face flushed, her naked body, burning hot, pressed against mine. Now, that's a feeling I could get used to. I stroke both palms down the length of her back, her butt, over her thighs, and reach once more between her legs, but she scoots downward out of my way, flicking her hair out of her face with one arm and pressing my chest down into the bed with her other.

What's she doing? She sits up, straddling me, and I get a full look at her, at her body glowing in the firelight. If we could stay like this for the rest of my life I'd be happy, but Em has other ideas. She tugs off my shorts. I'm not embarrassed. I lie there staring up at her as her gaze travels the length of me before returning to my face. She smiles mischievously and then dips her head and starts kissing me, starting with my lips before tracing her tongue down my chest. When she takes me in her mouth, I suck in a breath and have to focus on not losing control. It's my turn to twist the bedsheets into knots.

Every muscle in my body tenses as her fingers tease and stroke me. Before she can bring me close, though, I flip her off me. She cries out, but I quiet her with a kiss and pull her into my arms. Lying facing each other, our legs entwined, I reach for her again. She stares into my eyes as I slide my fingers inside her. Her mouth opens in a gasp and I bite her bottom lip. Her own hand grips me hard, starting up a rhythm that I match. We're both breathing hard and fast, blood pounding like lightning through me. Shit. Em's muscles contract sharply and I feel her start to come. I let go at the same time and we come together, both of us panting.

She's covered in a sheen of sweat and I pull her close against me so I can feel her heart smashing into my own ribs and I stroke her hair, breathing her in. She starts shaking hard and I wonder if she's crying, but when I try to pull back to see, her hands grip my shoulders tight, so I draw her closer and hold her as tight as I can.

"I'm here," I whisper.

She responds by curling into me. She's still shaking, and I pull back just enough to look at her face. I was right. She's crying.

I frown and wipe away a tear with my thumb. She smiles at me through her tears, and I realize she's not sad. She's happy. I kiss her, lightly, softly. She lets out a sigh, burrows once more into my shoulder, breathing in deeply, and that's how we fall asleep.

I wake up with Em's back pressed against my chest, my arm tight around her waist. For a long moment, I just lie there and listen to her breathe, enjoying the feeling of her body nestled against mine, the smell of her hair and her skin. At the memory of last night, my blood starts to rush a little quicker. I can feel her start to stir, her hips pressing back against mine, and my body responds. My hands inch down her body, enjoying every smooth inch of her. She sighs in her sleep.

I've got plans to wake her up in a way that will put a smile on her face, but unfortunately a loud crash followed by cursing interrupts me. It's the bachelor boys outside trying to light the gas stove and clearly failing. I peel my arm off Em and roll out of the bed, reaching for a T-shirt and pulling it on as I make my way outside. I really do not want to be blown up, today of all days.

The men all look up at my appearance, making their usual jibes, asking how my night was. I shrug, saying nothing, but Thor is straight onto me. "Look at that smile," he says. "You totally got some!"

I shake my head at him, but he's right, and the fact is I can't stop smiling.

I move toward the camp stove to make coffee, and that's where Em finds me a few minutes later. She creeps up behind me, and when I turn, I find her standing a little awkwardly, hair mussed from sleep, her face flushed—maybe from sunburn, maybe from embarrassment. Her lips look swollen, and I want to kiss them, but I'm conscious of the boys watching us.

"Here," I say, handing her a coffee.

She smiles and takes it. "Thanks," she says. She looks at me over the rim of the mug as she takes a sip and her eyes are dancing blue, filled with the kind of mischief that before, when we were kids, used to signal a dare coming my way and now seems to signal a different kind of dare altogether.

"Come back inside the tent," I tell her, in a voice quiet enough that the guys can't hear.

Her eyebrows rise. I walk into the tent. She follows.

This time as soon as she walks inside, I pull her into my arms. She hoists her leg over my hip, and I slide my hand along her thigh. She draws in a breath right by my ear, and I feel myself get immediately hard.

She kisses my ear. "Don't stop," she whispers hoarsely.

I grin and slip my hand once more between her legs and then inside her underwear. Guided by her moans, I increase the rhythm. She presses against me, then reaches her hand for me, but I nudge her away. I want to focus just on her. It's more of a turn-on than she could possibly know.

She's leaning against the table, and I watch as she throws back her head and closes her eyes. If only the bachelor party weren't outside and we could spend all day in here in bed. I want to make her come over and over, but instead I just have to make do with this one time. So I make it count. I build the rhythm with my hand until I see her bite down hard on her lip to stop from crying out loud, and then I pull her close and kiss her neck, even as I bring her to orgasm. She grips hold of my shoulders as she comes and I stop her mouth with my own, loving the way her body continues to jolt even afterward. Her legs are wobbly and weak, and when I set her down she falls against me.

"Oh my God," she whispers, her face flushed. "Wow."

I grin at her. She pushes me backward with her fists against my chest. "Stop looking so smug," she says. "Just wait until later." And with that, she runs her palm down my body before spinning on her heel and leaving.

The problem with what just happened is that while Em is happy and relaxed and cool as a cucumber for the next four hours, I am jumpy, frustrated, and so wound up that not even the freezing cold water of Puget Sound can cool me off or stop me from thinking about Em's naked body and what she might have in mind for later.

Em and I have to split up to make sure that we all get back to Bainbridge in one piece because the bachelor, after three days and two nights of drinking, twelve dares, and little sleep, is barely able to dribble, let alone paddle. I'm actually feeling sympathetic toward him, with his eyebrows shaved and with a permanent marker mustache drawn on his face, which is why I don't mind doing all the paddling while he rests, slumped forward in front of me. Besides, the paddle work helps me burn off some of the excess energy coursing through my body.

I glance across the waves to Em in the kayak just ahead of me. She's wearing just a bikini top, and I'm fairly sure she's trying to taunt me. She glances over at me, her face shaded by the visor of her cap, and grins. Yeah, definitely taunting me.

She's sitting behind Clark Kent, who's turned out to be the most athletic and fun of the whole bachelor party. He loves being on the water and seems undented by the drinking or partying.

Behind us, I can still hear Captain GoPro hollering at Thor as if they're in the Olympics.

I can't believe Em has to run trips like this all the time. It's great to be out and on the water, but having to constantly be at the beck and call of clients and in top form is tough. In just over a month, I'll be back at college, but Em will be here, doing this—until the weather turns too cold at least. I wish there were a way to bring her with me.

To distract myself from the thought of leaving, I think about all the things we can do in four weeks, all the places I'm going to take her, all the old haunts I want to revisit with her. I'm going to offer to take all Toby's shifts too, so I can get to work with her every day. I also figure that I owe him for his deliberate mess-up with the tents.

When we pull up on shore back in Bainbridge and hop out of the kayaks, I notice Toby skulking behind the door of the store, keeping out of sight, no doubt nervous that Em's going to blow his head off. As Em and I help the bachelor boys carry their stuff back to their car, he sneaks up to me.

"Hey," he asks. "How did it go?"

"It was great." I can't stop my eyes from sliding over to Em, who is locked in conversation with Clark Kent, whose real name we've discovered is actually Aaron. Em looks up at me as if she senses me watching and smiles. Maybe it's me, but she looks like a different person—lighter, glowing from within.

Toby fist-pumps the air. "I knew it! It worked, didn't it? The fire teepee! It totally worked!"

"What?"

"That place is a love den. You can't stay in the fire teepee without sparks flying."

I shake my head at him, bewildered.

"I even had to make two fake bookings," he tells me. "You totally owe me."

"I do," I tell him. "I'm going to take all your shifts."

He slaps me on the shoulder. "Well, at least now Emerson seems in a better mood. Thank Jesus for that." He's smiling at Em, who is now chatting animatedly to Aaron and scribbling something down in a notebook.

"Who's that?" Toby asks, observing them. "He's cute."

"He isn't Photoshopped either," I tell him.

"Excuse me a moment," Toby says, and strides toward him.

I watch him hold out his hand and introduce himself to Aaron. Em leaves them to it and strolls toward me. She rests her head on my shoulder, weary but happy.

"Good job," I tell her, kissing the top of her head.

"You too," she answers, putting her arm around my waist and leaning into me.

We wave off the guys after they tip us a huge amount of cash, which I insist Em takes. While Toby cleans up the kayaks, Em and I grab our bags and head toward the parking lot. I take her bag from her and throw it over my shoulder, then put my arm around her waist, drawing her near.

"So, can I see you later?" I ask.

She glances up at me, a small, sneaky smile pulling at the edge of her lips. "Yes."

I drop the bag and pull her against me. She fits perfectly, her arms looping around my waist. I slide my hands up her arms and take her sun-kissed face between them. She rises up on her tiptoes so she reaches my chin.

Electric current flows between us. This evening feels like a lifetime away. Her eyes close. Her lips part. I lean down to kiss her.

"Jake?"

My eyes snap open. I turn my head a fraction and freeze. What the . . . ?

"Lauren?" I say, as though I might be hallucinating the girl who's standing beside my rental car, arms crossed over her chest, lips pursed tight with outrage. She stares between Em and me, her eyes flashing furiously.

My arm drops to my side, and I feel Em pulling away to look between us.

What the hell is Lauren doing here?

Emerson

"Who the hell is she?" the girl yells, looking right at me. Jake's arm falls from my waist. I glance between him—standing there ashen-faced, lips half-parted—and the girl. Who is she? She's blond, pretty in a sorority way rather than a surfer chick kind of way, wearing spray-on jeans and a cashmere cardigan. Her hair is soft and silky and perfectly styled in a way mine will never be, and she's wearing immaculately applied makeup.

"What are you doing here?" Jake asks the girl.

"Who are you?" the girl asks, turning to me. I feel her eyes scour me from head to foot.

"Who are you?" I fire back.

She puts her hands on her hips. She nods at Jake. "I'm his girlfriend."

Jake glances at me—a desperate, apologetic glance. I can't compute. He has a girlfriend? My blood pounds in my ears. I snatch my bag from out of Jake's hand and in a blurry daze start walking fast toward my bike, past the girl, who refuses to move aside to let me pass, forcing me to walk around her.

"Em!" Jake shouts after me. He tries to follow, but the girl blocks his path. I hear him remonstrate with her, but an angry buzzing fills my ears and I can't make out the words. I don't want to make out the words. He lied to me. He has a girlfriend. I throw my bag on my back and climb onto my bike, blinking through a haze of tears I'm determined Jake won't see.

"Em!" Jake yells as I start to pedal off, but I'm deaf to it.

"I'm such an idiot," I tell Shay over the phone twenty minutes later.

"No, you're not," she argues.

But I am. How could he have lied to me like that? The way he looked at me, the things he said—all lies. And I fell for it. I'm never trusting anyone ever again. The thought of what we did together and the way Jake touched me makes me cringe. How could he? My body burns with shame.

He's the first person and only person who I have ever been that open with, who I've ever fully dropped my defenses with. He's the only guy I've ever even had an orgasm with, for God's sake. Rob never gave a crap about anyone's pleasure but his own. The first time he tried to touch me intimately, I froze—it threw up too many memories of what had happened. I wanted to make him stop, but then I forced myself to carry on, scared that if I stopped him he'd break up with me. I wanted to be normal, so I pretended for years that I was okay with sex, but I wasn't. Every time we slept together, I switched off. I went through the motions but never engaged. And Rob never made an effort to even ask me if I enjoyed it. It was only ever about him.

Frankly, I think he felt relieved that he never had to make an effort—or maybe that's being too kind. It probably never crossed his mind that he needed to.

Jake made me realize that it doesn't have to be that way, that there are some guys who will put you first. For the first time ever when kissing someone, my brain wasn't swamped by images of Coach Lee. I was fully there in the moment, with Jake, thinking only about him. He made me forget everything else. A surge of fury wells up. I hate him even more for that—for making me feel that way, for making me think it was something special.

Well, at least I didn't sleep with him. I suppose there is that. It's small consolation, however.

"What did she look like?" Shay asks, interrupting my thoughts.

"Pretty," I admit. "Really pretty."

Shay doesn't say anything, and I picture her pushing her glasses up her nose and pursing her lips. "At least let him explain," she says. "I mean, you guys didn't talk for seven years—do you really want to go back to that? Maybe hear him out."

I huff into the phone.

"You know I'm right," she answers in a cajoling tone.

Shay is always right, though I don't want to admit it. She was one of the smartest kids in school: has a full scholarship to NYU to study political theory and already has an internship lined up with a feminist think tank.

"Get all the facts before you make a decision," she tells me.

"You would say that," I mumble.

"I will see you tomorrow," Shay says. "Until then, don't do anything stupid."

"Stupid like what?"

"Like get-back-together-with-Rob kind of stupid."

"That's never going to happen. I swear it." Not after last night,

I want to tell her. There is no way I'd ever go back to Rob now. It's not even within the realm of conceivable.

I hang up and my phone beeps with a voice mail. I'm holding my breath, hoping that it's Jake, but instead Rob's grunting tones greet me. It's an old message from two days ago, when we were on Vashon and had no phone signal.

"Emerson," he says sullenly. "It's me. Listen, you like left some stuff here. I don't know . . . books . . . like a journal or something, and, yeah, some underwear. Let me know what you want to do with it all or I'll just go ahead and toss it."

Shit. I left one of my journals at his house. Oh my God. What if he's read it? It's not exactly a flattering read. I scrunch my eyes shut. No, I tell myself. What are the odds of Rob reading it? The only thing he ever reads is the sports section of the paper. I have to hold on to that hope . . . and get around there as soon as possible just in case he makes an exception to the rule. I'm already moving, pulling on my jeans, the phone still propped against my ear.

My voice mail beeps again. Another message from Rob. This time from this morning. "Okay, so I guess you're giving me the silent treatment," he grumbles. "Real grown-up, Emerson." I shake my head in disbelief. *I'm* the immature one? "So I'm sitting here and I've got your journal in my hand . . ." My heart thumps loudly, and I freeze, one arm through my T-shirt, one out. Nausea boils in my stomach and starts to rise up my throat. "Kind of an interesting read, Emerson," he says. And then he hangs up.

With my hair still wet, I fly down the stairs.

"Where are you going?" my mom calls after me as I rush out the door.

"To Rob's," I call. I catch her startled look, but I don't have time to explain.

I screech to a halt outside Rob's house ten minutes later, out of breath and in a blind panic. I throw my bike down on the lawn and race up to the front door.

Reid answers it.

"Is Rob in?" I ask.

His brow furrows. "What do you want with him? I thought you guys broke up."

"I just need to speak to him is all."

"How's things?" Reid asks.

I glower at him. "Is Rob in?" I press.

Reid glowers back, but then he turns and stumps off, yelling for Rob, who appears after a good long minute. One look at his face as he stalks toward the door tells me everything I need to know. I take a step backward. My stomach curdles. He's read it. The whole way around here, I was frantically wracking my brain to remember the details of what I'd written in that journal. I'm so stupid. Why on earth did I leave it here? I know that most of the entries are about Rob and me, about how unhappy I am—or was, about how angry I am about my dad's illness and my financial worries about the business. It's a journal. It's where I vent and rant and empty out all the raging emotions inside me that I can't ever vocalize, but I know Rob and I know that all he will have focused on are the bits about him.

"I'm shit in bed?" he hisses.

I cringe. Oh God. Why did I think committing to paper all the unsatisfying details of my sex life would ever be a good idea? "You read my journal?" I stammer in a whisper. But now that I'm facing him, anger starts to obliterate the embarrassment. "It was private. You shouldn't have read it."

"Well, if you hadn't left it lying around . . . ," he splutters, his face going red.

"No!" I shout back at him. "You still shouldn't have read it, so don't blame me if you read something you didn't like."

He snorts, his eyes narrowing to slits. "You know, Em, maybe if you weren't so frigid . . ."

It's my turn to snort. Lava-hot fury rushes through my veins. My hand curls into a fist. Normally at this stage in an argument I'd clam up tight—words would get twisted and tangled in my head—but not now. "Right!" I yell. "So it's my fault that you're a selfish lover who wouldn't know what to do with a woman even if she came with an instruction manual?"

Rob frowns. I shake my head at him in disgust. Three days ago, maybe I would have fallen apart at hearing him call me that. I would probably have believed him—believed that it was my fault he couldn't turn me on, that there was something wrong with me—but not now. I smile—I can't help myself; I'm remembering my night with Jake. "Just give me my stuff back, Rob," I say wearily.

"Can't," he answers, crossing his arms in defiance. "I threw it all away." He jerks his head toward the trash cans beside the house. And he slams the door in my face.

Asshole. I walk over to the trash cans and lift the lid, but one eye-watering whiff makes me drop it. I'm not wading through bags of trash to recover a journal. That chapter of my life is now officially over. And best left in the trash.

Jake

(Then)

I run all the way home from school. I don't even slow my pace after the junior that I punched and his friends give up chasing me.

When I finally make it, breathless and panting, through the front door, I find my mom ransacking the hall closet, suitcases piled up by the stairs.

"What are you doing?" I ask, wiping the sweat pouring down my face.

She barely glances at me. "We're leaving."

"What?"

"We're leaving."

"What do you mean we're leaving?"

"Your grandmother's had a stroke. She's in the ICU. We're flying to Toronto. Grandpa needs us." Her eyes are red-rimmed. It looks like she's been crying.

Shaken by the news, it takes me a few seconds to notice the number of suitcases. "Why have we got so much stuff? How long are we going for?"

My mom walks toward the kitchen, shrugging off my question. "I don't know."

I follow her. "Did you hear? About Uncle Ben?"

She pauses with her back to me.

"They're saying he attacked Em."

My mom's spine stiffens. She doesn't turn around.

"Have you spoken to him?" I ask.

"Yes." She turns to look at me. She looks like she wants to say more. Her lip trembles.

"Mom! What did he say?" I press her.

She shakes her head. "Just pack your things. And hurry your sister up. We're leaving in fifteen minutes."

She walks off and I stare at her departing back, my mind reeling. What? What the hell is happening? First Em and now my grandmother. It's like an earthquake has rocked through my world and now a series of aftershocks is destroying everything left standing.

"I'm not going!" I yell after my mom.

She doesn't answer.

My dad's on a business trip, so I can't talk to him about it, and my sister is only ten. I head upstairs to my room, grabbing the phone as I go. I need to talk to Em, find out what happened. But when I call her, there's no answer.

I throw my bag on the floor of my room and flop onto the bed, covering my head with my arms. The room is spinning. I don't know what to do to make it stop. He did something to her. My uncle did something to Em. I want to kill him.

I sit bolt upright. I'm going to go to his house. I'm going to confront him. And I'm going to . . . My door flies open. My sister, Beth, stands in the doorway. Her face is flushed.

"Did you hear?" she asks breathlessly.

"Hear what?"

"What they're saying about Uncle Ben?"

Damn, I think to myself. The gossip has already reached the elementary school playground, which means it must be all over the island.

"Get out!" I shout, all my frustration bursting out of me. I march to the door and slam it in Beth's face. Then I turn around and look around my room as though it's a prison cell I'm trapped inside of.

I kick the bed, swearing loudly. What do I do? I think about going over to my uncle's house to confront him and maybe punch him in the face. But that can wait. I need to see Em first. I need to know if she's okay. I pause, though. If I saw her, what would I even say?

"Five minutes, Jake!" my mom yells from downstairs.

Dropping to my knees, I empty my schoolbag onto the floor and grab my notebook and a pen. I'll write Em a note.

I scribble it fast. There's no time for a long letter.

I hesitate for a second, reading the letter back before scribbling one more line, and then I fold up the piece of paper and race down the stairs.

I'm halfway out the front door, letter in hand, when my mom appears, carrying my sister's suitcase.

"Where are you going?" she asks.

I skid around to face her. "To Em's."

"There's no time. And besides, I'm not sure it's a good idea."

"But . . ."

"No buts, Jake. Where's your bag? I need it in the car now. We're leaving!"

Jake

race around to Em's and pound on the front door. Her mother answers.

"Is Em here? Can I see her?" I ask, peering over her shoulder and up the stairs. I'm so impatient to see her that I almost barge my way inside the house and take the stairs three at a time.

"She's not here, Jake," her mom tells me.

"Where is she? Do you know?"

Em's mom hesitates a beat, and I look at her suspiciously. "She's gone to see Rob," she admits.

"Rob?" I exclaim. What?

Em's mom sighs loudly and shakes her head. "I don't know why. She rushed out of here like she had the devil on her tail."

I frown. Why would she go to Rob's? What's going on? The only thing I can come up with is that seeing Lauren and me has propelled her straight back into his arms. But no, that can't be right—can it? She wouldn't be so impulsive, would she? She hasn't even given me a chance to explain. But maybe she drew a conclusion, and it would be just like Em to want to hit back. Oh shit. I stagger backward off the veranda.

"I'll tell her you stopped by," Em's mom calls to me as I climb in my car.

I tear out of the drive, intending to go straight to Rob's, but I stop myself. Instead, I pull over on the side of the road and try calling Em again. Still no answer. I hang up without leaving a message. I need to speak to her face-to-face. Fuck it. I put the car into drive and head over to Rob's house.

There's no sign of Em or her bike, which is a relief, but I decide to knock anyway just to be sure she isn't there. Rob answers. He's wearing blue sweats and a T-shirt with the police academy logo on it. He takes one look at me and says: "What the fuck are you doing here?"

"Is Em here?" I ask.

"No." He grimaces like he's chewing on something rancid and foul-tasting. "Emerson is not here."

"*Was* she here?" I ask, trying to keep my tone even.

He narrows his eyes at me. "What's it to you?"

I stare at him. God, there's so much I want to say to him. Instead, I press my lips together and force it all to stay inside. I hate this guy. How could he be with a girl like Em and treat her the way he did? How could he let a girl like that slip through his fingers? The guy is the biggest jerk on the planet—after his brother, that is. But on the upside, I guess if he weren't such a jerk, I'd have more of a challenge on my hands winning her back, so thank God for small mercies.

I turn and walk away.

"Hey, McCallister?"

I glance over my shoulder.

"Good luck," Rob calls to me. "She's as frigid as an iceberg. You'll get more action from a corpse."

I come to a standstill, my heart pounding in my temples. My brain warns me to hold fire, but I can't. I'm already striding back up the drive. I'm so fast that Rob startles backward, but he isn't fast enough. I grab him by the neck of his T-shirt and twist it hard. His hands scramble for purchase on mine, but I'm stronger and I've got a tight hold on him. "You say another word about her," I hiss, "and it will be the last word out of your mouth with those teeth still in your head."

I'm so close to him, I can see the filigree of red veins road-mapping his eyes, can smell his sour breath. I let him go, shoving him backward, already furious at myself for letting him get to me, for not keeping on walking. He's not worth it. I know that. But I really want to tell him how wrong he is. I want him to know that it was not her. It was him.

"You know," I say, the words rushing out before I can stop them, "that wasn't my experience of Em at all. In fact, it was completely the opposite."

I let him go and he stumbles back against the door frame, glaring at me.

I wish I could tell him more—about how many times I made her come last night and again this morning, and the way she looked when she did. I want to tell him how open she was with me, how trusting, how giving, how alive and fucking beautiful she was. About how damn amazing it was being with her—but I'm not giving him that.

Rob's face crumples into a comical frown—all the parts rearranging themselves like a caveman cartoon, before clarity comes and his mouth drops open.

I smile at him, then swivel on my heel and walk off, laughing to myself. Let him stew on that.

* * *

I'm sitting on my deck the next morning at eight with a steaming cup of coffee. My phone sits beside me and I stare at it, willing it to ring. Em still hasn't returned my calls, and I'm not sure what to do. She always did need space to cool off, but I've given her that, so why is she still ignoring me? I left a message explaining that Lauren is my ex-girlfriend, emphasis very much on the "ex," but I need to explain to her face-to-face. And, as well as that, I need to tell her the whole truth about why I'm here.

"Hello, stranger."

I look up and almost spill my coffee down my front. I stand up and set the mug down on the window ledge.

"Shay! What are you doing here?"

She jogs up the steps and we hug. I pull back and hold her by the tops of her arms just to get a good look at her, still trying to process that it's Shay standing on my deck. She's still rocking the same dark brown hair cut in a bob and the same thick bangs she had at thirteen. She's updated her glasses, though, and is now wearing some tortoiseshell square-framed ones. She's accessorizing as she did when she was younger, with a string of pearls and bright red lipstick.

"I just got back," she says to me. Then she takes a step back and lets her gaze wander the length of me. "Wow," she says, nodding to herself. "She really wasn't lying."

"What?" I ask.

She grins at me. "Nothing."

"How'd you find me?" I ask.

She gives me an arch look. "Not difficult, Jake. I asked Toby."

"Wait," I say. "Does Em know you're back?"

She nods. "I spoke to her yesterday." She gives me a pointed look.

I take a deep breath. "So I guess she told you what happened?"

Shay nods. "Yeah." She glances over at my coffee mug. "So, what does a girl have to do to get a coffee around here? I'm so jet-lagged I could die."

I smile. I haven't seen Shay in years, but she's still the same: forthright, direct as a missile, smart as a whip too. I go inside and make her coffee, wondering what the real purpose of her visit is and feeling a little nervous, I have to admit. After it happened, Shay sent me a couple of e-mails basically bawling me out and telling me what a shit I was and that I had better never show my face in Bainbridge again. I never replied.

She follows me inside and I catch her glancing surreptitiously around.

"She's not here."

Shay gives me an innocent look, like butter wouldn't melt.

"That's why you're here, isn't it?" I ask. "To check that I'm not hiding a girlfriend in my closet?"

Shay shrugs and gives me a half grin. "Okay, maybe that's part of the reason I'm here. I told Em that she needed to hear you out, but I want to check that what she's going to hear isn't going to hurt her."

I turn to face her. "I'm not going to hurt her, Shay. I promise."

"So who's Lauren, then?" she asks.

"My ex-girlfriend," I say, handing her a mug of coffee. I lead us back outside to the deck.

"Definitely ex?" she asks.

"Yeah, definitely ex."

"So what was she doing here, then?"

"She thought we were on a break."

"And are you?"

"No. We were never on a break. We broke up before the summer. And I made it clear to her that I'm not available anymore."

Shay sneaks a smile in my direction. "Well, Emerson needs to know that too."

"I know," I say. "I've been trying to call her. She's not picking up and doesn't seem to be checking her messages, either."

"Go see her," Shay says.

"I'm going to. I tried yesterday, but she was out. At Rob's."

Shay looks up in alarm. "Seriously? She told me she wasn't going to do anything stupid."

"I don't think she has," I say. I put my coffee down and rest my head in my hands, sighing loudly. "What the hell did she ever see in him, Shay? Why did she date him?"

"Because I think she thought that was the best she could do."

I look up at Shay in disbelief. That's insane. But it also echoes what her father told me and the little that Em has mentioned too.

Shay shrugs at me. "And when she started dating Rob, people stopped saying shit about her."

"How bad was it?" I ask, bracing myself. I haven't wanted to press Em for details, but I need to know.

"How bad was what?"

"After I left. What was it like for her? She's told me a little, not much. I want to know."

Shay puts her coffee mug down and pushes her glasses up her nose. "It was awful, Jake. You know what school is like. Kids are fucking horrible. I'm amazed she didn't drop out, to be honest. People accused her of all sorts of stuff: of coming onto your uncle, of making it all up, of being a slut, of screwing the entire hockey team. They called her every name you can think of and then some. The bathrooms were a no-go zone—the graffiti was . . . inventive, shall we say. And when she wouldn't back down or change her story, it got worse. It's why she won't go near social media. The trolling was so vicious."

I stand up and kick the veranda post hard. Shit. I fucking hate myself for not being there for her. And more than that, I fucking hate my uncle. If he were still alive, I think I'd kill him. I kick the post again, pretending it's his head.

"No one stood up for her?"

Shay gives me a pointed look. "I did. Denton did."

"I would have if I were here."

There's a long pause while I try to imagine what it must have been like. I never knew it was that bad.

I turn to look at Shay. "I didn't want to leave—you know that, right?"

Shay doesn't say anything in reply.

"My grandmother had a stroke." I laugh quietly under my breath. "You know, I never put the two things together."

Shay cocks her head at me, not understanding.

"The stroke. It happened after she heard the news about my uncle. I never realized that's what caused it until years later."

Shay puts her hand on my arm and squeezes. "I'm sorry."

"You think it would have been any different if I'd been around?"

Shay gives a small shrug. Yes. I know that's what she's thinking. "Maybe," she answers. "Who knows? She really missed you, Jake, even though she wouldn't admit it."

"I missed her too. So much. I thought you all hated me."

Shay squeezes my arm again. "You're here now. You get to make it up to her."

We stand there for a moment, listening to the sounds of the forest.

"When she told me she broke up with Rob for good, I was so goddamn happy, Jake, I can't even tell you."

I glance over at Shay, who is now staring out at the trees.

"He's such an asshole to her. And she just puts up with it and takes him back every time. When she told me you were back and that Rob was out of the picture, I actually started to hope that maybe she'd seen the light. Finally." She turns to me. "So, please, I'm begging you, as her best friend, don't mess things up." She pauses. "Or I swear to God I will hunt you down and kill you with my bare hands. She's been through enough."

I give her a wry smile. "Can I ask you something?" I say after a moment has passed.

Shay nods.

"Why do you and everyone else call her Emerson now? Why isn't she Em anymore?"

Shay sets her coffee cup down, her expression solemn. "She made everyone stop calling her Em after it happened."

"Why?" I ask.

"Because she said it reminded her of him. He kept saying her name. While he was . . . you know . . ." She grimaces tightly and looks away.

My mug slips, splashing scalding coffee over my hands. "Shit," I whisper. I've been calling her Em this whole time without even thinking about it. I squeeze my eyes shut. I want to go back in time, change everything, stop what happened from happening. Why didn't I go into the goddamn locker room?

I'm so fucking frustrated that I kick the post again. Shit. I hop on one foot. I think I broke my toe.

Shay puts her arm around my waist. "Stop kicking the post, Jake, and make things right."

Emerson

There's a soft knock on my bedroom door. Before I can yell at whomever it is to wait, the door opens and Jake appears.

His eyes widen when he sees me standing in just a towel, my hair dripping from the shower. "Oh, sorry," he says. He closes his eyes and moves to shut the door again. "Your mom said to come on up."

"It's okay," I tell him. "You can come in."

Jake opens his eyes, frowning. "You sure?"

He turns around, giving me privacy, and I quickly pull on some clothes, catching him surreptitiously sneaking a glance in my direction. He looks away fast, embarrassed. As I dry my hair, I watch him taking in my desk and the shelf of books and journals above it.

I should have hidden them. Jake hasn't been in my room since we were thirteen. It feels weird, him being here now.

"I've been calling and calling," Jake says.

"I know," I say. "I'm sorry. Yesterday . . . I needed to get my head together."

After I went around to Rob's, I came home meaning to talk to Jake and hear him out like Shay had encouraged, but I found my mom struggling to wrestle my dad back into his wheelchair after a fall. We spent the day at the ER with him getting X-rays. I didn't have the energy to call Jake after that. I couldn't face the conversation. Not on top of dealing with my mom's worry about medical bills and my dad's depression as the doctor told him his symptoms were accelerating.

"Did you get my messages?"

"Yeah."

He turns around then. I'm standing there in just my jeans and a bra and I see his gaze dip to my chest before he looks up, flushing, apologetic. I almost smile as he turns his back again.

"She's not my girlfriend, Em."

I take a deep breath. I want to believe him. I really do.

"We broke up before I came back here."

I pull on a T-shirt. "You can turn around."

He does. We stare at each other awkwardly. I don't know what to do with my hands. Why, when he looks at me, does it feel like a drum circle is taking place inside my chest? It makes it hard to focus or think straight. But I remember what Shay said. I need the truth. "How long were you dating for?"

"Eight months."

Eight months. I swallow, my brain immediately assailed by images of Jake and her in bed together. Is that how he's such a good lover?

"Why is she here?"

Jake sinks down onto the bed, exhaling loudly. "She's not here any longer. She's gone."

My body sags with relief. "Why was she here, then?"

Jake looks at me sheepishly. "She wants to get back together with me."

"Oh." A lump rises up, blocking my throat. "Okay." Does he want to get back with her? Is that why he's here? To tell me that he's made a mistake with me? Why would he choose me, after all, over her? She's beautiful.

I walk toward the window so he can't see my face, which I'm pretty sure must look stricken, but Jake grabs my hand and turns me toward him. He rests his hands on my hips and holds me there, in front of him, looking up at me from the bed. His touch ignites a million signal fires in my body.

"Em. She's not getting me back. I don't want to be with her. I want to be with you."

The leaden feeling in my bones starts to dissipate at his words. Hope reignites, but as easy as it would be to link my fingers through his and fall on top of him, I hold back. I want to believe him. I want to trust him, but I don't know if I can. I pull out of his arms.

"What did she mean about you getting your shit together?"

Jake studies me carefully for a few seconds before he starts speaking. "When I left for the summer, I told her that I needed to deal with some things."

"What things?" I ask.

I can see him struggling with his words. He takes my hand and tugs me gently down onto the bed beside him. "Look, I haven't told you everything," he says to me, threading his fingers through mine.

The lead feeling returns—anesthetic creeping through my veins. What now?

Jake looks at me, suddenly shifty-looking. "About six weeks

ago, I went to a party," he says. "I'd just broken up with Lauren, and my head was a mess." He sees my jaw set and hurries on: "Not about her, about other stuff. Anyway, I got drunk. I don't usually drink, not during hockey season at least, not really ever. But all I could think about was how you were screwing everything up."

I pull my hand from out of his. "What?" How was I screwing everything up?

He shakes his head, wincing again. "I don't mean that literally. It wasn't you screwing things up. It was just . . . I couldn't stop thinking about what had happened. I couldn't stop thinking about you. I haven't been able to stop thinking about you for the last seven years."

I hold my breath, unsure where he's going with this.

"When my uncle died, I started having these nightmares . . ."

I stand up. Nightmares? He had nightmares after his uncle died. Am I supposed to feel sympathy or something? I was having nightmares every night until his uncle died. It wasn't until he was dead and buried that they finally stopped.

Jake's on his feet too. "Shit, Em. I didn't mean it like that," he says. "I'm saying this all wrong. I'd always thought that one day I'd get to confront him, you know? And then it was too late and I felt as if I'd failed you all over again. Why the hell did I wait?" He shakes his head. "I was so angry at myself. And Lauren—it was just too much. She kept wanting something I couldn't give her."

I pull away from him. Is that what it will be like with us, too? Am I expecting something from him that he can't give? Is it because he has to focus his all on hockey?

"So I broke up with her," he continues. "And then I went to this party and I got drunk, way too drunk. Someone offered me a smoke. I got high. I don't even remember the party. I just remember waking up on someone's floor."

Oh God. I almost want to cover my ears so I don't hear the next part. All sorts of things are crossing my mind.

"The next day, there was a random drug test, and I failed it."

My mouth falls open in shock. Jake gives me a grim smile. "My own stupid fault." He sees the question forming on my lips. "My coach agreed to keep it quiet if I agreed to sort out my shit over the summer."

"So this is why you're here, then?" I ask, looking down at my feet. "To sort out your shit? I'm your shit?"

"No," Jake says, then, "Yes."

I look up, vibrating with anger.

"Not in a bad way," Jake adds quickly, seeing my expression. "But yeah, I needed to see you again. I needed to make things right. Finally."

I nod, striving to contain my rage. "So do you feel better now?" I ask, and watch as Jake flinches away from the razor edge of my voice. "Have you made things right? Is your conscience salved? You got me to like you again. You good to go now?"

"No," Jake says, pained. "I can't ever make things right. That's the fucking problem, Em."

"I'm not some kind of pity project, Jake!" I shout. "I'm not here to help you get over whatever feelings of guilt you might have. I have enough to deal with on my own!"

"I know that," Jake says. He turns away, banging his closed fist against his forehead with frustration. "That's not what I mean. I'm sorry."

"You thought you could come here and wheedle your way back into my life and get me to forgive you so you could go away feeling better about yourself and get back into your coach's good books?"

"No!" he says, outraged, and I know that I'm not being fair, but I'm so angry and tired and frustrated. And a part of me is absolutely terrified of giving any more of my heart to Jake. It's easier to salvage what I can and push him away. And it's working. He moves to the door. "I'm going to go," he mumbles.

"Mmm," I say, laughing bitterly. Go on, then, go. It will make everything simpler if he does.

He turns around to look at me, one hand on the doorknob. His expression is so wounded and hurt that I almost feel bad. Almost.

"You know, Em—the reason I broke up with Lauren?" He pauses. "It was because she wanted me to say I loved her. And I couldn't."

He takes a giant breath in and then lets it out in a rush while talking. "And the reason I couldn't say it to her is because I'm in love with someone else and I always have been."

My breath catches. My anger evaporates like breath on a cold day. I don't want to lose him again. The thought lodges like a dart in my brain. Is he saying what I think he's saying?

I glimpse the scar on his chin, the one I gave him when we were kids. I glance at his hands, the ones that held me last night, that touched me in a way no one has ever touched me before or probably ever will again. I feel the invisible thread between us—that's always been between us—pulled taut and about to snap in two.

It doesn't have to be this way! a voice in my head yells. I can let the past go. It doesn't need to define me anymore. The choice is mine. I can speak up and stop this from happening.

But Jake's already out the door and striding down the hall-way.

I listen to his footsteps, willing myself to run after him. He's jogging down the stairs. If I let him go, it's giving his uncle even more power over me, letting him dictate even more of my life than he already has. My feet finally respond to my brain, and I rush out of the bedroom. I race down the stairs and yank open the front door. Jake's nowhere in sight. Where did he go? Panic flaring, I dart outside onto the veranda in my bare feet, ready to sprint up the road after him.

"Hey."

I spin around, heart racing. He's standing behind me in the hallway.

He didn't leave.

Before he can say another word, I throw myself toward him. He opens his arms and catches me, holding me so tight that I instantly feel safe, like I've found my home.

"Don't go," I choke out.

"I'm not going anywhere," he whispers, his lips meeting mine.

Jake

When Em heads off to the store for a shift that afternoon, I convene with Em's dad and Toby in the front room of the house.

"Here are the plans," says Toby, pulling up the CAD files on his laptop.

"Wow," I say, taking in all the detail. He's put in a lot of time. "This is incredible."

Toby preens and Em's dad leans forward in his wheelchair for a closer look.

"We can put in a mezzanine floor, and if we take out the whole side wall and replace it with French windows, it will get the afternoon sun. It'll be perfect," Toby explains.

"I like the deck. I think we should build it out another foot," I say. "What do you think? Add a wood-burning stove too?"

Em's dad nods, but he's frowning. I know why. "Forget about the cost," I tell him. "We've already agreed on the business model. I'll front the initial build costs, and then when it starts turning a profit, we'll figure something out."

"Interest," he slurs.

I shrug. "Whatever you're happy with."

It's awkward talking and wrangling over money with him, and I'd rather not talk about it at all, but I can't disregard his pride. The idea I had a few weeks back was to convert Mr. Lowe's old workshop at the far end of their property into a rental studio similar to the one I'm staying in. I figured it could become a sustainable income for them and help a little with their financial issues. Thanks to Toby's architecture skills, we now have a floor plan. The two of us are going to do all the build work on it ourselves, and I'm fronting the cost using the money from my modeling job. I'm not sure why I want to keep it quiet from Em. I want to surprise her, I guess, but I'm also wary of her reaction when she finds out I'm financing it.

"I think it will take about six weeks in total," says Toby.

"Can we manage it in four?" I ask. I want it done before I leave.

"If we get some help," he says. His face brightens. "I could invite Aaron for a weekend."

"Aaron?" I ask.

"Yeah," says Toby. "We've been in touch."

"In touch?" I ask, wondering how literally he means that.

Toby shrugs. "We're just having fun," he says. "I think I can get him over for a weekend."

"To work a construction site?" I ask skeptically.

"Hard hats, sweaty torsos, the promise of my company for a whole weekend—what's not to love about that idea?"

Mr. Lowe makes a coughing, choking sound. I turn hurriedly back to him. "So, what do you think about the idea for the bathroom?" I ask.

Emerson

Shay pushes open the door to the store and grins at me. In one hand is a plastic bag and in the other a statue of the Eiffel Tower.

"You bought me a statue of the Eiffel Tower?" I ask, stepping around the counter.

"And some cheese," she says, proffering the bag in my direction.

I laugh and we hug. "I'm so glad to see you. Why didn't you come by earlier?"

"I had a few things to take care of," she says mysteriously. "Where's Jake?"

"He's out on the water."

She turns around and scans the bay through the open door. Shay has a sexy-professor look going on that she works to the max. She's wearing a pencil skirt and a vintage silk blouse with heels. Beside her, in old cut-off jeans and a T-shirt, I feel boyish and nondescript, a look I've carefully cultivated over the years. But Shay's always been like this—wearing her grandmother's vintage designer dresses to school. She came to my eighth birthday party wearing a feather boa and a tiara, an actual tiara, studded with diamonds, which had belonged to her Russian great-grandmother.

The least sporty person in the school and one of the most girly, it was weird that we ever became friends, but we did. I'd been sent off the pitch during a soccer match for something— probably arguing with the referee or maybe for being too aggressive in my tackling—and Shay was already on the bench, having forgotten her gym kit for the third week in a row (she didn't actually own a pair of sneakers—still doesn't). We started a conversation about rules and how stupid they were and what a sexist pig the soccer coach was and about how Ice Cream Cherry Chupa Chups were the awesomest thing on planet Earth, and the next thing we knew, we were best friends.

She hops onto the counter and scours the Chupa Chup stand. I reach under the counter, where I've stashed the Ice Cream Cherry–flavored ones just for her. I hand her one and take one for myself.

"How's it going?" she asks. "Did you guys talk?"

"Yeah. He came by this morning."

"I told you that you just needed to hear him out. She's his ex-girlfriend."

I frown at her. "Wait . . . how did you know that?" I glance out the window, then back at Shay. "Did you speak to him?"

Shay shrugs and, grinning, chinks her lollipop against mine. "I might have."

Unbelievable. But she knows I'm not really mad.

"How's business been? Are things looking up?"

"Yeah," I say, thinking of the enthusiastic reviews from the bachelor party that have definitely helped bolster the business.

But then, after a second, I find myself frowning. Things are only good because Jake is here. When he leaves, I'm not sure what will happen. Maybe it will all fall apart when it's back to me providing all the customer service.

My gaze has drifted out of the door and across the water. Jake and the group are just dragging their kayaks out the water. Even from here you can see everyone is smiling. I can just imagine how he's got them eating out of his hand.

Shay hops down off the counter. She waves her half-chewed lollipop at me. "So, tonight, you around? You want to do something? I want to celebrate being back, and we've only got a few weeks left before I leave."

I bite my bottom lip, still staring out the door at Jake. "I can't," I tell her. "Jake's planning something. I'm sorry. But after?"

Shay follows my gaze, watching Jake walk toward us wearing just his board shorts, water dripping off his ripped torso. The Chupa Chup falls out of Shay's mouth and hits the ground, bouncing out the door. "Holy hell," she murmurs, "I hope he's planning what I hope he's planning."

Jake

She doesn't have any idea how beautiful she is, but when she looks up at me through her lashes, a small, almost shy smile playing on her lips, I almost blurt it out. I stop myself. I don't want to sound repetitive.

Em holds a forkful of chocolate cake out to me. "Try some?" she asks.

I take a bite. "That's good," I say. "Not as good as a s'more, though."

She grins and scrapes the chocolate sauce from the plate. I watch her. I could keep watching her like this for a year: happy, relaxed, laughing, eyes shining in the candlelight. Our feet are tangled beneath the table. All night I've been feeling this warm glow in the pit of my stomach.

I really don't want this night to end, but we're the last customers and the waiters are starting to clear the tables as well as their throats. Em's eyes widen when she sees we're the only ones left, and she bursts out laughing. "Oh my God, what time is it?"

"Nearly twelve," I say, waving over the waiter and handing him my card.

Em blushes and looks at the table as I sign my name on the receipt. "Em," I say. "I want to buy you dinner. I can afford it, okay?"

"Okay," she says, "but next time is on me."

I shrug. That's not happening, but I'll deal with that when it arises.

It's cold when we wander out into the night, so I slip off my jacket and put it over Em's shoulders. She leans into me and I put my arm around her waist. When we get to my car, I reach inside the inner pocket of the jacket she's wearing to get the car keys, my hand brushing against her side.

I feel her shiver in response and my hand lingers, tracing a pattern down the silk of her dress, feeling her rib cage rise and fall as rapid as a bird's against my palm.

I glance at her face, at her lips, then press my own against her neck. She tips her head back with an exhale that sends a shiver through me. The jacket falls open and suddenly I'm pressing against her, drinking her in. Her arms wrap around my neck and her hands run through my hair, tugging it, pulling me closer so I'm pressed up against the warmth of her body. I keep kissing up her neck, my heart pounding now in time with hers.

After a minute or two, I have to pull back to catch my breath.

Em's eyes burn like coal in the darkness.

I reach for the door handle. "We'd better go before we get arrested for public indecency. I want to get you home and get you naked."

"Not tonight," she whispers in my ear. "Shay's back. I promised I'd go see her."

I sigh. Damn. I'd forgotten about that. She slips inside the car and I close the door behind her, then jog around to the driver's side, taking a few deep breaths as I go to try to get my blood recirculating to my brain.

Em is curled up on the passenger seat like a cat, with my jacket still around her shoulders. Four weeks, I think as I start the car. Just four weeks. Then we'll be apart a whole semester, unless I can convince her to fly out to see me. If my coach lets me back on the team, which I think he will as we have some major games coming up, then I'll be busy every weekend and most of the week, too—between practice and academic work, I barely get a spare minute. How are we going to make this work? I have no idea. But I know that I'm determined to.

"What are you thinking about?" Em asks me as I drive.

I shake my head at her. I don't want to ruin the mood by telling her.

"Tell me," she wheedles, leaning over the hand brake and kissing my neck.

My hands grip the wheel tighter. She kisses the edge of my jaw.

"Emerson, I'm going to crash," I tell her, laughing.

She stops and sits back in her seat, frowning. "Why did you call me Emerson?" she asks.

"What?"

"You just called me Emerson. You never call me that."

I turn to stare out the window. "I don't know."

Em goes quiet.

"It's just that everyone calls you Emerson now, and I figured maybe you didn't like being called Em anymore."

"No," she says. "I like it when you call me Em."

"Okay," I say. "Em it is."

It's then I look up and see that I've taken a shortcut and it's leading us right by the ice rink. It's too late to turn around. Em's body stiffens beside me as we pass it. She turns away, staring out the opposite window, and the smile vanishes. I could ignore it, talk about something else, but I don't. Instead, I turn to her. "When was the last time you were on the ice?"

She doesn't answer.

"Sorry," I say quickly. "I didn't mean to bring it up." I've been doing my best not to talk about anything from the past, figuring that Em doesn't want to go there and I don't want to do anything that might upset her.

"It's okay," she says, swallowing nervously. "I haven't been back on the ice, not since then. The only thing I kept up with was track. I didn't want to do team sports after. And the track coach was a woman."

I nod, understanding.

"Do you miss it?" I ask after another pause.

Em doesn't answer for a while. "I never used to," she says finally. "But yeah," she says, and her voice cracks. "I miss it."

Emerson

Where are we going?" I ask.

Jake keeps his eyes on the road. "It's a surprise."

"Another surprise?" I ask. "I could get used to this." My stomach dances with butterflies. Are we heading back to his place?

I turn in my seat and watch Jake drive, taking him in, trying to memorize every detail and imprint him onto my memory. Even though we've talked about it and agreed we'll commit to a long-distance relationship, there's a little niggling doubt in my mind that refuses to quiet—an unspoken fear that when he leaves, that will be it—that he won't come back, that things will fizzle and die between us.

I brush the thought away, bury it deep, and watch him as he signals and turns right. I like watching him drive. Like everything he does, there's a certain easy, graceful skill to it.

Feeling me staring at him, he turns and smiles, but I note the smile doesn't quite make it to his eyes and that there's a furrowed line between them. He's worried about something. He signals again and pulls into a parking lot. I glance out the window and my heart does a double slam into my ribs before starting to hammer madly.

"What are we doing here?"

Jake pulls into a parking spot and kills the engine. His hands stay on the wheel, but he turns to face me. "Okay, you can tell me if you think this is a stupid idea, and maybe it is, I don't know, but I want you to get back on the ice."

Dumb with disbelief, I look out the window again and catch a glimpse of the skating rink sign and a billboard advertising the Bainbridge Eagles. My pulse starts to skitter and slide like a puck smashed across slow ice.

"Just hear me out," Jake says in a gentle voice. He takes my hands in his. "You were good, Em," he says. "And you loved it. And you had to give it up." I start to protest, but he cuts me off. "I get why you did. I totally get it. But isn't there a part of you that's angry about it?"

I scowl at him. "Of course there is," I hiss.

Jake gives a small shrug. "So take it back. Don't let him win."

He already has! I want to yell, but I stop myself. I glance out the window at the rain-lashed parking lot and the entrance, and my gut does a sudden loop the loop, relief shooting through me when I see the sign on the door.

"It's closed," I say, gesturing at the rink. "It's Monday." Lightness fills me up like helium.

Jake pulls something out of his pocket and waves it in my face.

"What's that?" I ask, pulling back, my gut clenching.

"The key."

"The key to what?" I ask.

"To the rink."

"How did you . . ."

Jake shrugs. "I still know the owner. And I promised to come teach a boot camp next weekend in exchange."

I open my mouth to say something, but nothing comes out. No words can make it up my throat because my heart is in the way.

Jake takes my hand again, his thumb stroking a pattern over my knuckles. "Come and skate with me," he says. "It's just going to be you and me in there. Just the two of us. Come on, we used to dream about breaking in and having the place all to ourselves." He's grinning at me, still a little uncertainly, trying to nudge me into it. His eyes have a low glimmer in them. "I dare you . . . ," he whispers.

I breathe in deeply, my body responding as much to his touch as to the look in his eye and the challenge he's just laid down.

"I don't know . . . ," I say. My gaze is tugged once again back to the door. And suddenly, out of nowhere, memories start to assault me, flickering thick and fast in front of my eyes: Coach Lee stepping toward me with that smile on his face, the echoing chill of the changing rooms, the metallic smash of my head against the locker doors, the stabbing of his fingers on my body as if I were made of clay and he was trying to shape me into something that was to his liking, the angry slash of his mouth.

"It's okay, breathe, just breathe."

I look at Jake, confused, then realize that I'm gripping his hand hard and hyperventilating, sucking in air, which doesn't seem to be filling my lungs at all.

"Em," he says. "It's okay. You're okay."

I rest my head back against the seat and Jake breathes with me, stroking my hair, trying to calm me.

"You know," I say to him after my heartbeat has gone back to normal and my lungs are cooperating once again, "for ages after it happened, I just wanted to forget about it. I actually wished that I could go back in time and change things. I wished that I had fought back. And even if I couldn't change what happened, I wished I'd kept my mouth shut or lied to my mom. I used to think that maybe if I had, everything would have just gone on being the same." I look at Jake. "You wouldn't have left. My parents wouldn't have been screwed financially. No one at school would have known. The teachers wouldn't have treated me the way they did. I might not have dated Rob." I pull a face. "Actually, there's no way I would have dated Rob."

Jake's scowl deepens.

"All those things could have been different if I'd just kept my mouth shut. But you know what, Jake?"

He shakes his head.

"I'm glad I didn't. Even though I had to go through so much crap," I whisper, "and no one believed me, even though there were days when I honestly thought about running away or, I don't know . . . giving up . . . I'm glad I told the truth. I don't regret it. Because it was out there, you know?"

He nods, still scowling.

"Even if no one believed me, at least it wasn't a secret. It felt like the only way to not be a victim was to come out and tell the truth. If I'd kept it a secret, it would have been worse in the long run."

"I just—I wish I could undo it all. I wish I could turn back the clock and make things right."

I laugh under my breath and dip my head to kiss his palm.

"I think we should get out of here. I'm sorry I brought you."

He turns on the engine, sticking the car into drive with an angry motion. He's mad at himself.

I grab for his arm. "No," I say.

He takes his foot off the gas and looks over at me.

"I want to do this," I tell him.

He studies me for a beat. "You're sure?" he asks. "Because we can just go. It's not important. We can go back to my place and just hang out."

"No," I say, louder, taking a deep breath and rolling back my shoulders. "Let's do this. I want to do this." Before I change my mind, I almost add.

Before he can say anything else, I'm out of the car. My legs feel wobbly, but I'm determined. Jake told me that it was okay. But it's not. It's not okay. I'm sick of feeling this way.

Jake takes my hand and steers me toward the door. I focus on his palm against mine, the solidness of his body—a barrier between me and the world—and try to banish the images jostling in my head.

Jake unlocks the door and we enter the echoing dark. I shiver instantly. I'd forgotten how cold the rink was, had forgotten the smell, too: sweat, ice, ripe foot odor, stale popcorn. It brings back more memories—of games, of practicing with Jake, of the euphoric buzz of winning.

Jake fumbles for the light switch, and when the fluorescents flicker and flare on, I blink. I'm primed to react—expecting to be hit by more memories—but actually the place looks so different that I can hardly reconcile it to the place from my memory. They've changed the layout of the reception area and painted it in garish reds and blues. It could be a different place altogether. I glance over toward the double doors that lead to the locker rooms, the place where Jake first kissed me. The doors are the only thing that is still the same.

"You okay?" Jake asks me anxiously.

I nod. He takes my hand again and leads me toward the doors. My body tenses. Jake feels it. He stops at the doors, barring my way.

"What?" I ask. I just want to get this over with. I've decided that this is like therapy, like climbing back on a bicycle or a horse after falling off. I just need to do it once—skate one lap and then we can go. Five minutes at the most. I'll have proven to myself I can do it and that I've won.

Jake drops his bag—which I realize now must contain skates—and takes my face in his hands. The world falls instantly away as it does every time he touches me. He takes it slowly, tauntingly, as if he's been given a do-over for that first kiss we shared five years ago right in this very spot, and, by the time his lips meet mine, I'm not sure if I'm floating or have my feet still firmly planted on the ground. When Jake releases me a few seconds or minutes later, I'm as dizzy as if I'd just done a flying sit spin on the ice.

"What was that for?" I ask, breathless.

"Old times' sake," he murmurs, his lips still brushing mine. "Come on." He picks up the bag and swings it over his shoulder. Then he pushes open the door, holding it open for me, and leads the way to the rink.

I stare at the ice—polished as a mirror—and I experience that loop-the-loop feeling once again, as if my stomach is on a spin cycle. I grin at Jake. He grins back, revealing his dimple.

"Here," he says, crouching down and unzipping his bag. He pulls out a pair of skates. "Your size," he says, handing them to me.

I stare at him in wonder. "You bought me new skates?" I ask.

He shrugs and nudges me back into one of the plastic seats lining the rink. He hands me some extra socks to put on, and when I've pulled on the skates and stood up, he also hands me an extra sweater. "Until you warm up," he tells me.

I pull it on. It hangs almost to my knees.

"It's one of mine," he says. "Sorry, it's too big."

He helps me roll up the sleeves. I want to bury my nose in the collar and breathe in deep, but I stop myself, at least until he's not watching.

Jake's wearing jeans and a long-sleeved T-shirt. I watch him pull on his own skates—an old, battered pair that he must use for practice—and start to feel a tingling feeling shiver up my legs, bubbles starting to simmer in my stomach. I used to feel like this before a game.

Jake jumps up when he's done with his skates and takes my hand. "Ready?" he asks.

I nod, so nervous I can't talk.

That first step onto the ice is as perfect a rush as our first kiss. With Jake's fingers linked through mine, it's easy. I realize that I'd been worried I might have forgotten how to skate, but I haven't. As we pick up speed, Jake skating backward, pulling me with him, the tingling feeling takes over, spreading down my legs and arms. "I can do this!" I shout in glee.

Jake lets go of my hands, skating out of my way, still facing toward me. I hunch down lower, and drive into the ice. It's good ice: cold, with no snow layer on it; easy to accelerate on. The speed is indescribable.

Jake takes the corners without even looking behind him. There's a light in his eyes—one I recognize from when he was younger—he comes alive on the ice. It's the same joyful, trium-phant, electrified look that he gets when he's daring me to do something. The same look I saw the other night in the tent when he was kissing me, and that time outside the restaurant when his hands were hovering against my sides, his fingers sliding over my dress.

That's what this feels like: sliding over silk sliding over skin. I'm laughing—it's bubbling up and out of me, and suddenly Jake's skating toward me, grabbing me by both hands, spinning me around. He digs his blade into the ice, braking, showering us both in a snowstorm of ice, and then catches me against his chest as we slam to a stop.

Out of breath, I look up at him. "Again," I say.

Emerson

(Then)

The phone rings.

"Don't answer," I hear my dad grunt angrily.

It keeps ringing, plaintive at first, as though begging us to answer, but then, when no one picks up, the ringing seems to become accusatory, before plain irate. I cover my head with the pillow and scrunch my eyes shut. Finally, it stops, and I let out a deep breath. But then a few seconds later, it starts up again. A pneumatic drill through my skull.

Before I can bury my head under the pillow again, I hear my dad stomping across the hallway, my mom's voice, soft and pleading, following behind him. The ringing is cut off abruptly.

"Bugger the hell off! We're not answering any questions," my dad yells before banging down the receiver. My mom mumbles something, and I strain to make out the conversation.

". . . another journalist?"

"I don't know. I'm going to unplug it."

"But what if . . ."

My dad's fuming. I can hear him pacing. His anger is a palpable thing—a force that makes me want to crawl under the bed and hide. I can't look him in the face. Looking anyone in the face has suddenly become impossible.

I keep wondering if I should have lied, though—told my mom I was fine. What if I had just stayed silent? Made something up? Told her that Coach had just bawled me out for attacking Reid?

No. No. No. You did the right thing. That's what my mom told me. That's what my dad told me too. That's what they kept telling me all night and all day, through the numerous interviews with the cops and a social worker. You're doing the right thing.

But why does the right thing feel so bad?

"I'm going to go there!" My dad's voice carries up the stairs. "I'm going to deal with this my own damn self. Goddamn cops. They're just sitting there on their asses doing nothing. Why haven't they arrested him? He should be in the county lockup, not walking around preying on—"

"Shhhh, shhhhh," my mom urges, hushing my dad, clearly scared I'll hear him. Too late for that.

He drops the volume to a whisper that still has the force of a tornado behind it. "What?!" he whisper-shouts. "I'm just expected to sit here and do nothing while they conduct some sham investigation? We all know he and the coach are buddies. It's his word against Em's, and we know he's denying it. Who's the sheriff going to believe?"

"Quiet!" my mom hisses.

"You saw they didn't believe her. They think she's making it up!"

I draw in a breath and something sharp as a screwdriver twists in my gut.

"She's not making it up," my mom says. "I was there. I saw."

"You didn't see it happen, though, did you?"

There's that pain in my gut again—twisting hard.

"Well, no . . . ," I hear my mom say. "But I saw her face. I could tell something had just happened." A pause. "She wouldn't make this up."

There's another, longer pause, and I find myself gripping the edge of the bed, heart pulsating like a frog in my throat. Doubt charges the air like static before a thunderstorm. He doesn't believe me. My dad doesn't believe me. It's as if someone has taken the screwdriver and punched it right through my rib cage into my heart.

"I'm going to kill that son of a bitch!" my dad yells, making the floorboards leap. The breath bursts out of me in a sob. My gut untwists as relief rushes through me. He doesn't doubt me. Of course he doesn't.

"No!" my mom shouts.

I don't catch the next few words she speaks, but I hear my dad mumble something and then my mom urging him into the kitchen, using the same placating, sympathetic tone she uses on him when his team loses the playoffs.

I slump back on the bed. I knew that the cops didn't believe me. It was obvious from the sideways glances they were sharing with each other and the patronizing tone they used to interview me, not forgetting the way they spoke over the top of my head, acting like I wasn't even in the room.

"Are you sure she wasn't imagining it?"

"You know, girls these days, they've got active imaginations."

"He's a good guy. I can't believe he'd . . ."

I glance down at my palms. I'm digging my nails in and they've made a row of crescent moons. But I don't feel anything. I stare at my arms. At my legs. They feel weird. My body doesn't feel like my own anymore but like a costume I'm being forced to wear. I press my fingers to my lips. They're dry and flaky. Nausea whooshes suddenly out of nowhere and a ball of vomit rockets up my throat. I swallow it with difficulty and then curl onto my side.

Jake's face appears in my mind's eye, and I try to blank it. I don't want to think about him. It makes me feel squirmy and hot inside. He must have heard by now. Everyone must have heard. My mom says I shouldn't worry about what anyone says because we have the truth on our side, but I can't help but worry because I know what the kids at my school are like. They're like snipers, always on the lookout for anyone to take a shot at. I'll be a prime target. I can just imagine them laughing, making comments, calling me a liar. I can picture the graffiti on the bathroom walls.

There's a projector screen in my head, and it keeps on playing back what happened on a loop. I've managed to partially block it out by forcing myself to recite poems and the lyrics to songs, but every so often my focus jumps to the screen—to Coach Lee moving toward me—to his face in my face and his hands . . .

The thought of other people—of Jake—imagining it is too horrible. It's his uncle. I sit bolt upright. It's his uncle, I think again. Jake worships his uncle. His uncle was once a national hockey player. Jake dreams of being a hockey player. He'll never believe me over his uncle. Why would he?

The knife is back—twisting, gutting, slicing, ripping.

I look around. The room feels suddenly too small to contain me. My body feels too small to contain the screams that are ricocheting around inside my chest like echoes trying to find their way out of a deep, dark cave. My mind is too small to contain the images flickering onto the projector screen. I need to get out. My legs twitch. I need to get out of here.

I need to disappear.

Jake

It's past midnight, and the ice is covered in a coating of wet slush. The nets are up at either end of the rink, and Em is facing me wearing my leg pads and gloves, glowering at me and gripping her stick like she's defending the Ark of the Covenant. I forgot what she used to be like when she played goaltender. She never used to get put in that position often because she was too fast to waste on tending goal, but now that I'm trying to slide one past her, I remember how fierce she could be when given the opportunity to play defense.

Unfortunately for her, she's now playing a pro, and though she took to the ice again like a duck to water, she's still a little off her game when it comes to hockey. I play gently against her at first, letting her have a few scores and saves, but now I've upped my play and she's frustrated, huffing at me.

I could back down, but something about her expression makes me not want to. I like seeing her this way: angry, obstinate, putting up a fight. It's the old Em. And though I'm not unappreciative of the ways she's mellowed and grown up (she's no longer threatening to throw a stick at my head when I get a goal past her, for one thing), I still think a little more fire in her belly would do her good.

"One more!" she yells.

I contemplate her and then shrug, shaking my head. "If you insist," I say, scooping up the puck with my stick and sliding it over the ice toward her. I pick up speed, racing toward her, seeing the faint flicker of alarm in her eyes as I get within ten feet of her with no sign of slowing. But instead of sliding the puck between her legs and into the net, I skid to a stop in front of her, pull her into my arms, and kiss her. Her cheeks and nose are cold, but her lips are warm enough to melt ice.

"What was that?" she demands, pulling out of my arms after a few seconds, looking unimpressed. "You were meant to take a shot."

"I thought you were asking for one more kiss," I say, laughing.

She whacks me across the shins with her stick—just lightly, which is good, as I'm not wearing shin pads. "Ouch," I say, skating out of her reach.

"Sorry," she says.

"Did you just apologize?" I ask her, skidding to a stop, just outside of hitting distance.

She makes a face at me. "Don't get used to it."

"Oh, I'm not," I say, laughing still, as I grab hold of the net and start dragging it off the ice.

"We have to go already?" Em asks, her shoulders slumping.

"Yeah, it's almost one," I tell her.

"Oh my God," she says, her eyes flying to the clock above the rink. She skates after me, her arm looping around my waist. "Thank you," she says as we step off the ice. "That was . . ." Her face glows from the exercise and the cold. "The best."

I smile.

"You are the best," she says.

"I'll take that," I murmur, my gaze falling like it always does to her lips. I pull her close for another kiss, this one longer and deeper. By the time I'm done, her face isn't cold anymore. Her skin is fire to the touch, and I think my own core temperature has risen so high the rink beneath us is in danger of turning completely to slush.

"Come on," I say, throwing my arm around her shoulders. "Let's get going. I've got more planned." I need to get her home. And I don't mean to her house. I mean to mine. She must be able to tell what I mean by "more planned," because she smiles up at me knowingly and sits down, in a hurry to take off her skates.

"Do you ever think it's weird?" she says as she undoes her laces.

"What?" I ask, sitting down beside her.

"Us," she says as she kicks off the skates. "I mean, us being together." When she says "being together," she keeps her head down, but I see the flush creep up her neck. "I keep getting flashes of you at thirteen. I keep being reminded of how we were friends, that we've known each other since we were babies. Sometimes I have to blink just to make sure it's really you. It feels like you're a stranger"—she squints at me—"but at the same time like I've known you forever. Do you know what I mean?"

I nod. "I think it's because we're getting to know each other all over again. There's a lot that's the same but a lot that's changed, too."

"How am I different?" she asks, pulling on her shoes.

"You're mellower and more guarded," I say, choosing my words carefully. "I can't read you like I used to. Not all the time, anyway." I drop the skates in the bag. "But I figure I'm getting better at it."

She smiles a little to herself.

"You're not as argumentative," I add. "Or at least, not *quite* as much."

She elbows me in the side. "Still violent, though," I say, grabbing for her fingers.

"I think you're the same," she says, pulling back to study me. "Maybe a little bigger."

"Bigger?"

"Taller."

"Just a little?"

"Yeah"—she smiles slyly—"just a little."

"The same, huh?" I'm not sure whether that's a compliment. I was a scrawny kid back then who didn't have a clue how to kiss.

Em strokes my hair back from my face, her eyes searching mine. "You still have so much good in you. You haven't lost that. Everyone always loved you. I used to envy you for that."

"Everyone loved you, too."

She whacks me with the back of her hand. "No, they didn't."

I snatch her wrists. "Well, they were kind of awed by you. You were fierce. You still are. It's what I loved about you. It's what I still love about you."

We both fall silent, and I quickly bend down and start zipping up the bag, aware of Em looking at me out of the corner of her eye.

"How long did you like me for?" she asks.

"What?"

"Back then, when you kissed me. The first time, I mean. How long had you liked me for?"

I shrug. "I don't know. A while." Oh God, I knew one day she'd ask me this, but I still don't have an answer prepared. I stand up, throwing the bag over my shoulder.

"Tell me! I'd been thinking about you for months. It was driving me crazy. I couldn't get you out of my head."

I blink at her in amazement. "Months? Seriously?"

She nods. "What about you? Come on."

"If I told you, you'd laugh."

"I won't."

I inhale deeply. "I liked you for years." Her eyes widen in both surprise and disbelief. What the hell, I may as well tell her the whole truth. . . . "Forever. I don't even remember a time I wasn't in love with you. There's never been anyone else."

Em offers me her skeptical face. "What about Lauren?" she asks.

"Yeah, okay," I admit. "There have been girls, but nothing serious."

"Eight months is pretty serious."

"What about Rob? You dated him for years."

She pulls a face, her nose wrinkling. "Don't remind me."

We start walking toward the exit. "Was it serious?" I ask, not wanting to know, but at the same time wondering if she ever told him that she loved him. She must have.

We've reached the door—the spot where we kissed all those years ago. This time it's Em who reaches for my hand and stops me. "No," she whispers. "It wasn't serious."

I drop the bag and run my fingers through her hair, pulling her toward me. Taking a deep breath, I press my forehead against hers. She takes a deep breath in too, and I feel her shiver against me.

"Not like this," I murmur.

She shakes her head. "No, not like this."

Em

Jake takes me back to his place. Neither of us talks in the car on the way there, but the atmosphere is so electric in the car, I think we're both scared to move or say anything in case the air ignites. Jake doesn't take his eyes off the road except to glance over at me once or twice, and the fire gleaming in his eyes makes my pulse leap. A warmth spreads through me at the thought of what's coming, an anticipation like nothing I've ever experienced.

We pull into his driveway and climb out of the car. It's quiet except for an owl hooting. The moon is full, and we can see the pinpricks of stars in the patches of dark sky between the tree-tops. Jake takes my hand and leads me in silence up the stairs to his apartment.

He fumbles with the key, and I wonder if he's nervous, which makes me feel slightly better because I am too, but not as much as I am excited. I never once felt excited about sleeping with Rob; in fact, I used to try to put him off as much as possible. I didn't even like him seeing me naked, but the way Jake looks at me makes it impossible to feel anything other than beautiful.

Jake shuts the door behind us and there's an awkward pause where we both just stand there. He hustles past me. "You want something to eat? Drink?" he asks.

I shake my head. There's only one thing I want. And it's standing right in front of me.

"Shower?" he asks.

I pause and then nod. I could use a shower after the skating, and it's cold inside. As if reading my mind, Jake kneels down by the wood-burning stove in the living room and strikes a match to get it going.

As soon as it starts to blaze, he gets up and walks toward me, taking me by the hand and leading me into the bathroom. He turns the shower taps on and then tugs me by the hand toward him. I let him. One thing I love about Jake is how safe I feel with him.

He pulls my sweater over my head and tosses it to the floor, then slowly unbuttons my jeans. I step back to pull them down as he watches. His gaze travels the length of my legs and then he pulls his own T-shirt off in one quick move. I can't help myself. I move toward him and rest my hands against his chest, stroking my palms over his shoulders and down until they rest over his heart. I can feel it pounding.

His arms loop around my waist and he pulls me closer, his hands sliding up my spine to undo my bra. He discards it with a trace of impatience and pulls me closer, his mouth hot—tracing across my skin, making me shiver. He draws me even closer against him so we're skin to skin, and an ache starts to build inside me until I'm as impatient as him.

I tear at his jeans and he takes over undoing his fly as I step out of my underwear. The next thing I know, Jake's stepping me backward and into the shower. Hot water drenches me, and I gasp as Jake presses me against the cold tile behind. He's against me, his hands stroking up my sides even as I pull him closer, raking my fingers through his hair, desperate to feel every inch of him against my body.

His mouth is on mine, his hands holding my arms above my head as he keeps kissing me until I'm breathless. Then he drops to his knees. I tilt my head, letting the water shower over my face, as Jake expertly finds the place that makes me moan.

He doesn't make me come, not yet, but I get close. I pull him back so we're face-to-face. "I want you inside me," I tell him, breathless. "Now."

He grins, water cascading down his body, and I let my own gaze fall the length of him, biting my lip in anticipation. He takes my hand and we climb out of the shower. I stumble on shaking legs and he catches me and wraps me in a towel, drying me off before he takes a towel himself and wraps it around his waist.

He takes me outside into the living room, where the fire has now warmed the room up enough that when Jake tugs my towel open, I don't even shiver. Or maybe it's his look that warms me. Either way, I stand there naked as Jake continues to stare at me.

"You are so beautiful," he murmurs, and a lump catches in my throat. He's the first person who has ever told me that. "You have no idea," he says, shaking his head as though marveling at a miracle.

"So are you," I say, running my hands over his skin, watching it contract in a long shiver. I strip his towel from his waist, and he smiles at me as I throw it to the ground, but the smile disappears when I push him backward hard and he lands on the sofa.

He narrows his eyes at me, but I straddle him before he can protest. "I want you to know something," I tell him as I lean down and kiss him on the lips. "I love you. And you're the only person I've ever said that to."

He catches my hands in one of his and forces me to look at him. His other hand curls around my neck. "Same," he whispers.

"And"—I smile, cheeks burning—"you're the only person who's ever made me come."

He frowns at me as he works out what that means. "Well, then you've got some catching up to do," he says, and he rolls me over onto my back and starts kissing me all over.

It's not until I'm aching so badly for him that I'm almost in tears that Jake tosses away the condom wrapper and finally pushes inside me. He rests on his forearms and he's as gentle as can be, but I let out a cry anyway. He stops, but I urge him on, wrapping my legs around him to pull him in deeper. He sighs against me and I can feel every muscle in his body taut as a wire, as though it's taking a monumental effort for him to hold back.

"More," I whisper, urging him not to hold anything back. I want him every bit as much as I can feel he wants me.

He hesitates, but when I urge him again, he moves inside me even faster, his fingers still touching me, stroking me until I think I'm going to lose total control. My fingers bite into his waist, drawing him into me, and I arch up to meet him, desperate to feel all of him. I had no idea it could ever be like this, that it could ever be this good. It's out-of-this-world unbelievable.

"Are you close?" Jake whispers in my ear.

I nod, feeling myself about to lose control. Jake strokes me with his hand as he drives into me even harder. I can feel his whole body starting to tremble. I bite my lip and suddenly I'm coming—a long wave of pleasure that rides through my body so hard that I cry out loudly. Jake's waited and as soon as he feels it, he comes too, collapsing down on top of me, breathing hard, his face buried in my hair.

Jake

My heart is going to burst out of my chest. I'm aware that I'm probably crushing Em, but I can't seem to make my muscles obey any command. Em strokes her hands down my back and I shiver, pressing my lips against her neck and her damp hair. I'm still inside her, and I take a second to revel in the feeling.

She hasn't moved or said anything, so, worrying that I'm crushing her, I slide my arm beneath her waist and roll her onto her side so we're lying facing each other. I have to brush her hair out of the way so I can see her properly. She's flushed, breathing fast, her lips bee-stung.

Her arms come around my neck and she presses against me and I breathe in deeply. That was the best sex I've ever had. I can't bear the thought of her sleeping with Rob, but at least I know that they had nothing on what we have. And I can safely say the same about any girl I've been with. I've told Em that there have been a few—hockey players don't exactly have to try very hard to get girls—but nothing serious, nothing that felt this intense or so right. No one who could ever hold a single light to Em.

Every nerve in my body feels as though it's being stroked, and the more that Em presses against me and traces her fingertips down my torso, the more shocks I feel zapping through me. If she keeps it up, then I'm going to be ready to go again in a few minutes, but by the sly smile on her face, I'm guessing maybe that's her plan.

"I like making you come," I murmur.

"I like you making me come," she answers, laughing. And there it is, that braying donkey laugh I've been waiting on.

I still can't believe that Rob never made it happen for her. What was the guy thinking? Why did she stay with him so long? It doesn't matter. She's mine now. And I'm never letting her go.

"How are you feeling?" I ask.

"Ready for second period." She grins.

I smile at her use of ice hockey terminology. "Yeah," I say, "but are you going to be ready for third period and penalties? I think there are going to be penalties. As well as overtime."

She's grinning so wide now that I can see all her teeth. She slips out of my arms and climbs on top of me, her thighs gripping my waist. "I hope you don't expect to beat me, McCallister," she says, scowling.

"Wait," I growl at her. "We're on the same team, Lowe."

She bends down and kisses me on the lips. "Yeah," she says, "you're right. Let's see how many goals we can score."

Em

I find my mom in the kitchen, sitting at the table surrounded by mountains of paperwork and a calculator. She looks up, flustered, when I walk in and pushes her glasses up onto her head.

"How was last night?" she asks.

I can't stop the grin from taking over. "Amazing," I say.

My mom raises an eyebrow. "You stayed at Jake's?" she asks.

Oh God, I realize she thinks I'm describing something else as amazing, which it was, but she doesn't need to know that. "No," I say quickly. "I'm talking about skating. Jake took me skating."

My mom gapes at me. "Skating?"

I nod, opening the refrigerator and grabbing the milk. My thigh muscles and shoulders are killing me, but it was worth it. So worth it. "Yeah," I say, pouring a glass. "He got us private access. We were the only ones there. It was so fun."

My mom shakes her head, smiling. "Have you told your dad?"

"No. Not yet. Is he awake?"

She nods. I lean over her shoulder. "You doing the accounts?" I ask.

"Mmm," she murmurs, shuffling some papers.

"How are things looking?" I ask.

She gives me a bright smile. "Better."

I narrow my eyes at her. My mom's a lousy liar. Out the corner of my eye, I notice a red stamp on one of the papers at the edge of the table and grab for it. My mom tries to stop me, but it's in my hand now. I read it, my heart tumbling to a stop.

"The bank is foreclosing?" I ask, my voice trembling.

My mom snatches the letter from my hand.

"How long have you known?" I ask.

"Em," my mom says weakly. "It's just a warning letter. I'm going in to speak with the manager today."

"But . . . ," I start to argue. "I thought things were picking up. With Jake and everything . . ."

"They are, but it's a little too late. I'm hoping to show them the new projections, though, and get them off our backs for a little while longer."

My shoulders sag. "It's always going to be this way, isn't it?" I ask. "We're never going to be in the clear. It doesn't matter how much we bring in when we have bills like these. . . ." I grab for one of the invoices from the health-care provider.

My mom sighs heavily. "We'll manage," she says, but she can't look me in the eye.

"How?" I ask, hearing the note of despair in my voice.

Just then we hear the sound of something smashing and my dad calls out from the front room. We both start for the door, but my mom takes my arm and pulls me to a stop before I can get through it. "Don't say anything to your father, okay?" she says.

I nod.

Jake

The phone wakes me at stupid o'clock in the morning. I'm groggy when I answer it, and it takes me a few seconds to understand what the person on the other end is saying.

I sit up. "Sorry? Say that again?"

"This is Jo Furness from ESPN. Could we get a quote?"

"What?" I ask, rubbing my eyes. I glance blearily at the clock. It's only 6:44 a.m.

"About the drug test that you failed."

Instantly, I'm wide awake.

"What does this mean for your career, do you think? Can you tell us why your coach covered it up? Is this indicative of a bigger issue at play in college league hockey?"

With my blood turning to slush in my veins and my heart hammering a thousand beats a minute, I hang up the phone and then sit there for five minutes, just staring at it in my hand. It keeps ringing—the number unidentified. I keep declining the calls. In the end I turn it off.

Shit. How did the media find out? I get out of bed, weak-kneed, and start pacing. What does this mean? I reach for my phone again. My first instinct is to call Em, but then I remember the time. No. I need to think straight. I need to speak to my coach, find out what's going on.

My pulse races ragged in my throat, making me feel like I'm about to throw up. It's only now that I'm faced with losing my career that I realize how much I want it. Yes, I told Em that sometimes I'm tired of hockey and the crap that goes with it, and I know that it's a short-lived career, but the thought of it all being pulled out from under my feet because of one stupid mistake is enough to send me into a spiraling panic.

"Sarge?" I say as soon as my coach picks up the phone.

"Who is this?" he barks. Coach Foster is an old hockey pro. He reminds everyone of a character from an old Vietnam War movie, the screaming sergeant—which is why we all call him "Sarge" rather than "Coach."

"It's McCallister," I say.

"What do you want?"

"I . . . ESPN just called me."

"What?" Sarge snaps.

"They know. About the drug test. About you covering it up."

"Shiiiiiiit," Sarge mutters.

I wait. He doesn't say anything for a while. "Who called you?" he suddenly demands.

"I don't know. I don't remember. A woman. She wanted a quote."

"Tell me you didn't give her one," he growls. "Tell me that."

"I hung up."

"Good. Keep your phone off. Give me a landline number or some other number I can call you on."

I think for a moment and then give him the number of the store. I'm supposed to be working there in an hour.

"Does anyone know where you are?" he asks next.

"Um, my parents," I say. "I guess maybe a few others. I don't know." My head is full of wool; I can't think straight.

"Right, here's what we're going to do," Sarge says, and I find myself calming down just hearing his straightforward, no-nonsense tone. He's got this. Everything is going to be okay. "You listening?" he barks.

"Yes," I say.

"You're going to not answer your phone, and you're going to keep a low profile," he warns. "I'm going to find out what's going on and who the hell leaked it, then I'll call you back."

I swallow. "Okay," I say. He hangs up and I sit there contemplating the shit I am. Shit I brought on myself. How can one stupid mistake count?

Because the stupid mistakes always do.

I'm first at the store. I'm covering a shift for Toby, who's using the time off to work on the construction site at Em's place. He's managed to turn the project into one he can get college credit for, so it's a win-win situation. I stand at the counter, staring at the phone, waiting for it to ring. When the door pings behind me, I jump.

"Hey," Em says.

I turn around. She's smiling, but her smile disappears when she sees my face.

"What's wrong?" she asks, freezing on the spot.

"They found out."

"What?" She scrunches her face in confusion.

"ESPN. The sports channel. They know about my drug test—that I failed it. A journalist called me this morning."

Em comes toward me. "What does that mean?" she asks.

I shake my head. She leads me to the stool and sits me down. "I don't know. I'm waiting to hear."

"It'll be okay," she says, putting her arms around me. I rest my head on her shoulder and try to breathe, but all I can think about is the penalty for a failed drug test. I know what it is. I've seen it happen before to other players. A suspension for the season, sometimes a total lifetime ban, depending on the type and scale of the drug abuse. The phone rings, jolting us apart. Em reaches for it, but I beat her to it, snatching it to my ear.

"Jake?" Sarge barks.

The fact that Sarge is using my first name makes my whole body sag. It's got to be bad. I collapse down onto the stool.

"I've just gotten off the phone with an old contact at ESPN. He gave me a heads-up. Someone leaked the news to them. Who'd you tell? Who knew about it?"

I wrack my head. Who knew? The people at the party where I passed out, I guess. But they don't know I failed the test. The only other people who knew about that were Em and . . .

"Lauren," I say in a whisper into the phone.

"Your girlfriend?" Sarge asks.

"*Ex*-girlfriend," I manage to say.

"She's gone and dropped you right in it. She sent them the actual proof, too."

"What?" I ask, my heart rate suddenly increasing. Then I remember. "Oh God, the letter was in my dorm room. In a drawer."

"Genius, McCallister."

"But what's going to happen now?" I ask.

"Well," he says with a sigh, "ESPN is running with the story. I tried to get them to drop it, but it ties into that big exposé they've been running on college sports—you know, the whole sex, drugs, and rock-and-roll lifestyle story."

"But that's not me," I hear myself argue, and it sounds like someone else talking, pleading. I hop off the stool and start pacing, aware that Em is standing beside me, tensed, listening in on the conversation.

"I know," Sarge says. "But you're the poster child for hockey at the moment. It makes a good story."

I run my hand through my hair. "What does this mean for my contract?" I ask—the question that's been running through my head like a siren wail since the phone call this morning. "Are they going to drop me?"

"I don't know," says Sarge. "I need to speak with your agent. But, Jake, that's the least of your worries right now."

I collapse back onto the stool. I can't even bring myself to ask the question.

"The college administrators are going to be on this."

The room starts to spin. I hadn't even considered that. My scholarship. My degree. It's all in the balance. If I'm kicked out of college, then I'm out of the hockey leagues. I won't even get my degree. My whole future will go up in smoke.

"But it was just some weed," I start to protest. "Everyone in college smokes weed. I do it one time and suddenly I'm out?" I think of all the other stuff I know that goes on in college. How the hell can this make the news? How can it get me thrown out?

"Let's not jump to conclusions," Sarge says, trying to calm me.

"But it's a possibility, right? That I'm not just booted off the team but I'm kicked out of school, too?"

Sarge doesn't say anything. I feel Em's hand on my back, squeezing my shoulder.

"Shit," I say, suddenly seeing that the dark hole I've been staring into isn't so much of a hole as it is a grave.

"Hopefully, it won't come to that," Sarge says, but I hear the note of uncertainty in his voice.

I laugh out loud at the ridiculousness of the situation—at my own stupidity.

"I'm going to fight for you, McCallister. All the way. But you need to get yourself a lawyer."

"What?" I say.

"The police are likely going to want to interview you."

"What? Why?" I say.

"Standard procedure when drugs are involved."

After a few more minutes of talk in which Sarge runs me through the rules and what he's going to do next, I hang up and look at Em, unable to think or talk. She opens her arms and I take a step toward her. She catches me, holds me, hugging me tight, like she's never going to let me go. "It'll be okay," I hear her say.

How can it be okay? I want to ask. I've just lost everything because of one stupid, reckless mistake.

"I need a lawyer," I say, pulling back, my head still spinning with the crazy. "Where do I get a lawyer?"

"Shay's mom," Em says, reaching for the phone. "I'll call her."

Em

I can't sit still. My foot is tapping. I jump up and start pacing the lobby of the police station.

"They've been ages," I say, glancing through the glass doors that lead through to the interrogation rooms and cells. "What's happening?"

Shay, sitting on a plastic seat by the door, gets up to join me. She puts her arm around me and hugs me. "It's fine. Don't worry. My mom will handle it."

I squeeze her hand. Shay's mom, who's a lawyer at the National Women's Law Center, came straight over on the ferry from work in Seattle as soon as she got the call about Jake.

"This is so absurd," I say. "How could she do this to him?"

"Who?" Shay asks.

"His ex-girlfriend!" I shout. "How could she do this?"

Shay shrugs.

The door to the station bangs open and we turn around. I'm half expecting it to be one of the reporters—one from the local paper and another from a sports radio station—who were hanging around earlier, having caught wind of the story, but it isn't.

It's worse. It's Reid Walsh. His father, the chief of police, is the one interviewing Jake right now.

Reid double-takes when he sees Shay and me in the police station reception area but then quickly recovers and swaggers over to us.

"Yo," he says.

I can hear Shay's eyeballs roll. She ignores him. I try to, but he isn't taking the hint. Vaguely it crosses my mind to confront him over the letter he never gave me, but right now I've got bigger things on my mind.

"What are you doing here?" he asks.

"Waiting for someone," I tell him.

"You get a ticket or something?" he asks.

"A what?" I ask.

"A parking ticket." He nods at the reception desk. "'Cause if you did, I could talk to my dad for you and sort it out. You know, get them to tear it up. He does it for me all the time."

Shay puts her hands on her hips, unable to keep up the facade of ignoring him any longer. "No, we didn't get a parking ticket. Now get lost before I file a restraining order."

Reid's face contorts into a scowl, which makes him look constipated. "Jesus, I was only offering to help," he snaps. "And I wasn't even talking to you, Shay. I was talking to Emerson."

"I think if Emerson ever needed help, you would be the last person on earth she'd turn to," Shay counters.

Reid glances my way, and I see the angry stubble rash across his chin flare even redder. "Whatever," he mumbles to Shay; then he bangs his shoulder against the door that leads through to the cells and interrogation rooms and disappears.

"Someone needs to ease off on the steroids," Shay remarks.

"I can't believe he just offered to do that."

"Yeah, I know. Nice to see corruption at work."

"No. I mean, why is he being nice to me? He's never nice to me."

Shay wrinkles her nose as though there's a bad smell lingering around us. "I'm telling you," she says, shaking her head, "it's the steroids. They're messing with his brain. And did you see the man boobs on him?"

"You think I should go after him and see if he can get his dad to let Jake go?"

"I don't think getting caught smoking pot is the same as a parking ticket," Shay mutters. "And do you really want to be beholden to Reid Walsh?"

She has a point, but I still can't stop wondering if there's something I could do to make this all go away.

Ten minutes later the door to one of the interrogation rooms finally opens and Rob's dad exits, looking mildly irritated, his mouth pinched and his eyes flinty. I take that as a good sign. Behind him follow Jake and then Shay's mom, who is dressed to kill in a black pantsuit and high heels. While she looks like an older, *Good Wife* version of Shay, Chief Walsh looks like an older, paunchier version of Reid, wearing a uniform that strains against his gut. He used to be a pro football player, but he's "gone to seed," as my mom puts it kindly.

Rob's dad has always been aloof toward me—he was one of the cops who investigated my assault, and he made it very obvious from the start that he never believed me. He was also one of the cops who arrested my dad when he punched Coach Lee in the middle of the supermarket frozen foods aisle. That was four months after it happened, when the investigation had been shelved and the charges dropped. My dad had been livid with fury. We were lucky that Coach Lee didn't press charges. We were lucky, my mom said, that my dad didn't kill him and end up in prison for life.

I've always tried to avoid Chief Walsh, even when dating his son, because he always made it clear what he thought of me. A priest has more respect for Satan than Chief Walsh has for me. When he comes through the door and sees me, I catch the sneer of distaste that tugs up his top lip, as though he's just stepped in dog crap. For the first time ever, though, it doesn't affect me, doesn't make my face go hot or my heart beat double time. His look bounces off me as though I'm wearing steel-plated armor.

Jake glances my way, but I can't tell anything from his expression. He looks completely shell-shocked.

Shay's mother stops and holds out her hand to shake Chief Walsh's. I see his knuckles blanch white as he grips her hand. She squeezes back just as hard until I see the chief's face tighten into a grimace and a muscle by his eye begin to twitch.

"If you need to contact my client, then you need to come through me," Shay's mother tells him coolly, offering him her card.

Walsh takes it, sneering at it in disdain. "Women's rights?" Shay's mom purses her lips.

I hear Shay grind her teeth behind me. "Neanderthal," she whispers in my ear.

Walsh looks at Jake. "You need to check in with me if you plan on leaving the island. I need to know your whereabouts. We clear?"

"Yes, sir," Jake says quietly.

Captain Walsh doesn't even glance my way again. He just strides back inside the station, letting the door slam shut behind him.

"What happened? How did it go?" I ask Jake the moment he's gone.

He shrugs, shaking his head, and looks at Shay's mom.

"He's lucky," she says, and bustles toward the exit.

"Lucky?" I ask, following her as she walks outside.

We stop beside her car and Shay's mom puts down her briefcase and takes out a sheaf of papers. "I think we can get the drug charge thrown out on a technicality," she says.

"What technicality?" Shay asks.

"They didn't give Jake due warning before the test."

"Huh?" I ask. I glance at Jake and he takes my hand and squeezes it tight.

Shay's mom holds out a piece of paper. "According to the rules, any random drug test administered to a college athletics student requires a minimum of twenty-four hours advance notice. They didn't give it to him."

"Really?" I ask Jake.

He nods.

"So, what does that mean?" I ask, a rush of relief building inside me.

"It means the test is inadmissible."

I burst out laughing. "But that's amazing news." I look at Jake. "Why aren't you smiling?"

"Because," says Shay's mom, "although it's inadmissible and his place on the team and in the hockey league are hopefully not in danger, the police are still investigating him on charges of possession of marijuana."

"But they don't have proof, do they?" Shay asks. "I mean, he smoked it."

Shay's mother sighs. "It's just Chief Walsh being an asshole."

My eyes widen at the insult.

"It's a power play, that's all," she explains. "He knows it's unlikely they'll be able to charge Jake, but he wants to show us he's the man. And"—she turns to Jake now—"don't forget that your college is bound by their own statute to investigate the cover-up. They'll be asking questions, especially about your coach and how and why he covered up the test."

Jake frowns down at the sidewalk and starts chewing on his lip.

"I don't think you're in danger of being kicked out of college," Shay's mom goes on, "but it's going to get a lot of press. You need to ready yourself for that and prepare a statement. I'll meet with you tomorrow morning to draft something, but until then don't say a word to anyone."

"Okay," Jake says. "What about my contract with the Red Wings?"

Shay's mother shakes her head. "That I don't know about. You'll need to talk to your agent." She holds up another piece of paper. "You've also broken the terms of your modeling contract. There's a clause in here about bringing the brand into disrepute. It's likely they'll drop you. Just hope they don't sue you too."

"What do you mean? There's no such thing as bad publicity," Shay scoffs.

Jake frowns darkly at the ground.

Shay's mom stuffs her papers back into the briefcase and unlocks her car. "You were lucky this time, Jake," she says. "Don't do anything stupid from now on. There's too much on the line."

"I won't," he says, finally cracking a weak smile. "I promise."

She smiles back at him and pecks him on the cheek.

"Thanks, Mrs. Donovan," he says.

"You're welcome, Jake."

Jake and I watch as she and Shay drive off.

"Come on," I say, taking Jake's hand. "Let's get out of here."
But just as we start walking, Reid Walsh strides out of the police
station. He sees Jake and me, and his expression darkens.

Jake sighs under his breath. I grip his hand tighter.

"Hear you got arrested." Reid smirks, sauntering over to us
with that stupid prison swagger walk of his.

"You heard wrong," I snap back. "They were just questioning
him."

It's Jake's turn to squeeze my hand. He's right. I shouldn't
even engage.

"Heard you're going to get kicked out of college," he says to
Jake.

"Yeah?" Jake asks with a sigh. "Where'd you hear that?"

"Guess you'll lose your place in the draft, too."

That gets to Jake. His jaw sets. A ripple of tension runs up his
arm as though he's holding on to an electrified fence. I start to
pull him away. I can see where this is headed, and it's nowhere
good.

"Come on," I say quietly. "Let's go."

Jake won't budge, though. He's glaring at Reid, who's glaring
right back at him, as though he's trying to telepathically challenge him to a fight. I wonder who would win? Reid looks like he
supplements six meals a day with steroid protein shakes.

Finally, Jake lets me tug him away. I don't loosen my grip on
him until we've walked a block, and then, when I glance over my
shoulder, I see Reid still standing in the same spot, watching us
with narrowed eyes.

Jake

My mom is standing with her hands on her hips, ordering me back upstairs to pack a bag.

"Jake! Come on. We don't have time for this. We're going to miss our flight. Move it!"

I glance down the driveway, clutching the letter to Em in my hand. I need to find a way to get it to her. My mom moves to shut the front door, but as she does, I spot Reid Walsh riding by the house on his bike.

"Hold up!" I yell, pushing past my mom and racing down the driveway, waving the envelope in my hand like a flag. "Reid! Wait!"

Reid screeches to a halt and stares at me, suspicious.

"I need you to do me a favor."

He sneers and starts to pedal off, and I leap in front of his bike.

"Jake!"

It's my mom. She's standing in the driveway and, judging by the tone of her voice, she's going to lose it any second.

"Can you give this to Em?" I say to Reid, shoving the letter at him.

Reid looks at the crumpled piece of paper. "Why?" he asks.

"Just . . . please? It's important."

"Jake!" my mom yells, really angry now.

Reid pauses, eyes narrowed, but then he snatches the letter from my hand. "Okay," he says.

"Thank you."

He cycles off and I watch him, realizing too late that I should have put the letter in an envelope. But it's too late now. I can't chase after him. The important thing is that she gets it.

I turn and dash past my mom, ignoring her flared nostrils. "I'll be one minute," I say.

"Hurry up!" my mom yells after me as I race up the stairs to my bedroom.

I grab a bag and hastily stuff it with a sweater, a pair of jeans, some clean socks, and my toothbrush and toothpaste. I raid my piggy bank, taking all 312 dollars and shoving it into my wallet.

Then I sneak back down the stairs, check that my mom is outside packing the car up, and hurry to open the closet under the stairs.

The tent my dad bought last year is in there. It's lightweight, folds up small, and sleeps two in close quarters. I pick up it and the sleeping bag and shove them into my rucksack, and then run into the kitchen and raid the cupboards for snacks. Noodles. Crackers. A bag of marshmallows.

"They have food on the plane, you know," my mom says, making me startle.

I nod, grab the bag, and dart past her into the hallway.

"Get in the car!" she shouts after me. "I'm just setting the alarm."

"Okay!" I shout back, but I don't get in the car. I run past it, past my sister, who is sitting in the back, ignoring her surprised look, and sprint down the street, taking the path that cuts past the Hollingsworths' house and into the woods.

I don't stop running until I make it all the way to the tree house.

Jake

We sit on the ledge of the tree house. Em's head is in my lap and I'm stroking her hair, watching as she scribbles in the notebook I gave her last week—a not-so-subtle hint for her to pursue her journalism dream—though frankly journalists aren't my favorite people at the moment. She's filled pages and pages already, and I'm glad that she's finding a way to process things. For me it's the ice. That's where I work out my shit. And the thought of losing that, of not being able to skate pro, is killing me inside.

We should be at the store, but Toby and Em's mom are covering for us. Apparently, the phone hasn't stopped ringing all day. Out here in the woods, up in the tree house, with just the scratch of Em's pen and the birds singing, it's easy to believe that the world beyond here doesn't exist—and right now that's how I want it to be.

I think about calling Sarge to check in with him, but I can't stand the thought of turning on my phone and seeing all the messages I know there will be, and I'm worried too about finding out what trouble he's in because of me. I'm also tempted to call Lauren and find out what the hell she was thinking, but Em's convinced me that would be a bad idea.

"What are you writing?" I ask Em, trying to distract myself from my thoughts.

She barely glances up at me. "Just something. A story." She pauses, chewing the end of the pencil. "No, not really a story— more like an essay."

"An essay?" I ask.

"Yeah."

"What's it about?"

She sits up and squints at the forest for a long moment before turning to face me. "It's about what happened."

"Can I read it?"

She hesitates for a moment, looking down at the notebook in her hands.

"Okay," she finally says. "It's messy, though. And it's just a first draft."

She hands me the notepad and then gets up, stretching her arms above her head. I long for a moment to pull her back down onto my lap, but she disappears inside the tree house and I turn back to the notebook and start reading. . . .

When I was thirteen years old, I was sexually assaulted by my hockey coach. One action by another—an adult in a position of trust—and I lost everything; my sense of self, my understanding of truth, my belief in what the world was, my faith in justice, my reputation, and my best friend. I lost the image of myself as a child in my parents' eyes. From that split second in time I became someone new.

*Someone I didn't recognize. A stranger to myself.
The man who assaulted me was never charged with
any crime. He was never punished. Instead, it was
me who was punished. For coming forward. There is
something wrong with a world in which a victim, a
child no less, is punished.*

*It took five years for me to learn that "victim"
is a word I can discard too. Just as I once discarded
the identity of champion hockey player, girl, friend,
winner. Just as memory bound me for so long,
memory also helped set me free in the end. Someone
reminded me of the person I used to be before it
happened, and with it came a glimmer of hope that
somewhere inside she still existed if I could just find a
way to set her free. . . .*

I keep reading, flipping rapidly through the pages, wrapped up in Em's story and her words, in the reality of all that happened, feeling as if I've opened a trapdoor into her mind and am finally seeing what it was like for her. All those questions I've had but never asked for fear of prying or upsetting her, are answered here. She details the hate mail, the insults, the time she walked into my uncle coming out of a coffee shop on Main Street and how he stepped aside to let her pass with a smile and a nod of his head. How she smiled back before she could stop herself and then spent three weeks playing over the episode in her mind, wondering whether he took that to mean she was complicit. I'm rapt by her account of turning around one day on a beach coming face-to-face with her past in the form of her ex–best friend and childhood sweetheart and how it opened up a Pandora's box of emotions, but that hope too was one of them. And how it took putting on a pair of skates to finally feel like her life was hers again.

I put down the notebook and let out the breath I'd unwittingly been holding. For a long minute, I stare at the tree branches, and then I get up and walk inside the tree house, ducking my head. I find Em crouched down on the floor with her back to me.

She turns her head and I see she's holding a penknife in her hand, and then I glimpse over her shoulder that she is carving something into the wall. I know what it is before I even step toward her. It's our initials.

I kneel beside her and take the knife from her hand. I finish the L as she watches, her hand resting on my shoulder.

"What did you think?" she asks me, casting a surreptitious sideways glance my way.

I put the penknife down. "I think," I say, turning to face her, "that you need to publish it."

She laughs. "What? No. It's stupid. It's just for me, really. You know, journaling, cheaper than therapy."

"Well, I think you should share it." She looks at me as if she can't tell if I'm joking. "I'm serious," I tell her.

She picks up the notebook and shakes her head.

I want to keep arguing with her, but I suddenly remember the time. I agreed to swap with Toby at the store so he could get to Em's house to oversee the plumber who's coming to fit the bathroom, and I'm late.

"I need to go. I'm covering for Toby," I tell Em.

Her face falls.

"Come with me," I say.

"No. I think I'll stay here. I want to finish this." She holds up the notebook.

"Okay," I say. "But I'll see you later, yeah?"

She nods and I pull her closer.

"At my place?" I ask.

She looks up at me and smiles sneakily. She stays over every night, but I don't take it for granted.

"Jake?" she says as I pull away.

"Yeah?"

"Thanks," she says, her fingers trailing through mine.

"What for?" I ask.

"For coming back." She pauses a moment. "And for the notebook."

Em

reread my essay, wondering if Jake's right about it being good enough to publish. I'm not sure I want to go public with this. It's like carving out a piece of my soul and offering it on a plate to the world. What if I'm laughed at or sent more hate mail? It can't be worse than what I've already experienced, though, and what if it helps someone else who's going through what I went through?

A rustling makes my head snap up. I'm smiling, expecting it to be Jake coming back for his sweater, which he left behind and which I'm now wearing, but it isn't. It's Reid Walsh. Great.

He steps out from behind a tree. How long has he been there? Was he waiting for Jake to leave? Has he been spying on me?

"What are you doing here?" I ask. My spine prickles, and my hands go clammy. From up here in the tree house, I have the advantage of height. But I'm also trapped, and it's not like I can pull up the ladder, either. Reid walks slowly toward the tree. Where's the boiling oil when you need it?

Reid rests his hand on the first rung of the ladder, and my pulse leaps and flies. I tell myself I'm being silly, but the last time I felt like this, something bad happened, so this time I decide to listen to my gut. I scan the inside of the tree house, my gaze landing on the penknife lying on the floor. I'm being stupid, paranoid, but something tells me—urges me—to pick it up.

Reid starts climbing up the tree. That's it. I move, darting toward the penknife. I hide it behind my back and as Reid heaves himself onto the ledge, I walk out to confront him. It's better to be outside on the ledge than inside, where I'm even more trapped. Why am I even thinking this way? I wonder. Why am I so paranoid? The problem with having been a victim of assault once is that forever after you judge every other situation by those terms. You lose all sense of proportion. Maybe I'm reading into things. But then again, I'd rather be paranoid than assaulted again. Not that I think Reid's capable . . . but yeah . . . once burned . . .

I watch Reid clamber to his feet, wondering if the platform can take his weight. He's got six or seven inches on me and easily made it to college on a wrestling scholarship.

Reid glances inside through the open doorway. "You've fixed it up. It looks great. Remember how we used to come here all the time as kids?"

I raise my eyebrows. He's smiling fondly at the memory. I guess he's remembering the porn magazine. I wonder if I can dodge past him to the edge of the ledge and climb down. Would it look like running away? An angry voice inside my head tells me to stand my ground, but then I realize that I'm not twelve and it doesn't matter. I can choose my battles.

I make for the ladder, happy to cede possession of the tree house to Reid for now.

Reid steps sideways, blocking me. "Where are you going?" he

asks. It doesn't seem to be a threat, more a genuine question, and it confuses me.

"I have to get back home," I tell him. "My dad needs me." I move once more to step around him, and this time he doesn't block my way.

"How is he?" Reid asks.

I freeze and turn to study him. He's not smirking, but why is he asking? "Why do you care?" I ask.

He shrugs. "I'm just being nice."

"Nice?" I ask, eyebrows leaping up my head.

"What?" he asks. "I can't be nice?"

I shake my head at his weirdness. "Nice" is the last adjective on earth I'd use to describe Reid. Up there with the words "thoughtful," "intelligent," and "sensitive." "Can you move? I want to go."

Reid stays blocking the ladder.

"Are you dating him?"

I pull back to look at him, frowning. What is he talking about now?

"Is that why you . . . you broke up with Rob?" he stammers, his face starting to flush. "Because Jake came back? That's what Rob thinks."

"No," I say impatiently. "I broke up with your brother because he's a jerk and I should never have dated him in the first place."

Reid grins. "Yeah, I know. Took you long enough to realize it."

That makes me pause. Is he messing with me? I'm not staying around to find out.

I push past Reid, sit down on the ledge, and start climbing as fast as I can down the ladder, but I'm in such a hurry to get away that I forget the rusting nail and catch my palm on it. Yelping, I miss my footing and fall the last five feet, landing on my butt on the soft ground at the bottom of the tree.

"Shit. Are you okay?" Reid calls down to me.

He starts climbing down the tree, landing beside me and offering me his hand to get up. I don't take it. Instead, I use the tree trunk to steady myself as I climb to my feet, rubbing my lower back, which is bruised from the fall. Without a word, I start walking away.

"Wait," Reid says, chasing after me.

I whip around to face him. "What? What do you want, Reid?"

"I'm sorry. I didn't mean to upset you," he says, holding up both hands in a defensive posture.

I shake my head again in confusion. "I don't get it, Reid."

Don't get what?

"Why are you being nice—apologizing, and . . . I don't know, trying to be my friend?"

He looks suddenly forlorn. "Aren't we friends?"

"Er . . . no." Is he crazy? Are all those steroids poking holes in his brain?

"But we used to be friends."

"Reid, you and I have never been friends." It's like explaining two plus two to a six-year-old.

"That's not true. We were always hanging out together."

"We were on the same hockey team. If you call practice 'hanging out together,' then yes, we hung out a lot, but it wasn't by choice."

His face falls some more, and now I really am starting to wonder if this isn't just a big joke. No one in their right mind would ever think Reid and I were friends, not unless they had a really warped idea of friendship.

"You were mean to me all the time," I say. "You were always teasing me and laughing at me."

He swallows. "I liked you."

I stare up at him, at the sweat trickling down his temple and the nervous way he is licking his cracked lips. "What do you mean?"

"I always liked you," he blurts, unable to meet my eye. "Like, *liked* you liked you."

Is he joking? I can't tell. The rash of acne on his chin flares even redder.

"I just . . . you know . . . didn't know how to tell you."

He lifts his gaze to meet mine—briefly. Oh my God. He's serious.

I burst out laughing. I can't help myself.

"Why are you laughing?" he asks.

"Reid," I say, shaking my head in amazement. "You bullied me for years. You told me that Jake thought I was a liar. I believed you."

"I was jealous of him," he interrupts. "You never noticed me. It was like I didn't exist. And then you start dating Rob and he treats you so badly and you don't even care. And I'm right here. . . . I've always been here. And I tried to be nice to you and you never even looked at me." He takes a step closer to me, swallowing dryly, and it's only then that I figure out that what Reid is trying to tell me is that he liked me back then and that he still likes me.

The shock is so enormous that a meteor could crash down beside us and I wouldn't notice.

Reid takes another step toward me, his expression pleading.

"I'm dating Jake," I blurt, stepping backward, away from him.

Reid freezes. Color floods his face—and his cheeks turn a mottled red. He shrugs. "Whatever. Like I care."

I raise my eyebrows. Confusion replaces the shock.

He makes a face. "You didn't think—that like, just because I said I liked you back when we were kids, I still like you?" He snorts. "Because, yeah . . . that's not what I was saying."

I take another step backward. "Okay, Reid, well, I'm going to go."

He looks like he might be about to say something else, but then he bites it back and gives me one of his trademark shrugs. "Fine."

I start running through the woods, my ears ringing from his words, my mind doing a loop-the-loop as I try to place this new information over the top of my memories and recalibrate them all.

Jake

He said what to you?"

"That he liked me."

I'm laying the wood in the stove on the deck, but I freeze and turn toward Em. "Wait, say that again."

Em hugs her arms around her waist. "He said he liked me liked me, but then he tried to walk it back when he didn't get the reaction he was hoping for."

I drop back onto my haunches beside the open door of the stove, lighter in hand. "Shit," I say, shaking my head that I never saw it before now. "It makes total sense."

"What do you mean?"

"You know they say that the boys in school who are the meanest to you and tease you are the ones who secretly like you."

"You were never mean to me," Em argues.

"Yeah," I say, lighting the paper beneath the wood and then slamming shut the door to the stove. "I was too scared. But this is Reid we're talking about. His only means of communication is being a jerk. I mean, look at his father. They had the perfect teacher."

I watch the flames roar to life inside the stove and walk over to Em. "What did you say to him?"

"I told him I was dating you."

I frown.

Em's smile fades. "What?"

"You shouldn't have to qualify your reasons why you don't want to date him. It's enough you told him no."

My instinct is to drive right around to the Walsh house and have a word with Reid. But I'm walking on eggshells at the moment, and the fact that his dad is trying to lock me up makes it kind of difficult.

"Jake," Em warns, reading my mind.

"I don't trust him."

I scan the woods. They're turning blurry and pixelated in the dusk light. "You think he was there in the woods?" I ask. "Watching, waiting until I left so he could get you alone?" The idea makes me feel sick with fury.

Em chews her lip. "Yeah, but I don't think he'd ever try anything. I mean, I made it very clear to him how I felt."

I grimace. That's probably the worst possible scenario. Most guys don't deal well with humiliation, especially not bullies like Reid Walsh. "Do me a favor," I say now, turning back to Em. "Don't go to the tree house by yourself."

Em pulls back. "No," she says.

"What?"

"I'm not going to give up one of my favorite places to hang out just because of Reid Walsh. It's our tree house. Not his. Besides, I mean, Reid's always been all talk and no action. Rob was the one with the big mouth who followed through."

I huff and stare at the crackling wood, most of it leftovers from the construction site in Em's house, which she miraculously still hasn't discovered. While I admire Em's defiance, and her decision not to let Reid threaten her, I'm not happy.

"I'm going to speak to him," I say, getting to my feet. It's the only way. I can't have her feeling intimidated or threatened. And I don't like the idea that he might follow her again or confront her.

Em reaches out and grabs my arm. "Jake, don't. It's not worth it. He's going back to college soon anyway. I won't have to see him again."

I glance down at her fingers circling my wrist, then up into her face. She's anxious, fearful, and I force myself to relax and calm down. I remember what Shay's mom told me about staying out of trouble and my coach's warning to keep a low profile. The chances are any conversation I have with Reid is not going to end in a handshake agreement and niceties. After all, I still have an argument to settle with him over the letter he never gave Em.

Em strokes her fingers up the inside of my arm, over my scar. "I shouldn't have told you."

My gut twists. I drop down by her side. "Don't say that," I whisper. "I don't want you to keep secrets from me ever. I'm glad you told me." I take her hand again and slip my fingers through hers. "I won't do anything, okay? I promise."

She studies me for a moment and then nods. "Good."

She gets up and I wonder what she's doing, but the words don't even make it past my lips before she sits down in my lap, facing toward me. I wrap my arms around her waist and she loops hers around my neck. Instantly, my senses are in overdrive. I watch Em reach back and tie up her hair. All thoughts of Reid Walsh scatter. If that was the plan, it's definitely working.

In the firelight, Em's skin glows and her eyes take on a wild cat gleam. I pull her toward me and let out a groan as she lets her fingers trail across my jaw and down to my chest. She bites my bottom lip between her teeth and that's it. I stand up, sweeping her into my arms. She wraps her legs around my waist, and I carry her inside.

"I love you," I say, looking her in the eyes as I lean over her. I want her to know it, really know it. I need her to know it. "I'm in love with you," I clarify.

She draws in a quick breath. "I'm in love with you too," she whispers.

And then she kisses me.

Em

I'm still daydreaming about Jake naked and all the things we did when I walk into the store the next day. Toby is already behind the counter, doing something on the computer. He looks up and smiles when he sees me.

"Someone had a good night last night," he says.

My hand flies instantly to my hair, smoothing it down. I flush under his scrutiny. Do I have stubble rash? I choose to ignore Toby and dump my bag and keys on the counter. "What are you doing?" I ask, looking over his shoulder at the computer.

Toby shifts a little to the side to give me a better view, and I see that he has a website open.

"What the—" I ask, pushing him out of the way and leaning closer.

"Hot, right?"

"Why is Jake on the store's homepage?"

"He agreed."

Confused, I stare at the store's website. It's been completely redesigned and now prominently features a photo of Jake standing beside a kayak, wearing a LOWE KAYAKING CO. T-shirt. He's gazing into the camera lens and he has a glint in his eye. The same look, in fact, that he was wearing last night right before he slipped my underwear off. Toby's right, though. It's hot. Extremely hot. Though I admit I'm biased.

"Who did this?" I ask, gesturing at the website.

"Aaron," says Toby with a grin. "Check it out." He hits a key and takes me through to the booking page, which has now been totally automated.

"No way," I say. "Aaron? The guy from the rafting trip?"

"Yeah. He did it as a favor to me. He's a web genius."

I'm still staring at the computer screen. We're finally out of the dark ages. Our website looked like it had been designed in the '90s—which it had. Now it's slick and gorgeous and looks almost as good as Jake.

"He must have owed you big-time for something," I say in awe, then cast a sideways glance at Toby, who smiles smugly.

"Guess who Aaron works for?"

I shake my head.

"Google! He's the guy who helps design their search algorithm."

"Shut up!"

Toby shrugs. "Well, something like that. I don't know. When he talks IT, I glaze over like a donut, but yeah . . . we're already at the top of the search rankings for Bainbridge Island. First place when you search Bainbridge and things to do."

"Really?" I almost squeal. We've always lingered on the ninth or tenth search page.

"Yeah, and we're the first thing that comes up when you Google Jake's name. The site almost crashed yesterday because of all the hits."

"Oh my God," I say. "How come?"

Toby looks guiltily away. "I got Aaron to SEO the heck out of the site. I mean, Jake's name is searched thousands of times a day . . . and, well . . . kayaking in Bainbridge is really not."

"What?"

Toby gives me cartoon innocent eyes. "Jake said it was cool. I checked with him. Honest."

When did they do all this?

"I'm telling you, the phone did not stop ringing yesterday," Toby says. "Mainly, it was journalists—who, by the way, your mom totally dealt with like a pro; the woman should get a job as the White House press secretary—but we also took two dozen bookings over the phone, as well as a dozen more online."

My eyes fly open. Toby is grinning at me. "Things are looking up, Lowe," he says. "And for Jake, too, by the looks of things."

"What do you mean?" I ask Toby, trying to sound casual.

"Apparently, he's now the next hot thing. Loads of designers are trying to sign him."

"What?" I stammer.

"For modeling. Everyone wants a piece of him. He's the bad boy with the chiseled cheekbones. They're beating down his door."

I close my eyes again and press a hand to my forehead. "I don't get it. How do you know all this?"

"His agent called the store yesterday when he couldn't get hold of him on his cell. I took a message. Didn't Jake tell you?"

No, he didn't. But then again, we were kind of distracted yesterday and last night.

"He'll be the next Tom Brady. Which makes you Gisele, I guess." He gives me a wonky smile and then goes back to staring at the screen. "Oh look, we got another booking!"

Jake

'm sitting with Shay on the deck of my place, our feet dangling over the edge.

"So you leave in three days, huh?" Shay asks me.

"Yeah," I say, contemplating a sparrow hopping along a branch.

"It's not that bad, Jake," Shay says. "At least you didn't get kicked out of college. What about your coach? What happened at the hearing? Did they fire him?"

"No," I say. "He argued that he covered up the test because he knew it was inadmissible."

Shay arches both eyebrows at me. "Is that true?" she asks.

I shake my head. "No."

Shay's mouth falls open in amazement. "So he lied and got away with it?" She shakes her head and laughs—snorting air through her nose.

"What?" I ask.

"Just that it sounds familiar. A sports coach lying and getting away with it."

I frown at the ground. I didn't want Sarge to get fired over my mistake, but on the other hand, Shay's right. Shouldn't we all pay for our mistakes? I feel furtive, like I've gotten away with something I shouldn't have, and I still feel as if I have an invisible noose around my neck.

"There are so many double standards in the world," Shay goes on, her voice getting louder. "It's so unfair. Like you getting all those modeling contracts. If you were a girl, I bet you'd have been destroyed by the press, totally vilified. You wouldn't have a career left at all. You'd probably have been thrown out of college, too."

"Yeah, you're right. I'm sorry. If it makes you feel any better, I've turned down all the offers."

"What?" Shay asks.

"Modeling is the most boring job in the world. You just stand around in your underwear staring into a camera all day being told to scowl as inside, your soul withers and dies."

"What about the money, though?" Shay asks.

I shrug. "I don't need it. If I could find a way to give the money to Em, then I'd do it, but she won't take it. I've tried."

Shay doesn't say anything.

I exhale loudly and kick the step with my foot, startling the bird, which flies off. "I don't want to go. I don't want to leave."

"I know. It's going to be hard on her. Us both leaving at the same time."

"It's just so unfair. I mean, Em's smarter than me. She's the one who should be going to college. She's the one who should be on a scholarship. I can't believe she didn't even bother applying."

"What do you mean?" Shay asks.

"For college."

"She did apply. What are you talking about? She got a place. At Washington State."

"What?"

Shay nods. "Yeah. You didn't know? She just didn't take it."

"Why?" I ask. And why didn't she tell me this?

"The money situation. They needed someone to run the business. And her mom needed help looking after her dad."

I frown. "But I've been through the business projections with her mom and Toby. The bank's agreed to give them another six months to get back on their feet. And it looks good. It looks like they'll be turning a profit if this place takes off and things keep going the way they are. So . . . couldn't she go now?"

"It's still a lot of tuition to pay," Shay says. "They had to use Em's college fund to pay for her dad's care."

The bird has flown back and is hopping along the branch again. I watch it for a moment. It's pointless. I kick the post. "I just wish there were something we could do."

Shay pats my arm. "You've done plenty, Jake."

Maybe—I sigh—but it's still not enough.

Em

This night is perfect. I lean back in the booth, feeling Jake's arm around my waist, and press myself closer against his side. I used to come here sometimes with Rob, but every time he'd sit at the bar, stuffing pretzels into his mouth, glued to the game on the giant TV screen. And I would sit beside him thinking that was normal and acceptable. What planet was I on? I don't even recognize who that girl was. She wasn't me.

"Are you okay?" Jake murmurs in my ear, shouting to be heard over the band.

I nod, shaking off the memory, determined to stay only in the present from now on. No more looking back. No more Emerson. I'm back to being Em.

Shay sits on my right-hand side. She's laughing at something Aaron has just said, but my mind isn't on the conversation; I'm just soaking it all in—this last night out together before Shay and Jake leave. At least, I think to myself, Toby will still be here to keep me sane. And Aaron, too, by the looks of things. He and Toby seem to be really into each other, are holding hands under the tabletop, sharing their drinks, and whispering into each other's ears like teenagers on a first date.

Toby suddenly glances across the bar area toward the door. "Look what the cat dragged in," he mutters.

I turn my head and feel my bubble of happiness prick. Rob has sauntered in and is standing in the doorway surveying the room. His gaze lands on me and he scowls.

Shay lets out a groan beside me. "Look who he's with."

My eyes flit to the person who's walked in behind him. Reid.

"Great," I mumble, feeling Jake's arm tense as he pulls me closer against his side.

"Oh my God, what's Tanya Hollingsworth doing with them?" Shay announces.

My eyes widen as I see Tanya—the most popular girl from school—sidle up to Rob and slip her arm through his. She flicks her hair over her shoulder and then catches sight of me. A smug, gloating smile takes over her face, and I laugh out loud. I always had a suspicion that Tanya liked Rob. Every time she saw him, she'd flirt with him, but then again, Tanya flirts with everyone with a pulse and a penis, and I thought she was just doing it to rile me. I never realized she actually had a thing for Rob.

"Tanya Hollingsworth and Rob?" Shay wonders aloud. "If they were on OkCupid, it would say 'one hundred percent match.'"

I laugh. I'm actually happy for them. They suit each other.

"Who is that scary-looking girl?" Aaron interrupts, glancing over at Tanya. "And why is she giving you a stare that could freeze lava?"

"She's nobody," I tell him. "Just some girl we know from school."

"Wow, she should audition for *Mean Girls*, the sequel." Aaron chortles.

"Do you want to go?" Jake asks me.

I turn to him. He's looking at me anxiously. "No," I say, feeling a warm buzz start to build in my bloodstream at the way he's looking at me: fiercely, protectively, like I belong to him.

"You sure?" Jake asks, his eyes searching mine.

"Actually," I say a little weakly, "yeah, I do want to go." I lower my voice and lean into him. "But not because of them." I whisper in his ear, catching a hit of his aftershave as I do. "I want you to take me back to your place." We've only got one night left, after all—best to make it count.

I pull back to watch the grin split Jake's face in two. Instantly, he's on his feet, pulling me up with him. "We're going to go," he tells the others.

Toby and Shay start laughing. "You have some kind of curfew, Lowe?" Shay asks.

"No," I stammer.

She stands up, grabbing her purse. "It's cool. I get it. You two love bunnies go enjoy yourselves. I have to get home and pack anyway."

"Wait up," says Toby, draining the last of his drink and standing up as well. "We'll come too." He catches my look of alarm. "No, not with you," he clarifies. "But we need to catch the last ferry."

Shay, Toby, and Aaron walk past Rob's table and out the door, but as Jake and I pass the table, I hear Rob say something under his breath, something aimed at Toby and Aaron.

Jake freezes and I grip his arm tight. "Come on," I say. "Let's just go."

"Yeah." Rob snickers. "Listen to your woman."

Jake's jaw tenses. I pull him toward the door.

"Slut."

Jake stops again and turns back to Rob. This time I feel the tension running in ripples through his body. His back stiffens and he pulls his hand from mine. Before he can do anything, I step up to the table.

"Last week I was frigid. This week I'm a slut. Make up your mind. You're pathetic."

I whip back around, take Jake by the hand, and tug him toward the door. He's resisting, but I hold on tight.

"Yeah, that's right, follow your little whore and her fag friends!"

I cringe as if he's thrown something at our backs.

Jake rips his hand from mine and, before I can stop him, takes a step toward Rob, who jumps to his feet at Jake's approach.

"What did you just say?" Jake asks in a low voice.

Oh God. I can see exactly where this is heading. I take hold of Jake by the arm and try to pull him away from the table, but he's a statue and won't budge.

"Jake," I say, but it falls on deaf ears.

Reid stands up now as well, and steps between Jake and his little brother, fronting Jake with an angry stare.

"Jake," I say again, loudly, pulling on his arm some more. "Just ignore them. It doesn't matter."

But Jake isn't listening. His hands are fisted and the energy is bursting off him like a crackling force field.

"Apologize," Jake says quietly, almost under his breath. "Both of you."

Reid laughs. Tanya is still sitting at the table—her eyes glued to the four of us—as the drama plays out.

"What do I need to apologize for?" Rob snorts. "She's the one who was two-timing me. And look at how she tried it on with Coach Lee, then acted like he assaulted her when he turned her down. If that ain't a slut, tell me what is."

His words hit me hard, knocking the air clean out of me, but they don't hit as hard as Jake's fist, which smashes into Rob's jaw with enough force to make his head snap back like a Pez dispenser.

I blink in shock, watching Rob go stumbling backward into the table, knocking over a bottle of beer, which spills all over Tanya's lap. Her screams pierce my eardrums. The bar roars to life, people yelling and rushing toward the fray. Rob's suddenly back on his feet and tearing toward Jake, who stands his ground and pulls back his arm, ready to lay another punch.

Reid throws himself out of the booth. Everything becomes a blur. Reid tries to get between Rob and Jake, but he trips. He falls toward Jake, who steps aside, and the next thing I know, there's a loud smack as his head cracks against the side of the neighboring table. He smashes to the ground with a thud. There are more screams. More shouts. Someone's shoving Jake back toward the bar, and in the jostling crowd I get pushed aside.

My head spins as I stare at Reid on the ground, surrounded by people. A man kneels and rolls him over onto his back. His head lolls. He's out cold. Blood oozes from a cut to his temple. I turn to Jake and see him scanning the bar. He's looking for me, and I see the wild fear in his face before he spots me and then the despair when our eyes meet.

Behind me, I can vaguely hear Tanya crying hysterically and Rob yelling at her to shut up. I turn, distracted, and see her flapping her arms and Rob kneeling over Reid as he starts to come around, stirring blearily and groaning.

I turn back to Jake in a daze. I can't believe he just punched someone. I've never seen Jake lose it like that before. I stumble toward him. He reaches for me and I wrap my arms around his neck. He pulls me closer, so tight it feels like he's drowning and I'm the only thing keeping him afloat.

"I'm sorry," he whispers hoarsely, burying his face in my neck.

"It's okay, it's okay," I say, kissing him, stroking his hair, holding him as tight as he is holding me.

I don't think he hears me, though, because the wail of the police siren drowns me out.

Jake

They've set a bail hearing for tomorrow morning."

I stare at Shay's mom. She's wearing jeans and a sweater, not a suit, probably thanks to having been dragged out of bed in the middle of the night. I'm so embarrassed I can't meet her eye. Instead, I look down at the cracked, coffee-stained table that's bolted to the floor.

"Jake, I need to warn you that Chief Walsh is going to ask the judge to refuse you bail."

I look up sharply. "What?"

"He's going to ask for you to be remanded into custody until the trial."

"Trial?"

Oh God. I rest my head on my hands. The room in all its yellow, peeling-paint, piss-stained glory starts to spin.

"You're being charged with aggravated assault."

I look up again, nausea shooting up my throat like a geyser. "What? What does that mean?"

Her mouth tightens into a straight line. "Rob's claiming you threatened to kill him and that you hit Reid when he leaped to his defense."

I shake my head and sit back in my plastic chair, thinking I must have misheard her. "What?"

Shay's mother gives me a long, hard stare. She doesn't believe me.

"He's lying!" I shout.

She shrugs. "It's his word against yours."

"Well, I'm telling the truth."

"Jake, I'm not interested in he said, she said."

"But Em was there," I say through gritted teeth. "She'll tell you what happened. She can back me up. They started it. And Reid tripped. I didn't lay a finger on him!"

Shay's mom sits down heavily in her seat. "That's not what they're saying. I've got your statement, Jake, and Emerson's, and I'll work with it as best I can, but, frankly, you chose the wrong people to pick a fight with."

I bite my lips shut and take a deep breath in, trying to get control over my spiking pulse rate. It doesn't work. The panic builds, becomes blinding. I didn't pick a fight with them. They picked it with me! "What am I looking at?" I ask after a pause. "Worst-case scenario."

Her mouth tightens into a line, and she shakes her head. "Worst case? They charge you for first-degree aggravated assault, which is punishable by up to life in prison."

I start laughing, but then stop once I see her face remains stony blank. "You're joking, right?" I hear myself ask.

She shakes her head at me. "You asked for worst case. It's highly unlikely the judge will accept a first-degree charge, though. Most likely what will happen is that if you plead guilty, they'll accept a third-degree assault charge."

It's as if I'm being slowly lowered into a vat of cold, wet

concrete. I can feel it climbing up my body, binding me rib by rib, paralyzing me. "What's the punishment for that?" I whisper as my throat starts to freeze up too.

"Worst case again: five years in prison and a fine of up to five thousand dollars."

My heart beats hollowly in my chest. Her words echo around my head. "Five years?" Prison?

"I'm going to try to get the charge dropped to a simple assault charge. If you plead guilty to that, if you act remorseful in court and pray you get a judge who doesn't play golf with Chief Walsh, you'll walk out with a suspended sentence. Maybe a fine. That's best-case scenario if you plead guilty. If you plead not guilty—"

"Not guilty?" I interrupt.

She nods at me.

"But I hit Rob," I say. "I am guilty."

Shay's mom tips her head to one side. "We can argue self-defense. I think it's your best shot. But obviously if Reid and Tanya testify for the prosecution and say you started it and it was an unprovoked attack, then that's going to complicate things. And their faces make quite a pretty picture for the jury too."

"Shit," I say. Tears burn my eyes and I blink them rapidly away. How could I have been so stupid? What was I thinking? I just saw red when I heard them say those things about Em.

"They called Em a slut," I say, looking up at Shay's mom. "Rob said she made up the accusation against my uncle."

Shay's mom reaches across the table and squeezes my hand. "Off the record, Jake, and while I don't condone violence in any form, I think I would probably have punched him for saying that too." She lets go of my hand. "But the fact is, you're now screwed."

Like Shay, her mother doesn't hold her punches. Given the situation I'm in now, I wish I had held mine.

"I'll fight for you to get bail," she tells me, "but if they refuse to drop the charges and we opt for a not-guilty plea, you need to prepare yourself for a trial. Once we know the exact charge, we can figure out the right defense move."

I rest my head in my hands and stare at the tabletop. How is this happening? I can't even bring myself to ask about what this means for my college place and my ice hockey career. They're both dead in the water whatever the outcome. Shit. I rest my head on the stained tabletop to try to stop the room from spinning. And what about Em? What must she be thinking?

"I'm sorry, Jake," Shay's mom says quietly. "Do you want me to call your parents and let them know?"

I shake my head and glance up. "They're overseas, on vacation."

She chews her lip.

"Can you tell Em?" I ask.

She nods. "Of course." She stands up and walks to the door.

"Tell her I'm sorry."

Em

Shay's words ring in my head. *Don't do it.*

I stare at the front door and feel my pulse leap into the stratosphere. A solid, sickly lump is wedged at the back of my throat and I can't seem to swallow it away. I need to do this. What other option is there? Jake's in jail. His bail hearing is later today. He might end up with a life sentence, which doesn't even bear thinking about.

I get off my bike and start walking toward the house. I don't head to the front door but veer to the left, to the basement door, instead. Taking a deep breath in and trying to calm myself, I knock.

Tanya answers, wearing one of Rob's football shirts and nothing else. I stare at her bare legs and her severe case of bedhead. She leans casually against the door and smiles at me through lids so heavy she looks drugged.

"Hi," I say, licking my lips, which are suddenly drier than sand. "Is Rob here? I need to talk to him." I figure talking to him is my best bet.

"Rob!" Tanya yells over her shoulder, not taking her eyes off me.

In the background I can hear the sports channel playing on the TV. After a few awkward seconds with Tanya standing with her nose wrinkling like I'm a bad smell, Rob appears. He's wearing a pair of sweatpants and a yellow college T-shirt that doesn't do much to flatter the purple shiny bruise around his eye. Tanya presses up against him. His hand rests on her ass as though she's his property, and she preens like a cat who's got the cream. I repress a giant eyeball roll.

"What do you want?" Rob grunts.

"I . . ." I stop, all the words I had prepared, erasing on my tongue before I can speak them.

Tanya laughs. "She's come here to get you guys to drop the charges."

My eyes flash from Rob to her, then back to Rob. He frowns at Tanya and then jerks his head at her, dismissing her. She glares at him but then follows his order and stalks off.

"That right?" Rob asks me, once she's gone. "You want me to drop the charges?"

"Jake never threatened to kill anyone. You provoked him. And Reid tripped."

Rob crosses his arms over his chest and glowers at me.

"I didn't two-time you, Rob. I got together with Jake after we split up."

His nostrils flare and two red spots appear on his cheeks. I know his pride has been dented, and that he probably hates Jake for a number of reasons, more to do with Jake's successful sports career than the fact he's dating me, but I have to believe that the person I dated for three years isn't a complete asshole, that he has some redeeming qualities . . . somewhere.

"Please, Rob. I'm begging. Speak to Reid. Please drop the

charges." I almost choke on the words. Having to plead with him is making me feel like hurling all over him, but right now it's all I've got.

Rob considers me and hope bursts from a spark to a flame. "Shame how it's going to affect his career, isn't it?" he says. "Guess the Red Wings will be dropping him faster than you can say 'game over.'"

My stomach clenches. "Rob . . . come on," I whisper. "If anyone knows what it's like to lose their shot at their dream, it's you."

Something flickers across his face. I think it might be empathy, but I'm wrong. It's spite. "He should have thought about that before he punched me." He moves to shut the door on me.

"I know," I say, quick to be conciliatory before he slams the door in my face. "It's just this could really screw things up for him. He'll lose his scholarship and get thrown out of college. He'll have a criminal record. If you ever cared about me, even the slightest bit, I'm begging you, please help. Talk to your dad. Tell him it was a stupid fight. Tell him that you guys started it." Rob's face turns thunder-dark. I backtrack fast. "I mean, tell him whatever you need to tell him to get the charges dropped. Please."

Rob weighs me for a moment, and then he nods. Hope fills me like helium.

"Break up with him."

I deflate immediately. "Excuse me?"

"Break up with him," Rob says, glaring at me defiantly. "Then I'll drop the charges."

I laugh. I actually laugh. Because he has to be joking. "What?"

"You heard me. Break up with Jake."

"No," I say, shaking my head.

He shrugs at me, then moves to shut the door on me.

"Why?" I finally manage to whisper.

Rob turns around. "Because."

Now I'm mad. All the rage contained within me all these years comes spewing out of me.

"Because why, Rob?" I yell. "Because it makes you feel like you're getting one over on him? Because you want to punish me? Or him? Are you jealous because he still has the chance to make it as an athlete? Are you pissed at me for breaking up with you? I didn't cheat on you, Rob." His face twists into a scowl and I know I've hit a sore spot. That is what he thinks. "You admitted yourself that you never loved me and you didn't care about me, so why does it matter if I'm dating him? You just can't stand him winning, can you?"

Rob scowls. I'm right. He knows it. That's exactly what it's about. Because Rob always wants what isn't his and he'll bully to get it. It's like the tree house wars all over again.

"You don't get to tell me who I can and can't date, Rob."

"Actually, I can." He smirks at me. "If you want to see your boyfriend ever again. And not in an orange jumpsuit with Plexiglas between you."

Shit. He's right. I have to stuff all the anger and rage back inside me. And from the gloating, smug expression on Rob's face, he knows he's got me over a barrel.

"How can you do this?" I whisper, fists clenched at my side.

"No. How can *you* do this?" he answers. "You want to be the one who's responsible for Jake going to prison? Because it's on you now."

Jake

I walk out into blinding sunlight, squinting and holding a hand up to shield my eyes.

"Do you need a ride?"

I turn to Shay's mom and shake my head. "Um." I glance around again, looking for Em on the off chance she's heard about my release and has come to meet me. The car parking lot is empty, though, apart from a white van.

"Okay," I say, trying to mask my disappointment.

Just then the door of the van swings open and a woman hops out. She's wearing a short black skirt and a white blouse and holding something in her hand. When she gets closer, I see it's a microphone. Tailing her is an overweight guy, panting to catch up, lugging a camera on his shoulder.

"Get in the car," Shay's mom orders me.

"What?" I start to say but am interrupted by the woman, who parks herself between me and the car.

"Jake McCallister, Jo Furness from ESPN. Would you care to comment on your arrest? Is it true you put someone in the hospital? What are they charging you with?" The questions come thick and fast as machine-gun fire.

"I—"

Shay's mom steps in front of me, holding up her hand to cover the camera lens. "My client has no comment to make at this time," she says in a clipped tone. She turns to me next. "Get in the car, Jake," she orders.

I reach for the door handle with a shaking hand. The reporter pushes Shay's mom aside and thrusts the microphone toward me.

"Witnesses claim it was an unprovoked attack. Can you confirm whether that was the case?"

I jump in the car and Shay's mom slams the door shut before walking around to the driver's side. The reporter keeps banging on the window, shouting questions at me through the glass. I stare straight ahead as Shay's mom starts the engine and tears out of the lot, leaving the reporter standing in our wake. I watch her in the mirror giving a report to camera. What is she saying?

"You okay?" Shay's mom asks me when we're a few blocks from the police station.

I don't answer. Instead, I wind down the window, my heart still beating hard from the run-in with that reporter. I take a few deep breaths. Freedom. It does have a taste. It tastes and smells of sea air and pinecones and the sweeter scent of huckleberries.

I close my eyes. It feels as if I haven't slept in fifty hours, which is pretty close to the truth. Just three hours ago, I thought my life was over. I was resigning myself to spending at least the next month in jail awaiting trial—for a goddamn punch, one punch—was going over and over in my head what it all meant, wondering what Em was thinking—but now I'm out. At least temporarily. My parents paid the bail money—are flying back from Europe early. I'm out, free at least until the trial, which could be up to three months away.

I feel relieved but also like I'm holding a ticking clock strapped to a bomb that may or may not go off in three months' time. That invisible noose around my neck has slipped even tighter.

When we pull into my driveway, I scan the parking area for Em's bike. I'm not really expecting her to be here as she doesn't yet know I'm out. I only just got my phone back—the cops had taken it off me when they put me in the cell—and the battery's now dead, but I'm desperate to see her. I almost asked Mrs. Donovan to drop me at her place instead of here, but I need to take a shower and change my clothes.

"Bye, Jake," she says as I get out the car.

"Thank you," I say again, shaking her hand. "I mean it. I'm really sorry for everything. I don't know how to repay you."

"We're not out of the woods yet, Jake. We need to work on your defense before the trial, okay? I'll be in touch. And you need to stay out of trouble until then. Curb that impulsiveness."

Nodding, I shut the car door and watch her drive away, then take a minute just to breathe in the fresh air and soak up the feeling of the sun on my face. It's amazing how special the small things become when you think you might be in danger of losing them. Finally, I move to the door, pulling out my keys as I go.

Before I even step in the shower, I plug in my phone. Ignoring the two dozen messages from my parents and Sarge and several unknown numbers, I try Em, but her phone is switched off. I wonder if she's with Shay, because I know Shay is leaving for New York this evening, but when I try Shay, she doesn't answer either. After a shower, I summon the balls to call Sarge.

"What the hell are you thinking, McCallister?" Sarge shouts the minute he picks up. "Have you got shit for brains?" I start to answer, but he cuts me off. "If those charges stick, you're off the team and out of school. I had to fight to even get them to let you play next season. They said it breaks the rules. I argued you were innocent until proven guilty. They find you guilty, though, in three months' time, there's nothing I can do. Say good-bye to your future."

"I know," I say, dropping my head into my hands. Does he not realize how much I know this already? Repeating it isn't helping any.

"Get your ass back here before you get into any more trouble. People in your position cannot take risks like this. What does your lawyer say? Can she get you off or not? You're not pleading guilty, are you?"

"I don't know yet. It depends on the charge."

"Don't be stupid. Plead guilty and you may as well quit now. You'll be out on your ear, no career, no future. There's only one choice here—plead not guilty. Come on, your lawyer must be saying the same."

"But—" I start to argue with him. I *am* guilty. I did punch him. It wasn't exactly self-defense, either.

"Listen," Sarge interrupts. "Get back here, get your head back in the game, McCallister. It'll take your mind off the trial and remind the Red Wings that you're worth holding on to."

"Okay," I say, though I think it's going to take a lot more than hockey to take my mind off the fact I might be in jail this time next year or out on the street but with a criminal conviction and no contract to play hockey.

"When are you leaving there?" Sarge asks.

"Tomorrow, but I have to be ready to fly back whenever they ask."

"Good. I want you where I can see you. You are on lockdown,

do you understand me? You are not getting into any more trouble."

"I won't."

"That's what you said last time."

"I swear," I say.

He grumbles something indecipherable, and I hang up and try Em again. There's still no answer. Something starts to niggle at me. Why isn't she picking up or returning my calls? I leave another message and then decide I can't just sit around anymore wondering and waiting for her to return my call. Fifteen minutes later, I'm knocking on the door of her house.

Em's mom answers. "Jake!" she says. "You're out!" She pulls me into a hug. "Are you okay? We were so worried."

"Is Em in?" I ask when she releases me.

She shakes her head.

"Do you know where she is?"

"She said she was going to the tree house and if you came by to see her that I should tell you to go there."

Jake

I keep expecting to see my mom marching down the path through the woods, screaming my name, but two hours go by and I gradually accept the fact that she's probably left with my sister to catch the flight to Toronto. Either that or she's called the cops and they're out searching for me. But I can't think about that. It's too late for regrets.

Where's Em, though? My ears are pricked for any sight or sound of her, but she doesn't appear. It's getting dark. Is she coming? What if she doesn't want to see me or she can't get out the house? What if she doesn't come?

Darkness falls like a shroud. The woods come alive with noises I never noticed when it was light—rustling and hoots and snuffling. I pull on a spare sweater and unfurl the sleeping bag to sit on, and then, because I'm starving, I take out the noodles, remembering too late I forgot the stove and a saucepan. Smart. Frustrated, and with my stomach growling in protest, I toss the noodles back into the bag and tear into the marshmallows instead, making a vague reminder to self to save some for Em.

I'm halfway through the bag when a snap of a branch has me jumping to my feet. Someone's coming. It sounds like a rhinoceros stampeding toward me. I stand up and lean over the railing to see, hoping it's Em and not my mom or the cops.

It's none of them. It's Reid Walsh. He appears, barreling into the clearing, brandishing a stick like a lightsaber.

"Where's Em?" I ask. "Did you give her the note?"

"She's not coming."

"What?"

Reid looks at me. I think I see a hint of smile crack his lips, but his eyes dart to the wilting wooden boards of the tree house. "Look, she's not coming, okay?"

"You're lying," I bark, stepping toward him. He holds his hand out, shakes his head.

"She wanted me to tell you to leave her alone and that she never wants to see you or hear from you again. Or from your uncle."

It's as if he's launched himself up the ladder and kicked me in the chest.

He snorts. "Guess you can't blame her."

His words ring in my ears long after he's run off.

Somehow, I'm sitting down with my legs hanging over the ledge, the darkness lapping all around. What a stupid idea, to think that Em would ever have wanted to even see me again, or speak to me, let alone run away with me. We were little kids the last time we planned to run away together. And we never followed through that time either.

I feel hot and squirmy inside when I think about what an idiot I've been. I climb to my feet, shaky but resolute. I just want to get away from here. If my mom has already left, then I'll catch the ferry to the mainland, then the train to the airport, and I'll buy a plane ticket with the 312 dollars I have stuffed in my bag.

That money was meant to buy Em and me tickets to the NHL playoffs this year, but I guess that isn't happening now.

Stiff and cold, I stuff the sleeping bag into my backpack and throw it onto my shoulder, taking one last look around at this place we built together, before I say good-bye.

Em

close my eyes and breathe in the damp earth. The trees block out the sun, painting bars of shadows across me, and it's so cold I wish I'd worn a jacket. I glance up at the tree house. I don't think I can do this. *You've got no choice.*

"Em."

I turn around and my heart slams like a rocket into my rib cage. Jake is striding toward me through the undergrowth, a smile on his lips but a question in his eyes. It's just like the time I saw him again on the beach, when he first came back to Bainbridge. He seems nervous, unsure of my reaction. He stops in front of me and moves to pull me into his arms. I dance backward on shaking legs.

He freezes, his eyes darkening, his arms falling heavy to his sides. "What's going on? When you weren't at the police station, I figured something was up." The look in his eye is so afraid that I find I can't speak. I just want to reach for him, kiss him, make it all go away.

"I'm sorry," he says, and his jaw pulses. "I know I shouldn't have hit him, but he deserved it—"

I cut him off fast. "Look, let's not talk about it."

"But—"

"No," I say, walking away, putting more distance between us. I need to do this fast. Get it over with. Get away from him. "I think we should break up."

I hear him take a sharp breath in. "What?" he asks quietly.

I turn to Jake, but my gaze rests somewhere in the middle distance, not on him. "I don't think it's going to work, Jake. I mean, you're going back to college and I'm stuck here."

"Seriously?" Jake asks, stepping toward me. It's as if he knows that if he gets close enough, I won't be able to think straight, that he will have the advantage, so I walk even farther away.

"Yes, seriously," I tell him, wrapping my arms around my waist. "I've thought about it a lot. You and me, we are never going to work. And I just have too much on my plate. I can't deal with a long-distance relationship as well."

Jake says nothing, but I can feel his eyes burning through me. I risk a glance up at him. He's been waiting for me to make eye contact.

"This is bullshit," he says, the word flying across the clearing like a bullet.

I startle. Jake doesn't swear. "I'm sorry," I mumble.

Suddenly, he's right in front of me. He takes my hand and when I try to snatch it away, he holds on tighter. "Look at me," he says, and I hear the thick layer of emotion in his voice. I glance up at him.

"I thought you wanted to be with me," he says. "I thought we had something—something real."

I shrug and wrench my hand from his grip. "Look, Jake," I say, "it was good. While it lasted. But all good things have to end. There's no point in dragging it out."

The confusion in his eyes is so real it's heartbreaking, but I'm able to stay cold, unresponsive to it. All I do is draw on all the tricks of the old Emerson—shutting down, closing off to all feelings and emotions. It's easier than I thought it would be.

"No point?" he asks. His hand falls to his side. "Of course there's a point. I love you."

Okay. Not that easy. I feel that like a slice to the heart.

"What?" he asks me. "Suddenly, you don't love me anymore? Because two nights ago that's not what you were saying."

"I made a mistake," I whisper, looking again at the tree house. Our tree house.

"A mistake?" Jake asks, and I hear the wounded note in his voice.

"Yes," I say, anger ripping through me. "It was a mistake getting involved with you. I should never have done it."

"I don't get it," he says. "Is it because of the fight?"

I turn away and start walking out of the clearing.

"No," I say.

He steps in front of me. "Then what? I'm sorry. I know it was stupid. I just reacted when he called you a—"

"You don't need to be my defender, Jake. I don't need you to stand up for me."

"I want to stand up for you," he says, his voice husky, his eyes filled with hurt.

"Why?" I ask. "Because it makes you feel better? Less guilty because you weren't around to stand up for me back when it happened? Because you ran off and didn't care a damn about me or what happened to me?"

I don't know why I've just said this last part. I didn't mean to. It just came flying out of me, and I wish I could take it back, but I can't. The words are hanging in the air between us like a bad smell.

Something flashes across Jake's face. "I've said sorry, Em. I told you what happened. I explained why we had to leave. I would have told you to your face, but you didn't want to see me. You made that perfectly clear. And I get it. I really do get it. I don't blame you."

"What are you talking about?"

He frowns at me. "I waited for you. At the tree house. You didn't show up. And I know why, but—"

"When?"

"The day after. I went there after school. I had this stupid idea." He laughs under his breath. "I was there for hours waiting for you to show up."

"Why would I have shown up?"

"Because of the letter."

"What letter?"

Jake blinks at me. The blood drains from his face as though a sluice gate has opened in his neck. "He never gave it to you, did he?"

"What? Who? What are you talking about?"

"Reid. I gave him a letter to give to you."

Jake bites his top lip and stares at the ground. Now he looks like a bull about to charge. I take a step toward him. He looks up and my feet freeze. "It doesn't matter now," he says.

"You're right," I say, taking a deep breath, forcing myself to be resolute. "None of it matters now. You should leave."

Jake stares at me for a moment and then he turns around and walks away.

I stay where I am, rooted to the spot, watching until he's out of sight, willing myself not to run after him.

The sound of clapping starts to echo through the damp woods. It gets louder. Rob appears on the path. He's climbed down from the tree house and is sauntering toward me, smiling while he applauds. It was part of the deal that I let him watch.

"Nice acting," he says.

"I did you what you wanted," I spit at him. "Are you happy now?"

He nods, still grinning. "Hell yeah. That was Oscar-worthy."

"I broke up with him like you told me to. I let you watch. Now are you going to drop the charges?"

Rob studies me, smirking. "I'll think about it."

I reel back and stare at him in disbelief. "Think about it?"

"Yeah, if I drop the charges, what's to stop you from running back to him?"

My mouth falls open. He's a bully—I knew that all along. But this is like a child pulling the wings off an insect, slowly, taking his time about it. I gave him a taste of power and control, and now he's desperate for more. Damn it. I should have known this is what he'd do.

I weigh him for a moment, a riptide of anger building inside me, and then I take a step toward him, fists coiling at my sides as I consider the giant target that is his head. There's a smug victory smile on his face, and it stops me in my tracks. For a brief second, it whips me right back to the locker room all those years ago. I saw that same smile on Jake's uncle's face right after he did what he did, both threatening and amused, both of them believing that my silence was a given.

Jake

The ice is torn up by the time I get off it and stagger my way to the locker rooms. It's past midnight. I'm the only person in the building. I collapse down in the darkness onto one of the benches, breathing hard, sweat coursing down my face. Gradually, my pulse rate starts to settle, but as it does, the ache in my chest expands. I smack my head back into the lockers. The only thing that helps me ignore the ache in my chest is being on the ice. I headed straight here from the airport, stopping only to dump my bag in my room.

Maybe I should have stayed in Bainbridge and tried to reason with Em some more, but I had a flight to catch and Sarge was yelling at me to get back before I got into any more trouble, and the truth was, after finding out that Reid never gave Em that letter, I was on the cusp of going over to his house and confronting him. I knew then I had to leave as soon as possible, before I made things even worse. Why did I ever believe him when he told me he'd given her the letter? Why did I believe him when he told me that she never wanted to see me again? Why didn't I just go over to her house and demand to see her? I was such an idiot. All those wasted years and wasted opportunities. Things could have been so different.

I thought Em and I were in a good place, though. I thought we had gotten past all her worries and fears and that I'd convinced her I was committed to her. Did I misread things so badly? Or was it because I punched Reid and she saw a side to me she didn't like? Or what if it's because she doesn't want to date someone who's most likely going to prison? I mean, I wouldn't blame her.

I pull off my shirt and undo my skates, then head for the showers. Beneath the scalding-hot jets, I bow my head, my thoughts spinning wildly. All I can see is Em's face when she told me she wanted to break up. She was so cold and so distant. She was Emerson again.

"There you are."

I jerk around, startled. It's late, and I didn't think anyone was around.

Lauren is standing in the doorway, smiling one of her seductive smiles. Her gaze dips to my chest, then even lower. Her smile spreads.

"Did you miss me?" she asks, stepping closer.

Em

The way he looked when I did it tore a hole in my heart. If I had ever doubted Jake's feelings for me, which I hadn't, that would have convinced me of them. And then there's the fact he wrote me a letter. And now I can't stop wondering how different things might have been if I'd received it. I want more than anything to know what it said. And why Reid never gave it to me. Though perhaps that's obvious.

I check my watch. He must have landed already. I need to wait until I know for sure he's on the other side of the country before I call him and explain. Maybe I should have told him the truth all along. But I was worried that if I did tell him and we playacted a breakup, Reid would know it was fake. Jake's the world's worst actor. I was also afraid that Jake would do something stupid if he found out that Reid was threatening me again, and jeopardize his career even more.

When I explain, Jake will understand. Hopefully, he'll laugh. We'll just pretend we've broken up. Reid won't find out, especially with Jake being away, and then, once he's dropped the charges and the case is closed, it won't matter. Reid might like to think he's controlling me, but he isn't. I'm the one playing him.

I pick up my phone and dial Jake. It's one in the morning, but I can't wait.

"Hello?" a girl answers.

I sink down onto my bed. "Who's this?" I ask.

"This is Lauren."

Lauren? "I was looking for Jake," I say, my heart thumping.

"He's in the shower," she answers, and I can hear the lazy smile in her voice. I swallow, glancing at the clock. It's almost one in the morning. "He's just had a very heavy workout." She giggles. "I can go get him if you like?"

"No, that's okay."

I hear a voice in the background. It sounds like Jake. "Can I take a message?" Lauren asks.

I hang up and sit there staring at the phone in my hand for several minutes trying to fit the pieces together. They won't fit. Or they will. But the picture they're making is so devastating I can't accept it.

All that bullshit about how much he loved me and it took him less than a day to move on.

Jake

"What are you still doing here?" I ask Lauren.

She leans up against my locker. "I wanted to see you, Jake," she says hesitantly. "I wanted to talk."

In the middle of the night?

"Excuse me," I say, indicating she move out of the way of my locker. She makes a big show of stepping aside. I yank open the locker door.

"You've been ignoring me," she says.

I keep my back to her, rummaging in my locker for my clothes. What the hell is she doing in here? How did she even get in? If Sarge finds out, I'm going to be in so much shit. No girls are allowed in the locker rooms. This is not what I need. She's already gotten me into so much trouble as it is.

"Why are you ignoring me?" Lauren asks.

I turn around, studying her in amazement. "Why am I ignoring you? Um, maybe because you sold me out to the press?"

Lauren's eyes go big and round. "What?" she says, her mouth forming a glossy O. "I didn't sell you out; what are you talking about?"

"Drop it, Lauren. I know it was you. No one else knew."

"Jake," she says softly, resting her hand on my shoulder. "Come on." She pouts at me. "Why would I do that? I love you. We're good together, you and me. You know it."

Her eyes are glimmering like a cat's in the low light. I put my hand on top of hers and lean down. Her lips part in anticipation. She presses her body up against mine.

"Go try it on with some other guy," I say. "I'm not interested." I take her hand and peel it off my shoulder, and then, grabbing my clothes and my phone from the bench where I must have left it, I walk back into the bathrooms and lock myself in a stall, resting my head in my hands. I wait ten minutes. When I walk out of the stall, Lauren's gone, but I double-check before I drop my towel and pull my hockey gear back on.

Picking up my stick, I head back out onto the ice.

Emerson

A loud bang makes me pull the covers off my head and sit up. I stumble groggily out of bed and over to the window. "What the . . . ?"

I dart from the room and down the stairs, fly through the kitchen, and dash across the lawn, barefoot and still in my pajamas, heading toward the shed.

"What do you think you're doing?!" I yell at the man in blue overalls who is carrying a toolbox across the lawn.

He freezes and looks at me and then looks back in the direction of my dad's old work shed. "Er . . . ," he says. "I'm the carpenter. I was just finishing off the wheelchair ramp."

"The what?"

He nods over his shoulder and I do a double take. The work shed no longer appears to be a work shed. How did I miss this?

"I'm just going to get started on the one by the back door," he says, and starts walking toward the house.

I watch him go and then walk past the bushes until I'm standing by my dad's old workshop. One side and the back—which has a view of the woods that brush our fence line—have been completely knocked out and replaced with French windows. There's even a deck where my dad used to keep the log pile.

"Oh, hey."

I look up startled. Toby is standing in the doorway looking like a burglar caught red-handed. He's holding a rolled-up piece of paper in one hand and a tape measure in the other.

"What are you doing?" I ask him.

He looks from side to side as if trying to find an escape route. "Um . . ." His face crumples. "Oh man, it wasn't my idea, okay? It was Jake's."

I peer past Toby's shoulder into the shed, which used to be where we kept the wheelbarrow and my dad's tools, but which now is . . . I'm not even sure what it is. . . .

"What's happening?" I ask Toby.

"It's a luxury rental unit. Jake had the idea. We've been working on it for weeks."

The mention of Jake's name is a karate chop to the chest. It's been a week since we broke up, since he ran back into Lauren's open arms, and the thought of it is a constant slow drip of acid on my broken heart.

"We?" I ask.

"Jake, me, Aaron," Toby says, giving me an apologetic shrug. He knows I never want to hear Jake's name ever again. "Your parents, too. Shay helped with the decorating."

My head snaps up. Shay was in on it as well? How did they do all this without me noticing? I know the shed is hidden behind a wall of trees and that I've been completely out of it this last week, but this has to have taken them months. I stare at the exposed beams in the roof, the cast-iron wood burner on the deck, the crisp white comforter on the bed.

"Jake wanted it to be a surprise."

Another gut wrench. Every second of every day, all I can do is think about him. I've tried to banish the memories—the silk on skin, the look in his eye when he pulled me to him that first time across the bed, his whispered *I'm in love with you.*

Clearly. So, so in love with me. He rebounded faster than a yo-yo on an elastic string. I haven't told anyone the details of the breakup because I'm too embarrassed for anyone to know what a fool I was. Everyone assumes we broke up because I didn't want a long-distance relationship and because of the bar brawl.

"I think he wanted to be the one to surprise you with it . . . ," Toby says. He breaks off and scratches behind one ear, looking away embarrassed. "Your mom's already taking bookings."

"Who's paying for it all?" I ask, staring at the flat-screen TV screwed to the wall. I know my parents can't afford all this—the fixtures and fittings alone look like they cost thousands.

Toby shrugs again and starts studying the floor.

"Is Jake paying for it?"

Toby glances up. "I think he's loaning the money, but your dad has cut some deal with him."

We'll see about that. I don't care if I have to take a loan or another job, there is no way that I'm letting Jake pay for all this. I turn on my heel and storm back toward the house.

"Does Jake know you still sleep in his T-shirt?" Toby calls out after me.

Jake

The door to the locker room flies open, smacking against the breeze-block wall. The rest of the team shove their way to their lockers in high spirits. The tension is trip-wire taut, though, beneath the joshing. This is a big game for us—the opening one of the season, against the University of Michigan. I pull on my sweater and reach for my skates and helmet, ignoring the clang of lockers slamming shut and friendly insults being traded all around me.

"Hey, Jake. Who're the girls? Did you bone them?"

I turn to Steve Tong, one of my teammates. He's half-dressed and holding a magazine, which he now shoves in my face. "They're hot, bro."

The others crowd around and start making comments about the girl in the photograph with me.

"How much they pay you for this?" Tong asks, leering over the photo. "'Cause I would have done it for free."

I don't answer. I just pull on my skates. The truth is they paid me a lot. And I'm due to earn a lot more. After I was arrested for punching Rob, the offers flowed in faster than Usain Bolt, which is so messed up I can't even get my head around it. My first impulse was to turn them all down, but then I thought about something Shay said. I can't give the money to Em, but I can do some good with it. I've been donating every cent to medical research for MS.

The magazine rips in half as the guys fight over it, and Tong starts yelling, but then the door swings open and everyone falls silent. Sarge strides into the middle of the locker room. He's got his Vietnam War look on his face, eyes lasering in on each of us in turn. Everyone gathers around him, ready for the prematch pep talk. He catches me still sitting on the bench and shoots me a death glare. I get up with a sigh and join them, but I barely hear his words.

It's been two weeks since I saw Em, since I last talked to her, but I can't stop thinking about her. I've thrown myself back into the game—putting in four, five hours straight at the gym after class, training on the ice until past midnight every night—but it's not enough. I can't get her out of my head.

I've stopped checking my phone for messages, stopped trying to call. Not even Shay has managed to speak to her or get her to answer an e-mail. Toby says she's okay but won't talk to him about anything. He did let me know that she's found out about the rental unit. But still not a word. It's driving me fucking crazy.

"McCallister?"

I startle. Sarge is looking at me, his mouth screwed up.

"Yeah?" I say.

"What'd I just say?"

I feel everyone's eyes on me. "Um . . ."

"I said we all need to be focused!" he barks.

I nod.

"This is an important game. All eyes are on you. Especially on you, McCallister."

I hold his gaze, hearing the snickers from my teammates. Does he think he's telling me something I don't know? All eyes have been on me since I got back; the media keep hounding me, and the college administration is watching my every move, scrutinizing my grade average and issuing me a warning that if one more toe steps out of line, I'm out. Sarge has been keeping me on the tightest leash imaginable—banning me from any parties or from leaving campus—which is fine because I've got zero interest in being social. The only thing keeping me sane is hockey. When I'm on the ice is the only time I can push away the thoughts of Em.

"Okay," Sarge shouts. "Let's win this game!"

Everyone roars their agreement. Except me. I'm channeling it all inward. Lockers slam shut. Everyone grabs their stick, their mouth guard, their helmet, and makes in a rush for the door. I can hear the screams of the crowd already assembled around the rink. I pick up my stick and go to follow the others.

"McCallister!" Sarge grabs my shoulder and stops me.

"Yeah?" I say, pulling out my mouth guard.

"Where's your head at?"

"In the game," I say, but even I hear the lack of conviction in my voice.

"Watch Koskela, okay?" Sarge grunts.

I nod. Koskela is a Finnish player who thinks the rules were made to be ignored—the player who once used his stick to block me and gave me the scar through my eyebrow.

"Don't sink to his level, Jake."

I nod again.

"I mean it. I see any sign of you losing it out there and I'm benching you."

"I won't." I start to turn, but his hand is still on my shoulder, gripping me in place.

"Why do you think you made it to the top of the draft?" he asks.

I shrug and stare at the ground. He shakes my shoulder, forcing me to look up at him. "Because you're a great player, Jake. When you rein in the impulsiveness. You don't quit. You play smart. Most of the time. You take risks, but normally they're calculated. And you give it your all."

I nod.

"Are you going to give it your all out there tonight?"

"Yeah," I say.

"Okay." He slaps me on the back. "Get out there, then, and win this game."

Emerson

I wheel my dad into the bar. He got it into his head that he wanted to get out of the house, and because it was the first time in nearly a year he'd wanted to go out, I couldn't exactly say no.

I park my dad's wheelchair at the table I sat at with Jake and the others before remembering and moving us to another spot. The barman recognizes me and nods his head, but I see his glance linger on my dad. My dad used to be a regular here—it's about the only place in Bainbridge that serves both a good coffee and a good beer. When I walk over, he smiles at me.

"What can I get you?"

"Um, just two Cokes," I say.

"You here to watch the game?" he asks.

"The what?"

"The game," the barman says, nodding at the TV screen at the end of the bar, around which a half-dozen people are crowded.

"Jake McCallister's playing. It's Michigan versus Boston College."

I turn to glare at my dad, who conveniently is looking

elsewhere. This is a total setup. Gripping the two glasses of Coke like they're grenades, I march back over to him. "You wanted to get out the house? You felt, suddenly, after a year of being stuck inside, like being social?" I ask, setting the Cokes down.

He looks guiltily up at me and then at the screen. "It's just about to start," he comments.

I shake my head at him and slump down in a stool with my back to the TV. The knowledge that I could turn my head and see Jake is pure torture. Now I have to sit here and listen to the crowd behind me yell and curse and comment on the players and the action.

"And McCallister, always first on the puck, has scored the first goal of the first period," the presenter announces.

My stomach flips at the sound of Jake's name.

"You don't want to watch?" my dad asks.

"No!"

"Why?"

He and my mom know I broke up with Jake but don't know the real reason—or real *reasons*. I shrug. I don't want to talk about it. And luckily, I don't have to, because the noise level in the bar is now too loud for us to have a conversation.

Though I keep my back resolutely to the screen and sip my drink, acting oblivious, my hearing is acutely tuned to the shouts and yells. I'm trying to zone in on the voice of the sports presenter, frustrated when the volume in the bar makes it impossible to hear the playbacks. I hear Jake's name several times, though, and from the shouts and cheers I can tell Boston is winning. Is Jake scoring?

I drain my drink and sit there for twenty minutes, foot tapping, wishing we could leave. My dad has no idea how hard this is; how every time I think about Jake or hear his name, all I can think about is Lauren answering his phone. Was she lying naked in his bed? Is she there at the rink in a front-row seat, watching him play? Will it be her he celebrates or commiserates with after the game? I grind my teeth and loudly suck up the last of my Coke, trying to drown out the latest round of cheering.

"And McCallister scores his third goal of this playoff game. . . ."

I can't bear it any longer. I get up and push my way through to the bathrooms, locking myself in a cubicle. I'll stay in here until it's safe to come out.

Jake

Koskela is trying to shut me down. He keeps back-checking me—trying to steal the puck from me every time I've got possession. He's playing aggressive like always, not afraid to throw his whole weight onto a player or dive to stop someone taking a shot on the goal. I've already had a half-dozen collisions with him, one that sent me headfirst into the boards. He's had one two-minute penalty for elbowing me, but the referee has missed or chosen to ignore the other cross-checking. He reminds me of Reid, and the unwelcome reminder of Walsh when I'm concentrating on my game injects me with a pure shot of anger.

I try to focus it on the game. I want to win. I want to show everyone I'm still the best player on the ice. I can't react to Koskela, no matter how much he's riling me. Everyone's watching: my parents in the stands, the university chairman, Sarge, my agent, the Red Wings coach. Is Em watching? The thought makes me play harder, pouring all I've got into the game.

Koskela appears suddenly on my left, slamming hard into my shoulder. He mutters something under his breath. He's trying to antagonize me. It's his play. He knows the minute I react I'll get benched by my coach, and that's what he wants. But then he's got possession of the puck, slicing it out from one of my players. I back-check him at full speed, putting my head down and driving down the middle of the ice toward our goal. I'm not letting him get a pass. He glares at me, swearing under his breath. Our sticks clash, his weight against mine. I can hear the deafening roar of the crowd as I manage to lift his stick, nudge the puck out of his control, and flick it across the ice to one of our defensemen.

I skate out of his way, throwing myself back in the play, putting myself between my teammate, who's driving toward the net, and one of the Michigan players, who's trying to check him.

But then suddenly I'm hit from behind by the weight of a freight train. I'm off the ice, in the air—a split second, an eternity, the thunder of the crowd filling my ears—and then the scarred, concrete-hard ice is flying up to meet me.

Emerson

'm walking out of the bathroom, driven out by the knowledge that I can't leave my dad just sitting by himself in a wheelchair while I sulk for another twenty minutes, when a deafening roar goes up.

People are on their feet, blocking the TV screen. A man in front of me has his hands on his head and is wincing.

"And McCallister's on the ice," the presenter is saying. "He's not moving."

I push through the crowd, listening to the gasps all around me, and when I get to the front, all I can see is a scrum of referees and players crowded around a figure lying on the ice, motionless.

"Michigan defenseman Koskela just earned himself a total season ban, I'd say. It looks serious. McCallister's not moving."

The picture jumps to a replay. It's Jake, recognizable even behind the helmet and face guard. He's intercepting a Michigan player, helping his teammate line up a shot at the goal. Then, from out of nowhere, another player is on him. Stick raised high, the guy leaves his feet and delivers a hard check, smashing what looks like both his stick as well as his whole weight onto Jake's back.

Behind me, I hear a woman let out a cry as Jake goes hurtling into the barrier before landing facedown on the ice, Koskela diving on top of him. I swear I hear the crunch of bones. The gasps around me are audible.

"Jesus," a man beside me whispers.

"What the hell?"

The playback stops and cuts back to the present moment. I can't see Jake anymore. He's surrounded by a team of paramedics. Panic shuts down my legs. I can't breathe. The view pans back across the ice, and I see Koskela buried beneath a scrum of Boston players who've launched themselves on him. Referees and coaches are trying to pull the opposing players off each other as fists and legs and skates fly and slash through the air.

"And they're bringing in a stretcher," the presenter announces. With my hands over my mouth I watch as the paramedics strap a neck collar to Jake and lift him carefully onto a stretcher. The paramedics are all over him. I want to push through the screen, force my way through the crowd to his side. A scream ratchets up inside me, trying to spring loose.

"The guy should be arrested!" someone behind me shouts.

Hand covering my mouth, I watch as Jake is carried off the ice. Someone puts their hand on my shoulder. "You okay?"

I blink. It's the barman. All I can do is stare at him. I don't have any words. Then I remember my dad. He's looking at me, anguished. He can't move, can't get over to me. I rush toward him.

"Go," he says, his arm jerking out toward the door.

I move in a daze behind him, ready to wheel him out the

door, my heart thumping, my gaze falling back to the screen. They've cut back to the fight. Koskela, bloodied and limping, is being helped off the ice.

GAME SUSPENDED flashes up at the bottom. BOSTON COLLEGE FORWARD JAKE McCALLISTER CRITICALLY INJURED.

I fumble for my phone. I need to call someone. I need to find out if Jake's okay and where they're taking him. But who do I call? I look at the phone's screen. There are three missed calls from Shay. She must have been watching the game too. My mom. My brain unfreezes. I need to call her. She needs to come and collect us.

"Go," my dad slurs angrily.

"I'm trying," I say, and I realize that I'm crying. I can't hit the right buttons to call my mom. My hands are shaking too much.

"No. Go to Jake," my dad says.

Jake

V oices cut in and out as if someone's playing with a TV remote, flipping the channel and messing with the volume. A panicked high note—someone yelling—blends with a screaming wail that rises and falls in pitch.

"Head trauma. Possible spinal injury. We need an MRI and a CT scan."

Who are they talking about?

Is it Koskela? Wait . . . What about the game? Am I still on the ice? I try to turn my head. I can't. I can't move anything. Can't feel my legs.

Where's Em? There's a ton of weight lying on top of me. Am I buried beneath a mountain of players? Is that why I can't move? Is that why I can't breathe? I try to suck in air, panicking, disco lights flashing in rhythmic bursts at the edges of the darkness, but it hurts too much to breathe.

I'm spiraling downward, slipping through ice, into the murky cold depths below. The voices grow fainter. The pressure in my lungs eases. The pain draws back.

In the solid blackness that I'm encased in, I try to turn my head. Where is she? I can't see anything.

Em?

Emerson

Koskela has been given a twenty-six-match ban and is likely to face charges of criminal assault."

It's the same woman from ESPN who ran the story of Jake's drug test fail—what's her name? Jo Furness. It's right there on the screen beneath her heavily made-up face. She's standing in front of the emergency room entrance, talking direct to camera, wearing a coat and scarf and a maniacal gleam in her eye. Ticker tape scrolls along the bottom of the screen: NEWS ALERT: JAKE McCALLISTER TAKEN TO UNI. MICHIGAN HOSPITAL . . . STAR NHL PROSPECT UNDERGOING EMERGENCY SURGERY . . .

"There's a real irony," she intones to screen, "to McCallister, Boston College's star forward and the ice hockey world's most feted star, being called the victim of assault."

I glare at the screen.

"It was only six weeks ago McCallister himself was arrested for aggravated assault after an unprovoked attack left an innocent man scarred for life."

I leap to my feet. "What the—" I yell at the TV.

My mom grabs my arm. "Calm down," she says, shushing me.

"McCallister, who is pleading not guilty to the charge, is due in court in less than a month, though it's looking like the trial date may now have to be pushed back given the severity of the injuries he sustained today in the match against the University of Michigan."

I sink back down onto the sofa. My mom clutches my hands in hers. On-screen, Jo Furness presses her hand to her earpiece.

"Initial reports suggest he's suffered internal injuries including a fracture to the spine, but we're yet to have confirmation of the extent of his injuries or what they might mean for this talented young player."

This can't be happening. What does it mean? A fractured spine? Is he going to be paralyzed? I wish I could reach through the screen, grab her by the neck, and throttle her until she tells me.

"It's too soon to say for certain, but it looks like McCallister's career, both as a professional hockey player and as a model, may be prematurely over."

I look up. No. How can she stand there and pronounce something like that as if she knows anything at all about anything? She's not a doctor. And his modeling career? As if he ever cared about modeling! As if any of it matters except him being okay! I want to throw something at the TV. I grab hold of a cushion and crush it to my chest.

My mom turns to me. "I'm going to book a flight."

"What?"

"You need to go to him. Whatever happened between you two, you're still friends, aren't you? If it were Shay, you'd go, wouldn't you? You would already be on a plane."

I close my eyes. Yes. I would go. No hesitation. And yes, I

want to go now. I want to be there right this second. This waiting, this not knowing, is torture. But his family is there with him. Lauren is there with him. He doesn't need me. He doesn't want me. He hasn't even bothered to call me, for Christ's sake.

"You need to go, Emerson. After everything Jake's done for us, it's the least we can do. I would go myself if I could."

I bite my lip. Should I go? Yes. I have to go. My mom's right. There's no other option. I can't just sit here waiting by the TV to hear what's happened to him. I can't leave it up to that vile reporter to update me. I'll go crazy.

They're replaying the game—the moment of impact—in slow motion and from every possible angle. Every time I see it, I feel like I'm going to throw up. But now it flashes back to that damn reporter again.

I take note of the name of the hospital, lit up behind her. If I can get a flight out of Seattle this evening, I can be there by the morning. I get to my feet. Now I have a plan. It gives me momentum. But as I move to the door, something suddenly catches my eye on the TV. On-screen, Jo Furness has just stopped someone who was walking by on their way to the ER.

". . . Jake McCallister's girlfriend, Lauren Willis . . ."

Lauren's tearstained face appears on camera. I stagger back as if I've been punched in the gut. My mom stands beside me frozen, with the TV remote in her hand.

"What?" she says, hitting the volume button. "What do they mean, his girlfriend?"

"Lauren, can you give us an update on Jake's progress?" Jo calls out. "Is he still in surgery? Have the doctors given you any indication of how severe his injuries are?"

Lauren turns away, holding up a hand to shield her

mascara-bleeding face, and heads toward the entrance to the ER.

Jo turns to the camera, then catches sight of someone else walking toward the ER. "And here, also just arriving, is the Boston College ice hockey coach." She thrusts the microphone into the face of a gruff, gray-haired man wearing a blazer and a cap.

"In your career as a coach have you ever seen an injury as bad as this one?"

He pushes the microphone away with an angry snarl. "No comment," he barks, and strides into the ER.

My mom switches off the TV. I stay staring at the ink-black screen. I can feel my mom looking at me, a silent question on her lips.

No comment.

Jake

burst through the surface with a violent jolt as though smashing my way through a thick layer of lake ice. A kaleidoscope spins on the back of my eyelids. I suck in a breath of air, but then, in the next instant, I'm tumbling back into the deep, pulled down this time not by the crushing weight on my chest or the blinding pain, but by limbs that are as heavy as lead.

I surrender, too tired to fight it, and let myself be tugged downward, through the gap in the ice and into the darkness below, letting it cover my mouth, my nose, my eyes. There's a rapid beeping noise and then a lightning bolt rips through me, yanking me above the surface again. And there I stay, suspended just above the hole in the ice, my fingers dangling over the edge, feeling the tempting numbness of the water. There's no pain down there. There's nothing. But up here, a hockey game is going on around me. There's so much noise. And a puck keeps slamming into my chest, and I can't move my arms to block it. What's happening? I try to struggle, and someone murmurs something.

The pain flares hot, excruciatingly hot—like I've been doused in gasoline and set alight. The hole beneath me widens as the ice below starts to melt. The cold snatches hold of my fingers and inches up my arm, extinguishing the flames. I roll toward the hole.

I want to disappear down there again, into the silence, into the cold.

Emerson

(Then)

I t's evening when I'm finally able to escape the house. The woods are dark as a grave and cold as one too. Not a sliver of moonlight breaks through the firs and alders. The dank, loamy smell of wet leaves and earth fills my lungs, and I draw it in deep as though I have been holding my breath underwater for the last twenty-four hours and have finally broken the surface.

I break into a run, stumbling over buried roots, ignoring the branches that whip my arms and face, ignoring the cold that slaps my cheeks and makes them sting, ignoring the damp that has soaked through my shoes and socks and jeans.

As I run, I can hear his voice echoing through the trees. He's chasing me, gaining on me. I run faster. I need to make it to the tree house. I'll be safe there.

"Em!" he calls my name again. This time closer. "Em!"

It sounds like he's right beside me.

I push on, sprinting now, desperate to escape him, but I can't because his voice is in my head and there's no running from it.

Fighting through a moat of ferns, I make it into the clearing, dart toward the tree house, and start scrambling up the ladder. A hand grabs my foot; another hand grabs my thigh. I yelp, kick out, almost fall, but manage somehow to keep climbing.

Dragging myself onto the landing, I lean over the ledge to look down. There's no one there. I'm imagining it all. It's not real. It's not real. It's only in my head.

I dig my fingers into the wooden boards I'm lying on—like it's the deck of a storm-tossed ship—and I hold on tight, until my breathing finally returns to normal and my heart rate begins to slow.

"Em?"

I jolt upright, scanning the forest floor, my heart bashing wildly against my ribs. There's no one there. Scrunching my eyes shut, I curl into a ball and press my hands over my ears.

"Shut up, shut up!" I scream at his voice in my head.

My skin prickles as if worms are crawling all over my body, leaving dirty, slimy trails in their wake. Another nest of worms writhes in my stomach. Why? Why? Why me? a voice mumbles over and over again, but there's never any answer. I must have done something wrong. That's the only thing I know.

Exhausted from crying and shivering from the cold, I finally open my eyes. My gaze lands on a half-empty packet of marshmallows. Have the Walshes been here? Or Jake?

A rustle in the undergrowth makes me jerk around in fright. Automatically, I cower backward into the shadows, holding my breath.

Is it my parents come looking for me?

Is it Jake?

Or . . . is it him?

Please let it be Jake. Where is Jake? Does he know? Would he believe me?

No one believes you; no one believes you, a sneaky voice in my head starts to whisper, quietly at first, getting louder, until it becomes a scream ricocheting around my skull.

I slump onto my side and lie there, not even curling into a ball, but just staring out into the darkness, letting the cold numb me, until I'm shivering so hard that I can no longer feel the worms crawling over my skin and my teeth are chattering loud enough to almost drown out the whispers.

Emerson

What if he dies? I try to shove the thought away, but I can't. Of course he's not going to die, I tell myself, but then the image of Jake lying on the ice motionless as a corpse spears its way into my mind and I curl up tighter, wrapping my arms around my chest and sob harder.

I lie there on the tree house ledge for an hour, maybe longer, staring out over the forest. I remember running here all those years ago, lying in the exact same spot, curled in a ball and crying, thinking about Jake. Just like then, I'm also scared. And alone.

I close my eyes, and I start praying. I've never prayed before. I don't believe in God—how, after what happened?—but now I find myself making bargains with a God I'm a stranger to, to please let Jake be okay. I will do anything, give anything, just so long as he's okay.

My phone buzzes in my pocket. My pulse spikes. Is it my mom? Is there news? I don't know if I want to know. Maybe I shouldn't answer. But it isn't my mom's number. It's Jake's. I stare at his name flashing on my screen, in mind-numbing shock. What? How? With a trembling hand, I hit OK and press it to my ear. "Hello?"

There's a pause, someone taking a breath.

"Jake?"

"No," comes a girl's voice down the line. "It's not Jake. It's Lauren."

The world stops moving, slams to a sudden halt. For a second, I contemplate throwing my phone into the forest.

"Are you there?" she asks. Her voice sounds thick from crying.

"Yes," I whisper as dread seeps into every muscle and cell.

"It's about Jake."

Don't say it, don't say it.

"You need to come," Lauren says.

Jake

Emerson

t's midmorning by the time I make it to the hospital, frantic, running on adrenaline—the kind that makes you feel like you're flying and fills your brain with buzzing.

Shay meets me at the airport. She's flown in from New York.

"Come on, let's find a cab," she says, taking me by the hand as soon as I appear at arrivals.

"Do you know anything? Have you heard?" I ask her. "Is he—"

Shay shakes her head and pulls me across the concourse.

The intensive care unit is on the top floor. We ride the elevator in silence, Shay gripping my hand. When we exit the elevator, she's the one who asks a passing doctor where to go. The doctor directs us to the end of the hallway, where a set of locked doors greet us.

"They won't let you in. It's just family."

We turn around. It's Lauren, though I barely recognize her as she isn't wearing makeup and her hair is greasy and lank, pulled back into an untidy bun.

"Hi," she says to me, warily.

"Are you Lauren?" Shay asks.

She nods.

"Is he okay?" I ask.

She nods again. "He's out of surgery. He was in there for six hours. I've been trying to get one of the nurses to tell me what's happening, but they won't."

"Why did you call?" I ask, frustration giving bite to my words.

"When he wakes up, it isn't me he's going to want to see. It's you."

I frown. "But—"

"You got the wrong idea," Lauren interrupts, glancing at me fearfully. "When you called that time. I . . . I answered his phone. But we weren't . . ." She looks away, embarrassed, twisting her fingers together in a knot. "Nothing is going on between Jake and me." Her shoulders slump and she looks at the ground. "I'm sorry."

Jake

*B*eep. *Beep. Beep.*

It's the first thing I become aware of. The repetitive beeping of a truck in reverse. *Just reverse already!* I want to shout, but my lips are stitched shut. I can't open my eyes, either. Sounds reach me, but they're from far away, as though carried across a stretch of water.

Water.

My lips are dry. I'm so thirsty. And now that I think about it, my head hurts too. It starts off as a sludgy kind of ache, but then the pain switches on like a light, hitting me with the force of an axe blade. If I could open my eyes, I think the pain would blind me. Where am I? I struggle to remember. And why can't I move my hands? Or my feet?

I try to focus over the buzz saw slicing chunks out of my skull, but no matter how hard I try, I can't make any part of my body move.

My pulse fires in response to the panic sweeping through me. The beeping becomes louder, faster. And then I feel the needle grip of fingers pulling me down; the buzz saw eases up, and the darkness grows thicker, denser, more suffocating. The beeping gets fainter and starts to slow.

Panic suddenly claws at me—I don't want to slide beneath the ice again.

I couldn't find Em down there.

Emerson

merson? Em?"

I look up, startled. I think I had been dozing. Jake's mom is standing in front of me, rumpled, pale, with dark shadows beneath her eyes. I almost didn't recognize her. She's holding a polystyrene cup of vending machine coffee.

"What are you—" she asks, staring at me in wonder.

"I called her."

Lauren is sitting opposite me on one of the plastic seats beside the water cooler. We've barely said a word to each other in the hours we've been sitting here. "I thought that Jake would want her here," she says, standing up.

Jake's mom studies her for a moment before looking back at me. "Yes," she says with a smile. "I think you're right."

"Is he okay? What's happening?" I ask, standing up myself, my legs as weak as two blades of grass.

Shay and Jake's coach have gone to buy us something to eat. But I'm wishing Shay would come back, because I really need someone to lean on.

"He's still not come round yet," Jake's mom says. "They're

keeping him under while they wait for the swelling to go down on his brain. It was putting pressure on his spinal cord."

"Is he going to be okay?" I ask again.

"Yes, I think so. He ruptured his spleen. He lost a lot of blood. And he had four broken ribs. One pierced his lung."

"And his spine?" I ask.

"It's fine," she says, giving me a weak smile.

"It's not broken? I say, feeling shaky, as though bubbles have been injected into my bloodstream.

"No."

Lauren collapses into a seat and puts her head in her hands.

"Do you want to see him?" Jake's mom asks me.

"Yes."

He looks so pale that at first I can't believe he's not dead, but then I see his chest rise and fall and all the terror that's been locked inside me comes pouring out and I think I'm going to burst into tears. I manage not to. Instead, I cross straight to the bed and take his hand. It's warm—familiar. I ease my fingers gently through his and squeeze. The only thing that's different is, for the first time ever, he doesn't squeeze back.

"Hey," I whisper. "I'm here."

Jake

(Then)

I'm riding my bike up Toe Jam Hill. The sun's out. I'm sweating, legs piston pumping as I stand up on the pedals and try to catch up with Em. She's riding ahead of me, looking back over her shoulder and grinning.

We reach the top, both of us out of breath. We turn around and stare down the almost vertical incline that drops off onto the beach and the water below. Em glances over at me.

"Dare you," she says, her eyes flashing blue as a kingfisher's wing.

"Double dare," I say back.

She grins wider. We both take hold of the handles of our bikes.

"On three," Em yells. "One. Two. Three!"

And then we both launch ourselves down the hill. Em's whoops are drowned out by the roar of the wind. We pick up speed—wheels spinning over uneven ground. The glint of water below is getting closer and closer by the second. Em is just ahead of me, but now touching her brakes, and I'm catching up with her, next second side *by side with her, brushing her arm, then racing past her and she's yelling at me. . . .*

"Brake!"

But I can't. I squeeze the brakes, but they don't work. There's no resistance. Uh-oh. I glance up. The asphalt rears up in front of me; the blazing blue of the water fills my vision.

Em's screams get louder.

I'm lifted over the handlebars and I'm flying through the air.

Em

Jake's mom and I sit on either side of the bed, listening to the steady shushing of the ventilator. We've been listening to that noise for almost twenty-four hours. I've started to wonder if it will be forever stuck in my brain, like a constant soundtrack of white noise.

"I'm sorry."

I look up.

Jake's mom is looking right at me.

"About what?" I ask.

Her cheeks turn pink and she looks away. "About what happened with my brother."

It takes me a full ten seconds to process what she's saying, and then I almost pass out in shock. She's bringing that up now? Here?

"I never wanted to believe it. He was my brother." Her voice is strained. She darts a glance up at me. "It was easier to think you were a liar."

My instinct is to stand up and leave the room, but a voice in my head tells me to stay and hear her out.

"It wasn't an accident, you know."

"What wasn't?" I ask.

"He killed himself. It wasn't a hunting accident."

I lean back in my chair and blink at her. "How do you know?" I ask, my voice sounding remote and faraway.

"He wrote me a note. A letter. He said in it that he couldn't live with the guilt of what he'd done to you."

The room spins. He admitted it.

"I'm sorry," she says again. "I should have come forward then. I planned to. But my mother was in a very bad state after he died. She'd already had a couple of strokes, and I was scared if she found out the truth, it would be the end for her." Tears fall down her cheeks and she starts to sob.

Does she have any idea of what I went through? I don't know what I'm supposed to say because I have no idea what I'm feeling right now: a mix of anger, shock, upset, and, weirdly, happiness.

She buries her head in her hands. "Em, I'm sorry. I'm so sorry. We can do it now. I'll speak up. I'll go to the police. Whatever you need."

Whatever I need? It's too late to speak up. It's too late to go to the police. It's too late. You can't rewind the clock, I want to scream. You can't undo what was done to me. But then I pause. There's a freedom to what she's offering me. If people were to hear the truth, it would be some kind of recompense, wouldn't it? At long last to be vindicated? What would Jake say?

"Does Jake know?" I ask her.

She shakes her head. "I'm going to tell him when he wakes up. He always knew he was guilty. I should have listened to him."

I stroke Jake's hand.

"He confronted him; did he tell you?"

What? I look up.

"Jake confronted him at Thanksgiving a few years ago. I thought perhaps it was time to all get together again as a family. He'd stayed away—Ben had—but he came to my parents one year. They invited him. Jake . . . well, Jake refused to stay in the house or speak to him, and when Ben tried to talk to him, Jake punched him. Broke his nose." She shakes her head. "He was always so calm and gentle as a little boy, but then he suddenly had all this anger raging in him with nowhere for it to go. He started getting into scraps. One time his school called us in because he'd gotten into a fight. Turned out that the boy he'd hit was two years older and had fought back. Jake ended up in the hospital with a fractured wrist."

I shake my head, confused. Aside from Jake's run-in with Rob, I hadn't seen that angry side to him.

"You want to know why he got in a fight?"

I nod.

"Some kid in his class was being bullied and called names by this older boy. Jake told him to stop. He didn't. So Jake hit him."

I frown. The scene sounds familiar.

"He was angry. All the time. I think he was so frustrated, and I think deep down he thought he was delivering some sort of justice." She chews on her lip. "He should never have hit Rob, though."

"No," I say glumly.

"But I'm glad he was standing up for you. I'm proud of him for that." She smiles fondly at him, and I can't help but do the same.

"He sounded different when he called me," she goes on, "over the summer. He was happy, back to being the old Jake. He was laughing again. I thought maybe he'd sorted things out with you, but also . . . I thought maybe he'd finally managed to deal with some of that anger and frustration."

Wow. I'd been so focused on me that I never stopped to think much about how Jake was affected too. Both of us felt angry and unheard. Only, my anger was buried so much deeper it couldn't ever erupt. I couldn't even give it voice until Jake encouraged me to start writing.

I begin to probe, gently at first. Is it still there? Usually, when thinking about Coach Lee, I get a clawing panic in my chest, a choking pressure inside my throat. My skin crawls. But now I notice the absence of any panic, of any pressure. I press harder on the memory, but it's as if a deep, ugly bruise has finally healed.

"Jake told me it was awful for you—after we left."

I turn back to Jake's mom, slowly, a little stunned. "Yes," I say, nodding. "It was bad."

Her expression is so pained, it makes me feel bad for her.

"I'm going to call your mom."

"I think," I say, after a pause, "she'd like that."

I stand at the window and look out. The lake sparkles in the far distance. I close my eyes, listening to the beeping of the heart monitor behind me, trying to summon images of Jake and me as kids: there's Jake smiling, running, skating, riding his bike. More recent memories force their way in: him spinning me on the ice, taking my face in his hands and kissing me, firelight flickering across bare skin, the touch of his hands, silk on skin on silk.

I open my eyes. The lake's still glinting in the distance, like a fragment of mirror someone's using to signal to me. I rest my head against the cool glass of the window and sigh. And then I hear a voice behind me.

"Hi."

I spin around. Jake's eyes are open. He's smiling at me—a broken, unsure smile.

"Hi," I say back, fighting the impulse I have to throw myself on top of him. Something holds me back—the same uncertainty I can see in his smile.

"How's the other guy look?" Jake asks.

I burst out laughing. "A lot better than you."

Jake laughs and then winces and groans. "How long have I been in the hospital?"

"Four days," I tell him.

His eyes widen. He looks around and sees the camp bed laid out on the floor and the sofa piled with blankets and cushions.

"Your parents are here. They've just gone to take a shower."

"You've been here the whole time? Sleeping here?" he asks.

I nod.

He frowns. "Why?"

"Because I love you, Jake McCallister, and nothing, not Reid Walsh, not Koskela, not fear of what might happen in the future, is ever going to keep me away from you again."

Jake smiles wide.

My feet unglue, and I rush toward him. No more push-pull, no more contradiction. The magnet inside me has finally figured out its charge.

Jake

My parents are sitting right behind me. So are Em, her mom, and Shay. Every time I turn around, they all smile at me reassuringly, but behind the smiles I see the anxiety they're struggling to hide. Em squeezes my shoulder.

Out of the corner of my eye, I can see Rob and Reid Walsh. Rob looks my way and shoots me a victorious smile like he already knows I'm going down. Reid doesn't make eye contact at all.

The doctors signed me off as I'm almost fully mended. I'm even back on the ice, though not playing hockey yet, as Sarge is paranoid and thinks I'm made of glass. I try not to think about that, though—about hockey or college or anything—because after today it might all be taken away from me.

The judge clears his throat and shuffles his papers.

Mrs. Donovan grimaced when she saw which judge we'd pulled. Judge Penrose is a close friend of Chief Walsh. I've been told this isn't "the best news." Basically, Mrs. Donovan is trying to warn me that I'm doomed and wants to prepare me for the worst, which will likely be a jail term as they're pushing for an aggravated assault charge.

Beneath the starched collar of my shirt, I can feel the sweat start to prickle. I tug at my tie, which is trying to strangle me.

"The prosecution would like to call Robert Walsh to the stand."

I grip hold of the defense table and watch as Rob crosses to the witness box.

He sits down, darting a glance in Em's direction and giving her a smug smile. Tension ripples like a tidal wave through the courtroom. Even the incessant scratching of Jo Furness's pen ceases.

Rob puts his hand on the Bible and swears to tell the truth, the whole truth, and nothing but the truth. I suppress the snort. The guy wouldn't know truth if it sucker punched him in the face.

Em told me how Rob blackmailed her to break up with me. My first reaction was that I wanted to kill him. But I'm working on my anger issues, particularly where they concern the Walsh brothers. My mom thinks it all boils down to my fourteen-year-old self's rage at what happened to Em and frustration at not being able to defend her.

Mrs. Donovan stands up and walks toward the witness box. She runs Rob through a series of questions about the lead-up to the fight. Rob answers politely, doing his best to appear like the wounded victim who did nothing to incite violence against him.

"And then he just walked over and punched me in the face."

"And you had done nothing to provoke the attack?" the lawyer presses.

Rob looks directly at me. "No," he says. "Nothing. He's just a total psycho."

There's a collective intake of breath. Every eye in the courtroom turns on me. I'm fried beneath the judge's eagle gaze.

"You neither said nor did anything to cause the accused to lash out and hit you?" the prosecutor asks.

Rob shakes his head vehemently. "No. I was just sitting there, minding my own business. And then he hit my brother, Reid, and knocked him out."

"Objection!" my lawyer shouts, leaping her feet.

I want to leap to my feet too and yell at Rob for being a perjuring asshole, but Em puts her hand on my shoulder and squeezes, reminding me to stay calm. The judge stares at me over the rim of his glasses. He scribbles something on a piece of paper. I've lost. I know it. Everyone believes Rob. I won't let Em take the stand in my defense because Shay's mom told me that they'll bring up what happened to her with my uncle and use it to discredit her as a witness. I'd rather go to jail. My mom has taken my uncle's suicide note to the cops, and the truth is finally out, which has made a huge difference to Em—I can see it in the new way she holds herself—head high—but I can't risk undoing the gains by having her credibility questioned in front of the entire town again by an antagonistic lawyer.

This is it, though. Any hope I had of winning this flies out the window. I'm going to have to come to terms with the fact I won't ever have a career as a professional hockey player, and how will I get a job or finish my degree with a criminal record?

Aware that there's a commotion going on behind me, I turn to look.

Reid is on his feet. Em is staring at him wide-eyed, mouth open, as are all the people around him.

The judge bangs his gavel down hard. "Order. Order. Please take a seat until you are called to the stand."

Reid doesn't sit back down. He glances at Em and then across at his brother. "It didn't happen like he's saying."

"Excuse me?" the judge barks.

Reid's face reddens. "Um . . ." He looks at the judge, then at Em again. "It didn't happen like he says it did." He jerks his head at his brother, Rob.

I lean forward in my seat, hearing Em gasp behind me. The courtroom starts to buzz as if a hornet's nest has been kicked.

Reid lifts his arm and points at Rob. "He's lying."

There's a mass intake of air. People start to whisper, and the whispers grow quickly deafening. The judge slams his gavel down on the block and roars for silence. The whispers recede.

"Go on, Mr Walsh," the judge orders Reid.

Reid takes a deep breath. "Jake didn't threaten to kill him. And he was provoked. The truth is Rob deserved that punch." He looks at Em, then at the judge. "And I tripped and hit my head on the table. He didn't lay a finger on me. It was an accident."

The judge swivels to Rob. "You understand you are under oath, Mr. Walsh? And that the statement you gave to police was also given under oath?"

Rob nods, shooting his brother a death stare that makes him flinch.

"And you understand that by lying under oath you are guilty of perjury, which carries a prison sentence?"

Rob starts to stammer and looks to his lawyer.

"We move to dismiss the case!" my lawyer shouts over the noise.

The judge calls for order again, slamming his gavel down repeatedly until a shocked silence falls.

"In the light of this new witness statement," the judge growls,

"I am dismissing this case. If the prosecution wishes to lodge an appeal, I suggest they think twice. I will be asking the district attorney to open up a separate case investigating Mr. Walsh for perjury and contempt of court. The witness is to pay all the defendant's costs."

And with that, he sweeps from the room.

Rob stays sitting in the witness box like a rabbit in a lab who can see the scientist coming toward him with a gigantic needle. His eyes skitter among us all in terror.

The courtroom is a chaos of noise and movement. I turn around, dazed. Em is already on her feet. She's grinning at me. I pick her up and lift her over the barrier, ignoring my mom's pleas for me to watch my back. Em wraps her arms around my neck and kisses me. I kiss her right back, hugging her tight. I was worried that I'd kissed her for the last time, so I make the most of the opportunity.

Over Em's shoulder, I catch sight of Rob Walsh's father angrily confronting him and Reid darting for the door. He looks back briefly and catches my eye. I nod at him. He nods back, then disappears.

Em wraps her arms around my neck and I kiss her again. I kiss her so hard that everyone around us cheers, and when Jo Furness sticks a camera in our faces, I don't even notice.

Em

The doorbell rings.

My heart yo-yos. Is he here? I glance at the clock. He's early. Jake's back today from Boston. We haven't seen each other in two months, and I'm so excited about seeing him again that it feels as if I have firecrackers going off in my bloodstream. I can't sit still.

Jumping up from my dressing table, I am halfway to my bedroom door before I remember that I'm only half-dressed and have no makeup on. Damn.

"Em?" my mom shouts from downstairs. "Someone's here to see you."

Oh God. I grab a T-shirt from the pile on the floor where I flung the contents of my closet earlier and race to the door. The makeup doesn't matter. I need to see him.

I fly down the stairs, barely noticing my mother's wide-eyed warning expression and certainly not registering it. I'm smiling, giddy, ready to bounce into Jake's arms, when I realize it's not him and pull up short.

"Reid."

The smile is wiped off my face. He's standing awkwardly on the doorstep, looking like he's tied to a post standing in front of a firing squad.

"What are you doing here?" I glance at my mom to see if she's somehow in on this, but she looks as confused as me. She backs away, though, and heads into the front room, probably to tell my dad what's going on. She leaves the door ajar—probably so she can listen in.

"Hi," Reid says.

"What are you doing here?" I answer, standing in the doorway, making no move to invite him in.

"I, er . . . ," he stammers, looking at the ground. His face takes on that eggplant hue. I notice, though, that the acne has cleared up, and he doesn't seem quite so Popeye. His neck is no longer the same width as his head. "How's things?" he asks.

It's my turn to stammer. "F-fine," I say, wondering what on earth is going on. It's not like we've had a conversation or even seen each other since the trial.

"Good," he says, nodding eagerly.

Okay. This is weird. I think about shutting the door on him, but before I can, he says:

"How's your dad?"

I open my mouth, ready to throw a snide answer back his way, before stopping myself. Maybe it's his tone or his stooped demeanor reminding me of a dog that's afraid he's about to be kicked. "He's okay," I find myself answering.

Reid nods again. "That's good. Great."

I frown. He's being nice. Why is Reid Walsh being nice? And more to the point, why is he even here?

He clears his throat, darts a nervous look at me. "Um, you might have heard about Rob."

I shake my head slowly.

"He got kicked out of the academy."

"Oh" is all I can manage. Is that why Reid's here? Is he trying to get me to feel bad? "Well, maybe he shouldn't have committed perjury," I say with a shrug. "I guess the police academy has standards."

Reid breaks into a smile. "Yeah. I just thought, you know, you might want to know."

"Right. Okay. Thanks." This conversation is so weird and awkward, and now I'm also hyperaware that time is ticking and Jake should be here any moment. I need to get ready and also I don't really want Reid standing there watching when Jake and I are reunited. "Well," I say, making to close the door, "I should probably go."

"Wait," Reid says.

I hesitate.

He looks at me with a hangdog expression. "I just wanted to say I'm sorry."

I bite my lip. Yeah, he should. For a moment, I consider letting loose on all the things I've thought about him and his brother and wanted to say to them, but then I realize I'm no longer angry about it. The past is in the past now. I'm too excited about the present and the future to be thinking or worrying about what happened. So instead, I take a deep breath and say; "Thanks. I appreciate the apology."

A look of absolute relief crosses Reid's face. He lets out a huge sigh and smiles. "There's another reason I'm here." He puts his hand into his pocket and pulls out a piece of crumpled paper, yellow and tinted with age.

My heart starts smashing into my rib cage, but it's no longer a yo-yo, rather a medieval mace.

I take the piece of paper with a shaking hand and open it.

Dear Em,
Meet me at the tree house.
Let's run away together.
Jake x
PS: I believe you.

I draw in a breath sharper than needles and look up.

"It's the note I should have given you all those years ago," Reid says by way of explanation.

My chest convulses as I try to swallow a sob. I draw in another breath and hold it. Can't seem to let it out. Jake never told me what was in the letter.

"I'm sorry I never gave it to you."

I can't speak. All I can do is nod. I read the note again and in my head I start imagining Jake at fourteen, writing it. I start imagining myself reading it, in tears, on my bed, feeling so broken but knowing I wasn't so alone.

"Why didn't you give it to me?" I ask Reid. My eyes are welling up, and I try to blink away the tears before deciding I don't care if he sees. I want to ask him if he has any idea what that letter would have meant to me. How much I needed it.

"I didn't want to," Reid answers.

"Why?"

"Because I liked you and I was jealous of Jake. Of what you guys had. I always . . . envied it. . . . It's no excuse. It's just an explanation. And if I could go back in time right now, I would. I'd fix things. I'm sorry." He looks at me half-wary, half-expectant.

What is there to say? I can tell he really is sorry, and although in one respect it's too late, it's also never too late to apologize, so I just nod at him.

"I'm not the only one you should apologize to, though."

Reid nods thoughtfully. "I know. I apologized to Jake already."

That takes me aback. "You did? When?"

"Today."

"Today?"

"Yeah, I just saw him. He came around to my place."

My lips part, and I blink at Reid a few times, trying to process this. Jake went around to see Reid before coming to see me?

"He wanted to talk things through." He backs away from the door, checking his watch. "You're going to be late."

I frown at him.

"He's waiting for you." Reid nods at the note in my hand.

I read it again. He's at the tree house? I look up and see Reid's turned and walked away.

"Reid?" I shout after him.

He turns. A flare of hope crosses his face that he doesn't try to hide.

I smile at him.

After a few seconds, he smiles back, and we stay like that, smiling at each other until he turns around again and walks off down the street.

Five minutes later, I run through the woods, still clutching the note in my hand.

Weak winter sunlight shimmers through the trees, giving the clearing an otherworldly feel.

"Jake?" I call.

I know he's here. I can feel it like I can always feel it when he's near me. A hot sun bursting in my chest.

He steps out of the tree house onto the ledge, and I skid to a halt at the sight of him.

"Hi," he says. Even from a distance, I see the dangerous glimmer in his eye.

Grinning in anticipation, I start climbing the ladder up to him.

He reaches a hand down and pulls me up the last few steps and I fall into his arms, wondering how on earth I forgot how good it feels.

Jake takes my face in his hands and kisses me hard on the lips. "God, I missed you," he murmurs.

Our breath fogs up because it's so cold, but I barely notice because his hands are so warm, even when they sneak beneath my jacket and sweater to stroke up my back.

"What's all this?" I ask, my gaze finally falling on the backpack lying piled at his feet.

Jake grins and gives me a shrug. "That night. When I wrote you the note. I was out here for hours waiting for you." Color rises in his cheeks. "I brought a tent and a sleeping bag. I managed to forget the camp stove. But I did remember to bring these." He reaches down and picks up a bag of marshmallows.

"You really planned for us to run away?" I can't believe he was serious.

He nods. "Yeah."

Wow. I try to imagine what would have happened if I'd have gotten the note. Would I have run away with him? Yes. I would have. Without a doubt.

"Where would we have gone?" I ask.

"Wherever you wanted to go."

"Wherever I wanted to go?"

He nods again, and my pulse quickens at the half smile tugging on his lips. For a brief moment, I picture the two of us living wild on Blake Island, fishing for our supper, sharing a sleeping bag, and toasting marshmallows over a campfire.

Jake brushes a strand of hair behind my ear.

"Emerson Lowe . . . will you . . . run away with me now?"

I take his hands and look up into his eyes. The smile is in his eyes, warming them, and a flurry of butterflies takes flight in my chest. "Yes."

He grins and dips his head to kiss me.

"Where to?" I ask.

"Actually, I booked us the fire teepee for three nights. I figured that we're older now and we can afford to run away in more style."

I sink to my knees, pulling him with me, and in the next second I'm straddling him. His arms come around my waist and he pulls me tighter against him. My hands slide beneath his jacket and his sweater, and I feel the goose bumps glide across his skin.

"Hey," he says now, pulling away from me, "I need to show you something."

He pulls an envelope from his pocket and hands it to me.

"Another letter?"

"Open it," Jake tells me.

I take it, smiling curiously.

"Don't be mad," he says.

My smile fades. What's he done? I glance down at the letter. It has a Seattle postmark, and it's addressed to me but care of Jake. I don't get it.

"Shay gave me the idea," he says nervously as I pull out the single sheet of paper inside and read what it says. Then I read it again. And a third time. Finally, I look up. "I don't understand."

"It's a scholarship," Jake says. "You won a scholarship. To Washington State."

"But . . . how?" I ask.

"Your essay. The one about what happened to you—your story. I took a copy of it and I sent it to the journalism school there. I told them about your situation. And they'd already accepted you, so . . ." He shrugs.

I blink at the page, but the words are all blurry. Jake grabs the letter from my hand.

"Look," he says, reading aloud. "They say it's 'one of the most powerful and honest accounts they have ever read' and that you 'have clear talent and demonstrate obvious potential.' Did you read it? They say they'll be honored to have your in their program." He hands the letter back to me triumphantly.

I take it, but it drops limply to my side. Jake notices. His smile falters.

"What?" he asks. "You can take this. You can make this work. I've already talked to your mom and dad. You can start next semester."

I look up sharply. "What about the store?"

"Aaron is going to take over for you at the store."

"What?"

"He hates his job. He loves being on the water. He and Toby are going to manage the place while you study. And you can go part-time. And now you don't need to worry about the cost or anything because they think you're brilliant, and so do I, and this is it, Em—it's what you wanted, and you can't not do it. . . ."

He breaks off to take a breath and I can see he's still waiting on my reaction, worried about what it might be.

"What are you scared of?" he asks me, and there's that look on his face, that teasing edge to his tone, as if he's daring me.

I glance again at the letter, still a little dumbfounded, before tossing it to one side.

Jake's face falls. I glower at him. His shoulders slump.

I put my hands on his shoulders and push him hard. He hits the deck, his eyes going wide, but then I'm lying on top of him, eliminating all the space between us. My hands slide beneath his jacket and his sweater. He breathes in sharply, and I lean down and kiss him, feeling the humming buzz of electricity shoot through me just like it did when he kissed me for the very first time.

"I'm not scared of anything," I whisper.

Author's Note

According to statistics*, one in five women and girls are sexually assaulted in their lifetime. Forty-four percent of them are under eighteen years old.

I have heard so many heartbreaking stories from women who were assaulted as teenagers and young girls—and it was these stories, as well as my own, that inspired me to write Emerson's story.

Each time I asked my friends if they regretted speaking up about what happened to them—given what it did to their families, their own reputations, their lives—and they all said no. By speaking up, they were adamant that they had reclaimed their selfhood, that they were no longer victims, forced to hold on to a secret they had never wanted to own. Speaking up became a theme I heard over and over, one that these women now emphatically preach to their own children: Never be scared to tell the truth. Do not let someone make you a victim.

I have my own story too—not as harrowing as most, but still ugly and upsetting, which left an indelible mark on me. I did not

*RAINN—the US's largest anti–sexual assault organization.

speak up when it happened. I was a vocal, strong, empowered young woman, and yet I could not find my voice, not during the assault and not after it happened. It took me years to realize what happened to me was sexual assault because I believed that I had allowed it to happen. I think this is typical. It took me fifteen years to realize that I was innocent, that no person has any right to touch me in a way I do not ask for or actively consent to. I wish I had spoken up then. Writing this book is my way of doing that now.

If you've been the victim of sexual assault, know that you are not alone. What I discovered is that once you start talking about your experience, you discover just how many other people have been through the same thing and that talking about it, sharing it, kick-starts the healing process.

Acknowledgments

Enormous thanks and gratitude go to:

My wonderful girlfriends Lauren, Asa, Nic, Becky, Rachel, and Vic, who keep me sane, keep me laughing, and inspire me daily.

The wonderful men in my life: my husband, John, my brother, and my dad.

My amazing agent, Amanda Preston.

Nicole Ellul at Simon & Schuster, whose brilliant editing skills and suggestions really helped shape the novel.

All the brilliant people at Simon & Schuster who have worked so hard to make this book look so good and to get it out there, into your hands. I'm so grateful to you all.

At eleven, Jessa first
met Kit Ryan.

At fourteen, her crush began.

And now . . .
she's fallen in love.

Read on for a sneak peek of Mila Gray's
Come Back to Me.

A whorl in the glass distorts the picture, like a thumbprint smear over a lens. I'm halfway down the stairs, gathering my hair into a ponytail, thoughts a million miles away, when a blur outside the window pulls me up short.

I take another step, the view clears, and when I realize what I'm seeing, *who* I'm seeing, my stomach plummets and the air leaves my lungs like a final exhalation. My arms fall slowly to my sides. My body's instinct is to turn and run back upstairs, to tear into the bathroom and lock the door, but I'm frozen. This is the moment you have nightmares about, play over in your mind, the darkest of daydreams, furnished by movies and by real-life stories you've overheard your whole life.

You imagine over and over how you'll cope, what you'll say, how you'll act when you open the door and find them standing there. You pray to every god you can dream up that this moment won't ever happen. You make bargains, promises, desperate barters. And you live each day with the murmur of those prayers playing on a loop in the background of your mind, an endless chant. And then the moment happens and you realize it was all for nothing. The prayers went unheard. There was no bargain to make. Was it your fault? Did you fail to keep your promise?

Time seems to have slowed. Kit's father hasn't moved. He's standing at the end of the driveway staring up at the house, squinting against the early morning glare. He's wearing his Dress Blues. It's that fact which registered before all else, which told me all I needed to know. That and the fact that he's here at all. Kit's father has never once been to the house. There is only one reason why he would ever come.

He hasn't taken a step, and I will him not to. I will him to turn around and get back into the dark sedan sitting at the curb. A shadowy figure in uniform sits at the wheel. *Please. Get back in and drive away.* I start making futile bargains with some nameless god. If he gets back in the car and drives away, I'll do anything. But he doesn't. He takes a step down the driveway toward the house, and that's when I know for certain that either Riley or Kit is dead.

A scream, or maybe a sob, tries to struggle up my throat, but it's blocked by a solid wave of nausea. I grab for the banister to stay upright. Who? Which one? My brother or my boyfriend? Oh God. Oh God. My legs are shaking. I watch Kit's father walk slowly up the drive, head bowed.

Memories, images, words, flicker through my mind like scratched fragments of film: Kit's arms around my waist drawing me closer, our first kiss under the cover of darkness just by the back door, the smile on his face the first time we slept together, the blue of his eyes lit up by the sparks from a Chinese lantern, the fierceness in his voice when he told me he was going to love me forever.

Come back to me. That was the very last thing I said to him. *Come back to me.*

Always. The very last thing he said to me.

Then I see Riley as a kid throwing a toy train down the stairs, dive-bombing into the pool, holding my hand at our grandfather's funeral, grinning and high-fiving Kit after they'd enlisted. The snapshot of him in his uniform on graduation day. The circles under his eyes the last time I saw him.

The door buzzes. I jump. But I stay where I am, frozen halfway up the stairs. If I don't answer the door, maybe he'll go away. Maybe this won't be happening. But the doorbell sounds again. And then I hear footsteps on the landing above me. My mother's voice, sleepy and confused. "Jessa? Who is it? Why are you just standing there?"

Then she sees. She peers through the window, and I hear the intake of air, the ragged "no" she utters in response. She too knows that a military car parked outside the house at seven a.m. can signify only one thing.

I turn to her. Her hand is pressed to her mouth. Standing in her nightdress, her hair unbrushed, the blood rushing from her face, she looks like she's seen a ghost. No. That's wrong. She looks like she *is* a ghost.

The bell buzzes for a third time.

"Get the door, Jessa," my mother says in a strange voice I don't recognize. It startles me enough that I start to walk down the stairs. I feel calmer all of a sudden, like I'm floating outside my body. This can't be happening. It's not real. It's just a dream.

I find myself standing somehow in front of the door. I unlock it. I open it. Kit. Riley. Kit. Riley. Their names circle my mind like birds of prey in a cloudless blue sky. Kit. Riley. Which is it?

Is Kit's father here in his Dress Blues with his chaplain insignia to tell us that my brother has been killed in action or that his son—my boyfriend—has been killed in action? He would come either way. He would want to be the one to tell me. He would want to be the one to tell my mom.

Kit's father blinks at me. He's been crying. His eyes are red, his cheeks wet. He's still crying, in fact. I watch the tears slide down his face and realize that I've never seen him cry before. It automatically makes me want to comfort him, but even if I could find the words, my throat is so dry I couldn't speak them.

"Jessa," Kit's father says in a husky voice.

I hold on to the doorframe, keeping my back straight. I'm aware that my mother has followed me down the stairs and is standing right behind me. Kit's father glances at her over my shoulder. He takes a deep breath, lifts his chin, and removes his hat before his eyes flicker back to me.

"I'm sorry," he says.

"Who?" I hear myself ask. "Who is it?"

Three months earlier . . .

Oh dear God, who in the name of heaven is he?"

Didi's grip on my arm is enough to raise bruises. I look up. And I see him. He's staring at me, grinning, and I have to bite back my own grin. My stomach starts somersaulting, my insides twisting into knots.

"Kit," I say, half in answer to Didi, half just for the chance to say his name out loud after so long. My eyes are locked with Kit's, and when he hears me speak his name, he smiles even wider and walks across the living room toward me.

"Hey, Jessa," he says. His eyes travel over me, taking me in, before settling on my face. He rubs a hand over his shorn head, a self-conscious gesture that makes the somersaults double in speed. He's still grinning at me but more sheepishly now.

"Hi," I say, swallowing. I'm nervous all of a sudden. I haven't seen him in nine months. I wasn't sure he was going to be here today, and though I've run through this moment dozens—hell, thousands—of times in my head, I find I'm completely unprepared for it now it's actually happening. In all those imaginings I never once factored in the way he'd make me feel—as though

I've just taken a running leap off a cliff edge. I'm breathless, almost shaking, finding it hard to hold his steady blue gaze.

He looks older than his twenty-one years. His shoulders are broader, and he's even more tanned than usual, both facts well emphasized by the white T-shirt he's wearing. I can feel Didi squeezing my arm with so much force it's as though she's trying to stem an arterial bleed, and I know if I turn around I'll see her drooling unashamedly. She might go to a convent school, but Didi's prayers center around asking God to deliver her not from trespassers but from her virginity.

"Happy birthday," Kit says now. He hasn't taken his eyes off me the whole time, and my skin is warming under his relentless gaze. I can feel my face getting hotter.

"Thanks," I manage to say, wishing I could come up with a better response, something flirtatious and witty. I know I had something planned for this moment, but my brain has chosen to shut down.

"Hi!"

It's Didi. She has let go of my arm and now thrusts her hand out toward Kit. "I'm Didi, Jessa's best friend. You must be Kit. I've heard a lot about you."

Plenty of emphasis on the *lot*. I make a mental note to kill her later. Kit glances over at me, clearly struggling to contain his amusement, before turning his attention fully back to Didi. He shakes her hand, introducing himself properly, and it gives me a chance to mentally pull myself together and really get a look at him. He's six foot but he seems taller, maybe because he's standing so straight. I recognize the ink marking on his arm, poking out from beneath his sleeve. It's the same tattoo that Riley has. A Marine Corps emblem. My fingers itch to trace it. Oh God. For months I've been telling myself to get over Kit, ordering myself to forget him. Didi rolls her eyes at me every time I mention his name. She's even added my name on Urban Dictionary under the word *pathetic*. But now, as I watch Kit casting his spell over her, I can see she may finally be ready to cut me a break.

She's firing questions at him like she's a Chinese match-maker, asking all about his job and his uniform. I wouldn't be surprised if she starts asking him next how much he earns and whether he has a girlfriend. I would interrupt, but I'm still try-ing to gather my wits and formulate a sentence, and, truth be told, I'm kind of hoping she does ask him whether he has a girl-friend. Though another, bigger part of me doesn't want to hear the answer. Because what if he does? Taking a breath, I remind myself he's been in Sudan for the last nine months living with a bunch of guys, sleeping in a room with a dozen other men, eat-ing in a mess hall. It's not like he's been going to parties or out clubbing every night, so it's highly unlikely he's managed to find himself a girlfriend in that time.

Kit answers Didi's questions politely, nodding and giving the standard-issue responses that they're trained to. In other words, no detail whatsoever. All I know is that he and Riley have been in Sudan along with the rest of their marine detachment, protecting the US embassy in Khartoum. That's all. They only got back yesterday.

As I listen to Didi and Kit talking, Didi telling him all about how she only moved to Oceanside six months ago and how her big ambition is to finish school and move to LA (thankfully she omits to mention her other big ambition—to lose her virginity), I realize I'm fixating on Kit's lips, imagining what it would be like to kiss him.